The Shadows of Rutherford House

CE Rose is the pen name of Caroline England, the author of psychological thrillers *Beneath the Skin*, *My Husband's Lies*, *Betray Her* and *Truth Games*.

As CE Rose, Caroline has written gothic-tinged domestic suspense novels, *The House of Hidden Secrets* and *The House on the Water's Edge*. As Caro Land she has written the legal suspense drama series, Convictions and Confessions.

Also by CE Rose

The House of Hidden Secrets
The House on the Water's Edge
The Shadows of Rutherford House
The Attic at Wilton Place

THE
SHADOWS
OF
RUTHERFORD
HOUSE

c e rose

hera

First published in the United Kingdom in 2022 by

Hera Books
Unit 9 (Canelo), 5th Floor
Cargo Works, 1-2 Hatfields
London SE1 9PG
United Kingdom

A CIP catalogue record for this book is available from the British Library.

Print ISBN 978 1 80436 183 2
Ebook ISBN 978 1 80436 182 5

This book is a work of fiction. Names, characters, businesses, organizations, places and events are either the product of the author's imagination or are used fictitiously. Any resemblance to actual persons, living or dead, events or locales is entirely coincidental.

Cover design by The Brewster Project

Look for more great books at www.herabooks.com

Printed and bound in Great Britain by Clays Ltd, Elcograf S.p.A.

For Rita, Gerry and the Lanigan clan.

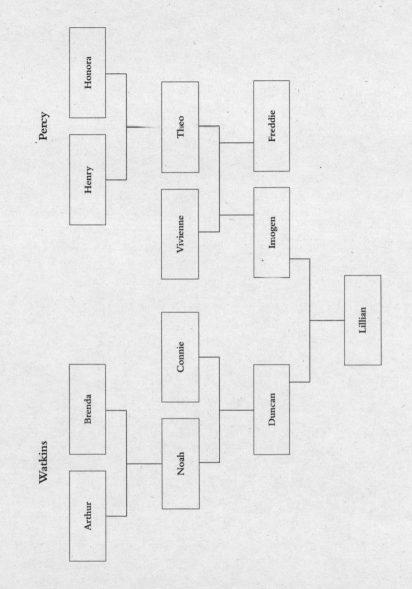

Prologue

Present Day

It's heavily raining tonight, the wind whipping the windows behind the closed shutters. As ever, the midnight darkness is inky black, but that makes no odds to me. I know every inch, nook and cranny of this old manor like the back of my hand; even with my eyes closed, I could find each remnant of its former glory in seconds, the oil paintings depicting the haughty Percy line, the exquisitely shaped standard lamps, the Romanesque pillars and busts, the ornate marble hearths, brass grates and antique fire tools.

It wouldn't be appropriate to be seen wandering Rutherford House as though I owned it, so I like this quiet time to explore the ancient corridors and chambers, to take in the aromas, the textures and vibrations, and tonight is no exception. I trace my fingers along the walls and feel the nap of velvet wallpaper, ridges of stucco trim and knots in fine hardwood. The panelling hasn't been polished for years, and yet I know each room's distinctive, waxy smell. I know which floorboards creak, which chairs have broken springs, which handsome tables have woodworm, the crystals missing from the showy chandeliers, the locks and latches which no longer work.

Remembering a spring ball I once watched from the wings, I dance across the marbled floor of the domed hallway. The worn carpet of the sweeping staircase is rough beneath my toes, yet it still has the elegance, the grandeur of the past, especially when I pause to listen to the rock 'n' roll echoing from the dance floor below. Humming at the memory, I sashay up the steps, and when I reach the open landing, I stop again to new noises which pierce the silence. Babies, of course, the joyful bleats and shuffles of all the newborns brought into the world under this very roof. I brush by the balustrade and make my way through the shadows towards the warmth and the sound, but as ever, a hand slips into mine, insubstantial but undoubtedly there. And though I long to turn back the clock and wipe out my one and only guilt, history can't be changed, so I pull away and cover my ears to block out the inevitable.

Yet I still hear it. A thud and the crack of broken bones.

Chapter 1

Milly

I had no intention of going into service like my mother, Maggie Shaw. All that fawning and servility, the bowing and scraping I'd watched from a distance. Not that she would see it that way. As housekeeper, she liked to think she was a cut above the other staff, a friend of the family, almost.

I was left with my gran, and she wouldn't half laugh when Mother deigned to visit us in the village with her 'airs and graces'.

'The worst type of fool is one who fools themselves, Maggie. Mark my words, if the going got tough, the Percys wouldn't give you the dirt beneath their fingernails,' she'd say.

As it happened, the going had got tough. Like many country manors during the Second World War, Rutherford House had been requisitioned by the government as a maternity home for evacuated pregnant women. The exquisite furniture was stored in the east wing, the paintings and paraphernalia removed, the velvet-lined drawing room and library boarded up, and provision made for a dormitory of thirty in the west wing. My mother astonished Gran by not only embracing her new role of midwife-cum-nanny, but growing a 'bun' of her own,

3

namely me, Millicent Shaw. She never did disclose the identity of the father, but Gran had her own sucked-in-cheek theories.

'With a house full of women and only a couple of men on leave, it wasn't Greek to work out,' she'd say. Whatever that meant.

I didn't have the honour of being born at Rutherford in 1943. It seems Mother hid the pregnancy beneath her stern smile and layers of white aprons, then eventually pushed me out in her childhood Scawsby bedroom with a stick for the pain and Gran's 'told you so' eyes. Gran agreed to house and feed me but said if anyone asked '*There'd be no lies*', especially as my grandad had died many years before in the 1926 Thorne Colliery shaft accident. She didn't think it fair for folk to believe she had a fella on the side when it was actually '*Pure as pure flaming Maggie*'. But nobody did ask. I was one of those quiet and studious children no one noticed, save for Gran, and my invisibility continued at school. Unless the alpha kids were bored and needed someone to pick on, of course, and what better reason than a face full of freckles and the colour of my hair.

Rutherford House was – and indeed still is – the seat of the Rutherford-Percy family. Back in the day it was a splendid, bustling Palladian-style manor with a hefty gaggle of employees. The female staff ranged from a variety of maids to a cook, a head nurse, a governess and a nanny, not to mention the dependable, prudent, sensible and honest housekeeper, who was then a fiery woman in her eighties. The male line-up included a butler, a valet, a groom, a coachman, a gardener, a gamekeeper and an estate steward. The numbers inevitably dwindled as a result of conscription during the war, but after it ended and the evacuees finally left, the staff pyramid slowly crumbled due to 'finances'. Apparently the *weak and witless* Henry Percy had left matters of money entirely in the hands of his steward, who'd managed to leak or steal or imbibe a huge chunk of the family fortune. Thankfully, on Henry's early death at the age of fifty-three, his widow Honora was a little more savvy. She dismissed the 'hangers on' and rewarded her loyal staff with the honour of promotion rather than an increased salary. As a consequence, Cook became 'Chief Cook', and my mother was upgraded to 'Mrs' Shaw, housekeeper. In return for the rather magnificent hunting lodge, Watkins was given the role of gamekeeper, groom and gardener and any other 'male' role the poor man was allotted, which included managing the sixty-acre estate.

Around this point my mother called upon me to perform my daughterly duties. I didn't know the ins and outs of it – indeed I had no interest in the Percy family at all – but apparently the son and heir, Theo, had found a wife. The fiancée was of good stock – with money presumably – so Honora decreed that it wouldn't do for her to start married life at Rutherford without a lady's maid. According to the 'housekeeper', I was the perfect candidate: I'd turned sixteen, Gran was frail and the cottage tenancy would go with her when she died; I didn't have any suitors on the horizon and, needless to say, I was guaranteed by her to be a cheap employee.

I'd always been a clever girl and had hoped to stay in education to take the Higher School Certificate, so the thought of tending to the whims of a spoilt, posh princess-type, like my mother had before me, was frankly abhorrent. I tried to rail against it as much as was possible when Maggie's mind was set, but even Gran was all for it.

'I haven't much time left, love. Seems you prefer books to boys, so how else will you get a roof over your head? Do it for me, love. When I'm not here to fret about you, you can do as you please.' She peered at me with milky eyes. 'And as for learning, I'm told Rutherford's library is the best in all the land, let alone South Yorkshire, so it wouldn't be all bad...'

So, in 1959, I duly packed a small case and veritably stomped across the long driveway that cleaved the walled parkland of my new residence. I'd never visited before, but I was determined not to gush or have my head turned like my mother. Yet as Rutherford House came into sight, I couldn't help but stop and stare in awe. Surrounded by immaculate lawns and flanked by its two wings, the white elevations and handsome windows wouldn't have been out of place in ancient Rome. And far from Gran's description of it being a 'trophy home' built with tasteless wealth, it looked graceful, understated and classical. But I soon reset my jaw, made my way around the back to the servants' entrance, pushed open the heavy door to the scullery, and entered the warm, sweet-smelling kitchen.

Cook glanced over her shoulder. 'You must be the girl from the village,' she said. She looked me up and down. 'Mrs Shaw runs a tight ship here and doesn't put up with any silliness. Let's hope you're up to the task.'

As it happened, Gran outlived her daughter and held onto her tenancy until she was ninety-three, but ultimately that didn't matter one jot. Between general dull chores, I spent the first weeks at Rutherford stealthily exploring every nook and cranny of the house – the domed Venetian-style hallway and elegant parlours, the lofty, well-stocked library, stately rooms and chambers, their opulent furnishings, gilt-framed oil paintings and crystal chandeliers. Then, when the housekeeper was distracted by her projects and plans to ensure everything was 'shipshape' for the new Mrs Percy, I'd escape outside. I explored the stable block and gardener's bothy, the walled and flower gardens, the orchards, the meadows and woods beyond, and gradually, very gradually, my hostility thawed.

–

After I'd had a month of waking at dawn in a fusty attic room and dreading the prospect of a mistress and a life of subservience, Theo and his new bride returned from their honeymoon. Though only a handful of staff, we duly lined up by the steps of the twin perrons and watched Theo's convertible approach. Grinning and waving at his mother, he propelled his new BMW around the circular driveway several times. But of course, we had no interest in the foppish heir to the throne; our eyes were on his princess. Apparently unperturbed by the centrifugal force of her new husband's ridiculous driving, she smoothed back her blonde hair, opened the door and slipped out her long legs. Then, greeting each servant with a graceful, gloved hand and a stunning smile, she asked who we were.

When it came to my turn, I was almost holding my breath, yet I could still smell her delicate scent. 'Millicent. Or Milly,' I managed to mutter. 'Lady's maid.'

'Milly it is. What a lovely name.'

My emotions didn't take long to adjust this time. In truth, I was instantly smitten.

Chapter 2

Christie

'Morning, Lillian. How's tricks?'

Her arms folded, Lillian doesn't reply. She's still in bed and picking at what's left of her nails.

I ignore her stubborn silence, open the curtains and peer at the misty February morning outside. 'The sun's trying for a smile. We could venture out for a walk to the village if you fancy? Buy some sneaky ciggies?'

It's a dance we have played over the few weeks I have worked at the Devonshire. We connect, and we chat, and we smile like good friends, then I break for a holiday, the weekend or change shifts, and she retreats to her room, refusing to come out or cooperate with any of my colleagues.

'Madam has been playing up and refusing to join in for meals,' Sunia commented the moment I arrived this morning. 'Her grandma came yesterday and brought the usual goodies, but that's pretty much all she's eaten.'

Sunia finds Lillian draining, and I really don't blame her. Nursing staff are the core of the caring profession, and central to their role is the development of effective relationships with the individuals they support. Yet it isn't always that easy in the mental health sector. Sure, we start the day by doing nurse-type things, such as talking to them to see how they're doing, checking their medication and filling reams of paperwork. But close observation, where patients need to be kept within sight, or even at an arm's reach at all times, doesn't make for an equal partnership. We don't like to term it 'suicide watch', but that's what it is.

I didn't work here when Lillian was first sectioned, but I don't believe she is a suicide risk any more – if, indeed, she ever was. After boarding school from the ages of ten to eighteen, her sixteen-hour days on the investment bank floor, then her six months with us, I think it's more a case of being so institutionalised that she's afraid to leave here, that she'll grasp at any loophole or grounds to persuade us she should stay. Any reasons other than the actual truth, I suspect. Which is why she intrigues me so much.

Perhaps a new face has helped, but it seems I have managed to 'click' with Lillian where others have failed, to slowly open the clamped shell and peek inside. But she's still intensely private. Her granny travels from Doncaster to visit every Sunday, and she's a mystery too. Though clearly well into her seventies, she sports a black Mary Quant bob that surely is dyed. Petite, slim and yet somehow sturdy, she's the polar opposite of her fair, willowy granddaughter. My attempts to engage with the woman have been wholly unsuccessful, but when I've hovered outside Lillian's door, her clipped, authoritative tone has softened, and occasionally my patient's laughter has echoed out.

The prospect of cigarettes usually animates Lillian, but I've been off for a week, visiting my dad, who decided to 'retire' to his childhood Scottish village at the ripe old age of fifty-five. Though I'm thirty-one, his leaving – or perhaps his *wanting* to leave Yorkshire and me – has hit me far harder than I'd thought. Is it single child syndrome, like Lillian? Perhaps, but over the years, my dad and I have been through a lot.

'I guess it's a final closure thing,' he explained when he made his surprise decision. 'I think a clean start somewhere else will help.'

I now sit in Lillian's armchair and take the next step of our dance. Sharing personal information with a patient is not condoned – indeed it can be dangerous with some mental health conditions. However, I take the view that self-disclosure can have a beneficial effect on therapeutic alliance and treatment outcomes. Besides, patient or otherwise, I'm always careful with what I'm willing to share.

'So, my hot Saturday night date I told you about...' I begin.

I sense the tension ease from Lillian's shoulders.

'In two words – a disaster.' I pull out my mobile. 'Want to see profile pic versus real-life mug?'

She finally looks at me, wide-eyed. 'You're joking! You took a photo of him?'

'On the QT, of course. Come and look.'

She pads over and quietly perches on the desk chair. 'They're not exactly Cecil Beaton standards, admittedly,' I say, showing them to her. 'But I was checking my phone for messages, as you do, and quickly took a couple.'

'Sure,' she replies vaguely.

If Lillian owns a mobile phone, she doesn't have it here, and I still haven't learned whether she's ever had a significant other. From her records, I know that her mother died shortly before she was bundled off to boarding school, that she was a high-flyer, attending university in London, then joining an investment bank under a graduate scheme and staying. I'm also aware that she was a loner who worked all hours and had bouts of severe anxiety but was finally floored by her father's early death.

'So what do you think of the hairy beau?' I ask her. 'Is he your type?'

Two spots of pink colour her pale cheeks. 'Not really. For as long as I can remember, I had a crush on someone, and no one else seemed to measure up.'

I try for nonchalance at this surprising revelation. 'Oh yeah?'

'We were in the same class at primary school, but he pretty much ignored me there.'

Ah, so a male. I chuckle. 'As boys do when anyone else is watching…'

'But he was mad about horses.' She faintly smiles. 'So that was my leverage. Ollie.'

I'm not sure if 'Ollie' is the boy or the horse, but she clearly went riding. Maybe even had her own pony. More new information. 'Do you still ride?' I ask. 'Well, did you ride until you joined us here?'

Lillian shakes her head, so I try another tack. There's a photograph album in her bedside table, which she hasn't yet shared with me. I gesture to the pic of my date again. 'Your guy doesn't have a yeard, I take it?'

'A yeard?'

'Growing out your beard for an entire year without touching it? Even trimming, grooming, combing it.' I snort. 'At least that's what it looked like on Saturday night.'

She rubs the chair arm. 'Not that I know of. And at ten, a beard is unlikely…'

'That's true. So you haven't seen him since then?'

'Only from a distance. I was sent away to St Hilary's, so...'

'Ah, of course. What about when you came home in the holidays? Didn't you meet up then?'

'No.'

'That's a shame. Any particular reason why not?'

She turns to the frost-covered view from the window, and for moments I don't think she'll reply.

'Something horrible had happened, and he wanted to talk about it,' she says eventually. As though batting the memory away, she sharply shakes her head. 'But I didn't.'

Chapter 3

1987

Duncan

Duncan bends to the mirror and fluffs his blond hair.

'Don't worry, you're looking good,' Stiggy, his house-mate, says from behind him. 'Not sure what she'll make of the boots, though. What are they? Cowboy?'

Duncan looks down to his footwear. Thank God they're black. He asked his mum to buy him boots for Christmas, and they're not what he had in mind by a long shot. He tried to persuade her to give him the receipt, but she was having none of it.

'They're knee-high and leather, like you asked,' she snapped. 'You'll keep them and be grateful.'

He smiles and shakes his head. His intransigent bloody mum.

'*I've told you, university isn't for the likes of me*,' he always said when she nagged him about studying all hours to get the right grades.

'*Well, you're going. You'll work hard and get a proper job.*'

It was rich coming from a woman who'd started serving behind the bar of The Mallard at eighteen and still works there now. Of course, she had a break when he was born and living with his dad at the Ridings, but she's never been one for changing her mind once it's set. He can clearly remember his dad's look of bewilderment during the summer holidays when he was still at primary school. With a tut of annoyance, his mum had answered the telephone during breakfast. When she returned to the table, her face was linen white.

'That's it, that's proof,' she said, putting a hand to her ample chest.

'What's "it" and "proof"?' his dad, Noah, asked.

'Me and the lad, we're going to Mum's.'

At only nine, he'd been completely baffled, too, especially when his mum raised her eyebrows meaningfully at him before reverting to his dad. 'I'm not risking it.'

'That's just people talking, Connie. I've said this before. There's no truth in tittle-tattle or folklore.'

'Well, you're urgently wanted at Rutherford, and you'll be thinking twice when you get there.'

'Why, what's happened?'

She opened her mouth as though to speak but clearly thought better of it and smoothed his hair. 'Go up and give your room a tidy, Duncan, love,' she said.

He looked from his mum to his dad. Something was clearly going on. Connie loved a good gossip, but rather than her usual hand-on-hip intrigue, her voice was tremulous, her whole being a little shaky. Why on earth would they be going to his grandma's house in the village? Sure, his gran had recently moved into an old people's home, but the bungalow was being sold, and there was an estate agent's sign in the front garden. Even more strange, he hadn't yet finished his scrambled eggs, and his mum was a stickler for a polished plate.

Always hungry, he considered objecting, but his dad spoke. 'Go on up, son. You can polish that off in a bit.'

He later learned about the shocking news at the big house, but he never worked out what his wide-eyed mum had been rabbiting on about, nor why they went to his gran's – not just for that night or even the week – but forever. Connie basically upped sticks from their home and moved lock, stock and barrel to the bungalow. Though it was a nice enough modern building and closer to his school and his mates, he never got over the rupture from the Ridings and his dad, or ever quite forgave his mum.

Still, she was on the money about university. He still intends to go back to his dad and the land at some point, but he's only twenty years old and there's no rush. He didn't fancy more studying after his dreary A levels, but an agriculture degree is right up his street, so lectures and learning aren't a chore. Besides, education isn't really what he's here for.

'Do it, lad. Go to Newcastle and have fun. Chat up some pretty girls,' his dad said when the offer came through. His lips twitched. 'Maybe even attend a class or two. Your job and the Ridings aren't going anywhere. They'll be here when you're back.'

Duncan now comes back to his boots and Stiggy's guffaw. 'They're supposed to be trendy,' he says.

'If you say so. If they don't catch Jana's attention, nothing will.' He gives Duncan a playful shove. 'Come on, chin up; tonight could be the night you drag her away from Sheena. Word has it she's getting bored with him "Working Nine to Five".'

Ignoring the usual pun, Duncan gives his fringe a last tweak and inhales deeply. Bloody hell, he hopes Stiggy is right. He's followed his dad's advice and chatted up plenty of pretty girls over the last year, but one woman in particular is proving elusive. She's so damned attractive; he struggles to say anything remotely interesting and can't even maintain eye contact for more than three seconds. And though his mates soften the blow by taking the piss and calling the guy 'Sheena', it really doesn't help that Jana already has a cool musician boyfriend.

Chapter 4

1960

Milly

When my mother was Honora's lady's maid, her duties were traditional – helping her mistress with her appearance, applying her make-up or putting up her hair; laying out her clothing, her jewellery and shoes; repairing and altering garments; running her bath. Mine didn't apparently encompass any of those things. Though I appeared in Vivienne's bedroom each morning with a curtsey and offered my services, I was wafted away with a 'No thanks. I'm sure Mrs Shaw can find you something to do.'

Mrs Shaw did indeed find me plenty to do, and it finally dawned that the title 'lady's maid' had been somewhat disingenuous, a more palatable version of a scullery-cum-laundry-cum-housemaid. Part of me wanted to march back to Gran's and my books, but Vivienne's presence in the house made it feel glamorous and exciting. In truth, that frisson of delight upon first meeting her was still tight in my chest, so I took far longer than was necessary to collect her clothes, change her bedding and clean her bedroom, in the hope she'd still be there. Then if she was, I'd covertly watch her style her hair, artfully paint her face and dab perfume behind her pretty ears before leaving with a peculiar mix of adoration and rejection swimming in my belly. But in fairness to her, I was a surly teenager who didn't bother to hide my dissatisfaction as I went about my chores, whereas she was a sophisticated twenty-one-year-old woman perfectly capable of looking after herself.

I had no idea what an exquisite creature like Vivienne saw in yet another 'weak and witless' Percy. Theo was handsome enough, I suppose, but he'd clearly been spoilt and cosseted by his mother, his nanny and governess. Though he was twenty-four, he still had a childish, stubborn air about him, and everyone treated him accordingly by pandering to his whims. It both frustrated and disappointed me. Save for Watkins and his son Noah over at the Ridings, Rutherford was a house of strong women. Why did they – including my mother – indulge him and allow him to do everything to excess and fritter what little money there was?

My relationship with Mother was strictly on a Mrs Shaw and Millicent basis, so I rarely had an opportunity to talk to her on a personal level. But Gran had her theories, which she'd eagerly convey on my visits: 'The Percy men have always died young, so it won't be forever. They're on God's earth to sire an heir, then when they do, they expire from the effort like one of those marsupials. The silly toff won't be long for this world, mark my words.'

As it happened, the impasse with Vivienne was broken because of that very subject. After several months of my morning routine, I asked the usual question:

'Is there anything I can help you with today, Mrs Percy?'

She wasn't in her dressing room or perched at her table but sitting on the rather uncomfortable-looking baroque walnut sofa and gazing out through the huge, panelled window.

'Yes, there is, actually,' she replied.

Surprised, I stopped in my tracks and turned to her. She inhaled deeply and smiled a wobbly smile. 'It's fine to call me Vivienne in here.' Then, 'Would you do something for me?'

My heart contracted, not just at the offer of her Christian name but because she'd obviously been crying.

'Anything. Always,' I replied, the words popping out before I could stop them.

'You're sweet,' she replied. She gestured to the four-poster bed. 'It's a bit of a mess, I'm afraid. I think the sheet will need soaking. Or perhaps even throwing out?' She pulled in her lips. 'And I fear the mattress might be stained and need a good scrub.'

'Don't worry, I'll sort it.' Her time of the month, I immediately thought, but when I carefully gathered the four corners of the cloth, it was apparent from the amount of blood that this was more than the curse.

'Don't tell anyone,' she whispered from behind me.

I bundled the linen into my basket. 'Of course not.' Then on impulse, I knelt and took her trembling hands. 'I'm so sorry for your loss. I'm sure there'll be a next time.'

She clapped her palm over her mouth. 'Will there? It's the third occasion I was sure I was…' Her cornflower-blue eyes searched my face. 'Because that's the deal between me and Theo. A respectable marriage in return for children, which I dearly long for too.' A sob escaping, she gestured around her old-fashioned surroundings. 'Why else would I imprison myself in this godforsaken place?'

Chapter 5

Present Day

Christie

I attend Lillian's session with her new psychiatrist, Doctor Finnegan. Her lilting Irish accent belies her old-school, no-nonsense approach.

'It's time for you to stand on your own two feet, Lillian,' she says. 'Your mental health has improved, your Section 3 has ended, and you don't need us any more. I understand this has been your home and safety net, and it won't be easy, but you're an exceptionally smart, resourceful young woman.'

She peers at me over her half-moon spectacles. 'Did we have any Section 17 leave?'

I glance at Lillian and give her a reassuring smile. Despite now being at the Devonshire voluntarily, she has refused all offers to break free from the unit, even for a weekend.

'Not yet,' I say.

'That's where we'll start, then.' The doctor removes her glasses and addresses her patient. 'Leave of absence is accepted as an important part of your treatment plan. It promotes recovery and helps us assess suitability for discharge.' She rifles through Lillian's file. 'You have Granny in Doncaster, I believe?'

As still as an effigy, Lillian stares at the scars on her arm and doesn't reply. She hasn't self-harmed since she's been in my care, but her notes say past episodes have coincided with the expiry of her Section 2 and Section 3 Mental Health Act orders. Clearly this was a woman who wanted to stay.

'And she'd be happy to have you for a few days?' Dr Finnegan rustles her papers some more. 'At your own childhood home, it appears, so that's nice. Isn't it?' She gazes at her truculent patient, then eventually sighs. 'Of course, you should be fully involved in the decision but in my clinical view—'

The scrape of Lillian's chair interrupts her. 'How very civilised. I had no say about coming here in the first place, but now you want to throw me out, I'll be consulted, will I?' She lifts her chin. 'Well, I'll politely decline, thank you.'

When the door clicks to, Doctor Finnegan wafts me away. 'If you could encourage her to…'

I stand and nod. 'Of course.'

–

Rather than immediately go to my patient, I return to the staff room and allow her a few minutes to gather her thoughts. To assemble my own too. Sure, I've witnessed Lillian's sulky stubbornness before, but this is the first time I've seen her eloquent anger, and it feels like a breakthrough somehow. If 'Granny' is to be involved in any visits, she'll have to be consulted, but only if Lillian consents. From her white-faced refusal just now, I know I'll have my work cut out.

Curious about her resoluteness, I flick through her records. Why is a highly intelligent thirty-three-year-old professional woman so opposed to staying with a grandma she apparently likes? When I take her a coffee, I decide for a more direct, albeit humorous, approach.

'So, Doncaster,' I say, blowing on my mug. 'I've never been, but I believe it was voted the worst town in Britain or the like.'

'So I've read.' Though her expression is deadpan, I detect a twitch around her mouth. 'It's the birthplace of Thomas Crapper, the bloke who invented the flushing toilet.'

'Does your grandma live in a smelly pre-Crapper hovel with no sanitation, then?'

Lillian snorts but doesn't answer.

'Ah,' I continue. 'I feel I'm getting to the *bottom* of your reluctance to visit.' When she makes no comment, I try another tack. 'As it happens, I still live in my childhood home.'

As ever, she's intrigued with me as much as I am her. 'How come?'

I don't say that me and my dad stayed there in case Mum ever decided to come back. 'Well, I'm sure that you've gathered how rubbish I am at men and relationships. I tried living with a couple of guys in my twenties, but ultimately I preferred my dad as a flatmate.'

A shadow passes through Lillian's eyes and she stands. Berating myself for my insensitivity, I stare at her narrow back, but to my surprise, she steps to her drawer and pulls out her photo book.

She sits cross-legged on the bed. 'What's it like?' she asks me. 'The house you grew up in?'

I picture my pretty stone-built home. 'A terrace half an hour away from here,' I reply, not really giving it the credit it deserves.

She flips open her album and hands it to me. 'This is mine.'

I gawk for several beats. Set in a manicured lawn, and something between a mini manor and a very large cottage, the beautiful old house is a far cry from the Doncaster hovel I described.

'Wow. Gorgeous,' I say. 'It's just lovely.'

'I know. It was once a huntsman's lodge.'

Goosebumps spreading, I peer more closely. Is that the face of a woman in an upstairs window? But when I blink, she's gone, just like my mum had always gone before I could catch her, vanished in a crowd, at the playground or in Sainsbury's.

I take a breath to blow away the usual stab of grief, but Lillian turns the page. 'And this is the other.'

'Another?'

'Yup. Growing up, I never knew which one I'd wake up in.'

I gaze, confused. The image is of a three-storey stately house flanked by handsome buildings on either side. It's clearly a smallish country estate, the sort of pile the landed gentry used to inhabit.

Wondering whether she's pulling my leg, I turn to look at her. Her expression is odd, but she clearly isn't joking. 'This is your home?'

She shrugs. 'It will be, one day. Both will, I suppose.'

I go back to the photograph. No one, surely, lives in such a huge dwelling these days? The maintenance, the bills, the staff. 'So has it…' I begin.

Lillian seems to read my mind. 'Nope, it isn't separated into flats or become a museum or a nursing home. My grandmother lives there.'

Hoping I'm not gaping, I simply stare. It's hard to equate the strident little woman who visits on a Sunday with the mistress of all this. And why, when there's clearly so much wealth, has Lillian been housed in the Devonshire, a basic NHS mental health unit on the outskirts of Sheffield, rather than in a private psychiatric facility?

'There's no money,' she says, answering my thoughts again. 'The two wings were boarded up years ago.'

'Well, it still looks absolutely glorious. Just those steps to the entrance and the sweeping driveway...'

I inhale to ask my question, but Lillian beats me to it. 'I'm not going back, Christie.' She takes a shuddery breath. 'I won't go back because it's... because it's haunted.' Her eyes luminous, she looks at me fixedly. 'It's haunted by my dead mother.'

Chapter 6

1987

Duncan

Duncan never tires of looking at Jana's face – her glossy skin, sculpted cheeks, chestnut eyes and those astonishingly long lashes. And, of course, her full mouth, which breaks into a grin so easily, so beautifully. But today he's watching for her reaction. He still can't believe she dumped Sheena for him, and though they've only been dating for six months, he knows, absolutely, that she's *the* one. Stiggy and his other flatmates never tire of telling him what a soft dolt he's become, but he spends all his free time hanging out with Jana at uni, and right now he's desperate for her approval. One day his father's house will belong to him and – though he'd never actually say it out loud – when that happens, he wants her by his side.

'Eyes on the road, Duncan!' she's now saying with a smile. 'Though I'm not sure "road" is the word. More a wide walkway or a path? Exactly how big is this estate?'

He's actually taking her the long way around, but he wants her to see the Ridings from its best vantage. Thank God he has the car; thank goodness he could afford it by working all those teenage summers from dawn to dusk, helping his dad with various chores on the parkland, from fixing fences to fertilising, from painting benches to mowing lawns. Anything other than inside the big house. Even though years had passed since the tragedy, his mum still forbade him to go in.

'Look at you. Exhausted and smelly with sweat!' she said when he returned to the bungalow and flopped in front of his dinner each evening. 'I hope this'll teach you that being a glorified gardener isn't for you, Duncan. That you need to work hard at school, go to university and do something better with your life than your father has. And particularly earn more than a bloody pittance!'

'I know; you're right,' he always said to appease her. He didn't bother to point out that his dad had been more savvy than that. Sure, his grandfather had been in awe of the Percy family, dutifully doffing his cap and slaving all hours for the honour of working for them and living rent-free in the Ridings, but when Noah took on the mantle, he asked for either a proper salary to reflect his status as estate manager or the title deeds to the Ridings. Of course, he knew more than anyone there was no money to be had, so the Ridings was transferred, mortgage-free, to him.

Still, Duncan reminds himself, his mum was right about him going to university. Giving her a mental salute, he glances again at his girlfriend. Without Newcastle, he wouldn't have met someone so wholly different to the girls he'd dated from the village; he wouldn't have met his spectacular Jana.

'Ready for the big revelation?' he asks her.

She chuckles. 'It had better be good after this build-up.' The smile falls from her face as the house comes into view. 'Wow,' she says. 'From what you said about it being a former hunting lodge, I expected some sort of cabin made of logs, but it's so much bigger than I'd thought and, well, very stately and handsome.' Her eyes glint with humour. 'It's a comedown from Mum's council house in Leeds, but not bad.'

'You like it, then?'

'Absolutely. Who wouldn't?'

'Other than my mum?'

Her look turns to concern. 'God, yes, sorry. It must have been tough when she left your dad.'

'Don't be sorry. He still turned up at the bungalow for his dinner every Friday – and clearly "pudding" when I'd gone to bed, much to my embarrassment. And they're supposed to be moving to the Costa Blanca when he retires if Mum gets her way.' The old hurt fires in. 'What was far more challenging was her taking me with her rather than leaving me where I was settled and happy.'

'Yeah, Connie was talking about that at lunch.'

He pulls up the car on the gravelled drive. 'Before she was pissed or afterwards?'

'Aw, don't be mean. She was enjoying herself. It's nice to be spoilt, and she's quite a character. I really liked her.'

As they're backpacking to Europe for the summer, the time felt right to meet each other's parents. This weekend it's the Watkins' turn, so they set off from Newcastle first thing, collected Connie and took her for a meal in a pretty country pub. After drinking too much wine, she regaled Jana with her various complaints about his dad and the Percy family, but he'd heard them all before, so he sipped his pint and tuned out.

'So what was the story this time?' he now asks. 'My dad's long working hours and him never being around for her, I'm guessing? Which was hardly going to improve by her moving the two of us out.'

'Yeah that, but—'

'But what?'

Jana's forehead creases. 'Well, it was a bit out there, but she also said she did it for your safety.'

'My safety?'

'I think so. In fairness, she was getting a little worse for wear, so maybe I misheard…'

'Go on.'

'Something about not wanting you to be you tainted by the Percys or the like.'

Duncan laughs. 'What? Having my head turned by stiff-upper-lip tradition and money?'

'No. It seemed more nebulous than that.'

'Really?'

'Yeah. She said all men in the big house die young. She called it the Rutherford curse.'

Chapter 7

1960s

Milly

Though Honora still ruled the household behind the scenes – duly assisted by my mother – Vivienne maintained the dignified role of mistress, donning stylish but sensible attire and attending the expected social gatherings on Theo's arm. At least when he wasn't away from home and spending her inheritance on some investment or other, which was generally abroad and always, ultimately, a disaster.

I suspected less-than-reputable sorts could see Theo and his naive, egocentric ways a mile off. He was a sucker for flattery, so it only took some sharp chap a few minutes to persuade him of his financial genius, and the next moment the money was gone. Watkins tried to rein him in with income earned from the estate, but Theo seemed to consider Vivienne's assets a dowry, available to him to spend on a whim, and so he did.

Despite Vivienne's pained expression when another 'unfortunate collapse' of any given shares or speculation occurred, I never heard her complain, and when I once dared to touch on it, she looked at me with hollow eyes.

'How can I possibly complain about his failures when I'm doing the very same?'

I still stripped her bed and laundered her underwear, so sadly I had no answer to that.

–

More than anything, I wanted my mistress to be happy, but in truth Theo's losses were my gain. He increasingly disappeared to far-flung places to 'check on business progress', and when he was home, he drowned his sorrows in brandy. Vivienne continued to do her wifely duties when Theo was up to the task, and she joined local committees, became patron of various causes, opened the village fete and seconded for Honora when she didn't feel well enough to do the monthly tour of the estate grounds with Watkins. Where appropriate, I duly attended and assisted as her 'companion', but behind closed doors, we were 'Milly and Viv', and I was her confidante and friend.

The wings at each side of the quadrant had been boarded up during the war, but when Vivienne and Theo wed, Honora moved into the west annexe, so the main house was theirs. Viv soon discovered that Theo was as ineffective at saying 'no' to her as everything and everyone else, so she organised a rejig of the first floor before her money ran out. Theo's dressing room – which had more often than not been his bedroom – was moved to the back corridor 'to give darling more room and more privacy', and the area was converted to a comfortable sitting room, where Viv and I could hide from the housekeeper's sharp and disapproving eyes.

Almost as devoted to Rutherford as I was to Vivienne these days, I regularly stood at the panelled windows, took in the stunning view of the driveway and grounds, and thanked my lucky stars, but the splendour of a country estate was nothing new to her. She was from a traditional landed family so she had adopted all the stiff-upper-lip and keeping-up-appearances-for-the-proletariat attitudes instilled by her parents, but in private she was a thoroughly modern woman who was embracing the Sixties.

Though five years older than me, Viv was more the teenager when it came to music, fashion and popular culture. I have no doubt she'd have plastered the ancient walls with posters of Elvis Presley, the Beatles or the Rolling Stones if decorum had allowed, but she brought in several items of modern furniture – including a somewhat psychedelic orange velvet sofa – upgraded the 'gramophone' to a stereo record player, introduced me to 'rock 'n' roll' and tried to teach me to dance.

More miscarriages came, so I was glad to make her laugh. 'You're hopeless!' she'd say, swapping one LP for the next. 'Let's try again, and remember rock is a fast dance that requires rhythm. Listen to the tempo of the music. It's a four-beat rock. You just have to let your arms do all the work, then the legs will follow.'

I loved the intimacy, Viv's touch, her smile and her smell, but there was no doubt that rhythm was not my natural forte, nor was make-up, fashion or hairstyling. Books were still my thing – any reading matter I could get my mitts on, from educational to classic literature to trashy romances – and Viv allowed me to stash a few in her sitting room and snatch half an hour here and there to read them in her leather swivel armchair.

'Thank goodness I didn't need a lady's maid,' she often said with raised eyebrows. She'd wink in the mirror or do a twirl in a lovely new two-piece. 'Otherwise, I wouldn't look like this.' Then sitting me down by the shoulders,

'Come on, Milly, it's your turn. You already have gorgeous hair, but let's see what else we can do to transform you too.'

In truth, save for powder over my freckles, there wasn't a great deal even Vivienne could do to change the fundamental me. And at the end of the day, my mother was in charge of the Victorian-style household; I was still a servant with various domestic duties, so when I left my exquisite escape, I had no option but to don my apron and cap and revert to being the 'girl from the village'.

Chapter 8

Christie

Lillian clammed up when I tried to ask more about her mother's death, but the 'haunting' stays with me all week. God, I know about that. Not a pallid-faced ghoul wearing a white burial gown, not even a human-like hologram or apparition, but the real, living person who was once my pretty mother. Though the sightings are few and far between these days, I still catch her face when I least expect it – in a hospital bed or on a walk, in the queue for the post office or at a bustling market stall, and it devastates me afresh. Which is all very silly when she's wearing the clothes she left in twenty-three years ago.

With a sigh, I load the tuna on tonight's jacket potato and take it to the kitchen table. Before Dad moved to Scotland, we rang the changes every night for dinner, but these days a different topping on my spud is as far as variety goes. Dad brushed shoulders with drug-fuelled rock stars, exotic models and acting luvvies during his career, yet he's a steady traditional sort, so his meals always involve frazzled meat and two overcooked veg. That was pretty much the only good thing about his leaving, and I said as much to him with a wobbly smile before he left. But he squeezed my hand.

'I need this, love. I need to move on and live my life. You're thirty now, so you do too.'

He was referring to that old chestnut called closure, of course, far easier said than done. Because that's the trouble when a person goes missing and they – or their body – are never found. One doesn't know what happened, where they went, what they're doing. Whether they're alive in a dungeon or suffering from amnesia, whether they're dead from killing themselves or accidentally falling off a cliff, or from a person brutally ending their life. Or if they absconded because you'd been naughty or said something wrong. Or simply because they'd stopped loving you.

I picture my dad in the tiny front room of his dour Aberdeenshire terrace. I truly hope he's getting that closure. Love and happiness too. A plump, rosy lady knocked when I last visited him. She presented a wicker basket that smelled of fresh baking.

'For Ally,' she said, a name my mum never called him. 'You must be Christie. He said you were coming up. I'm Ruthie. A long time ago now, but me and Ally once sat at adjacent desks.'

Though I felt a small stab of sorrow in my heart, I was duly polite. 'Yes, I am. Pleased to meet you. Would you like to come in?'

My phone dings a notification, so I methodically shovel in my dinner and look at the message. The hairy monster guy clearly didn't see last week's date in the same light as me as he's asked to meet again. Should I give him a second chance? Suggest I have a rare allergy to beards, but if he'd kindly dispose of it or even trim it three inches, I might be persuaded to down a bottle of Malbec? But what is the point? I already know my shortcomings; I can't sustain a long relationship. I very much like the chase, the passion and sex at the start, but once that wears off, I get the 'ick' and quickly end it.

In short, I'm as fickle as my missing mum.

Rolling my eyes to the heavens, I groan. How do I know that? Why am I so sure she left us rather than died? Why am I certain she's still *somewhere*? That she wasn't abducted on that bright summer's day? Is it really just deep feelings of abandonment and insecurity that anyone suffers in circumstances such as ours? After all, I was only eight years of age. Could a young child really detect something *off* about a person?

Though I've never breathed a word to anyone, the answer is yes. After Dad had left for work that morning, I happened to peep into my mum's bedroom. As I watched from the doorway, she dropped the towel she was wearing and stepped to her full-length mirror. Clearly admiring her own reflection, she smiled and swayed, then donned a bra and panties I'd never seen before. But it wasn't just her black, sexy lingerie that caught my breath, it was the barely concealed excitement in her eyes.

'What are you doing today, Mummy?' I asked her at the school gates.

'Seeing Auntie Marsha, remember?' She adjusted her silky scarf, the leopard print one I'd always coveted. 'So don't forget you're going to Heidi's for tea after school.'

I sigh at the memory. If my mother did catch the bus to visit her sister, she never arrived.

Chapter 9

1987

Duncan

Inhaling the smell of Christmas pine from the tree in the Riding's hallway, Duncan stretches and watches the flames dance in the open hearth for a few minutes. He's stuffed, slightly pissed and inordinately contented on the comfy old sofa.

Back in November, his dad telephoned his university digs. Probably because he never gets a word in edgeways when Connie is around, Noah isn't a great conversationalist, so Duncan's mind thrashed for reasons for the call. He still felt a little guilty about spending the summer inter-railing with Jana rather than helping out on the Rutherford estate, but as his dad put it at the time, 'Don't you worry; I can get a lad in from the village. Rest assured, long working hours will come if it's still what you want. Be carefree and have fun while you can.'

After a few questions about his course and his housemates, Noah cleared his throat and got to the point. 'How's your love life going?' he asked.

Unlike Connie's brazen questions about the specifics of his 'love life', including whether he's using reliable contraception, it was his dad's subtle way of checking whether he was still dating Jana. Which he was and still is. There's no chance he's letting her go, and by some miracle she seems to feel the same way.

'Great, thanks,' he replied. 'Jana's right here and says hi.'

But he needn't have worried about the rare communication. His dad was thinking ahead about Christmas. Did Jana want to join them for a night or two at the Ridings? She'd want to be in Leeds with her own folk on Christmas Day, no doubt, but seeing as she was a Yorkshire lass, she wouldn't have too far to travel.

Duncan now rocks his head towards the 'Yorkshire lass' in question and takes her hand. Perhaps being from God's Own Country has swung it, but his dad seems to enjoy her company very much. He never realised how important Noah's approval would be to him, but it is.

Though his dad went upstairs a good ten minutes ago, he decorously pecks Jana's lips.

'I do like you, you know,' he says in a low voice. 'And you're great with Dad.'

'Why wouldn't I be? He's lovely.'

'You bring him out of himself and actually listen.' He laughs. 'Guess what he said earlier?'

'Go on...'

'That you and my mum are both as pretty as a picture, but that's where the similarity ends. Or something along those lines.'

'He loves her, though?'

'Yeah, I think he does.' He pulls a face at the thought of those Friday night 'puddings' in the bungalow with its paper-thin walls. 'Or still fancies her, at least.' He glances at the smiley wedding portrait on the mantelpiece. 'I've never worked out which year they got wed, but I suspect she might already have been—'

'Pregnant with you?'

'Yeah.'

'Shotgun, eh?' Jana chuckles. 'So, if I got up the duff, you'd whisk me off to church and make an honest woman of me?'

'In a heartbeat,' he immediately replies.

'Really? The full vicar and bridesmaid malarkey?'

'Yeah, why not?'

'You're not going to confess you're a religious wacko after eleven months of keeping it under your hat, are you?'

'Haven't I shown you my mitre yet?'

'Seriously though, marriage isn't mandatory, is it? People live together, or they bring up the kid separately. Some consider a termination if the time isn't right. And astonishingly, others go through with the pregnancy and give the kid away for adoption.'

'Yeah, I get all that.'

Though he knows a couple of girls on his course who've had abortions, he's never considered what he would personally want. Having a kid straight out of university isn't something he'd plan by any means, but if it happened... He laughs at the surprising self-revelation.

'Yeah, maybe not a religious ceremony, but I'd definitely want to do the honourable thing, even without a pistol in the small of my back. If, of course, the object of my affections wanted to get hitched to me.'

Jana nestles into his shoulder. 'Good to know,' she replies.

'Does that make me a wacko?'

Sitting up, she gives him a lingering kiss. 'Probably,' she says. 'But I still love you.'

Chapter 10

1967

Milly

Though 1967 turned out to be a year of unexpected change, Vivienne's childlessness didn't alter. She was clearly able to get pregnant; keeping the baby was the problem, and as time passed, she developed a weary acceptance of 'another failure', as she put it to me. I'd quietly deal with the soiled clothes or bedding, kiss her cheek and whisper 'next time', but I could feel the weight of responsibility on her shoulders. Neither Theo nor Honora said anything out loud – they were the landed gentry, after all – but my mother would corner me with questions: What was going on in the master bedroom? Was the mistress menstruating? Were she and the master copulating? It was their duty to procreate and continue the Rutherford-Percy family line!

'I couldn't say, Mrs Shaw,' I'd reply.

'Don't play games, Millicent. Are they having marital relations?'

That expression made me laugh. My mother had managed to conceive me without any wedding in sight, and she still hadn't publicly acknowledged our relationship. 'I don't think it's my place to say, Mrs Shaw.'

'Just tell me!' she'd hiss. 'I am your mother, after all.'

Sometimes I really hated that woman. 'That's news to me,' I'd reply.

I deplored the thought of Theo stumbling into Vivienne's bedroom worse for wear and pawing her, but I did want a baby to grow and thrive, so I set about attending the public library in Scawthorpe on my days off to read up on anything – from medical causes to diet or herbal remedies – that might help her situation.

False rumours didn't particularly bother me, but it felt a little ironic when the librarian – a contemporary of my mother – clocked the tome I was reading on pregnancy and birth. She looked at my ring finger pointedly. 'I know it's the swinging Sixties and that things are done differently these days, but I can't say I approve.' Then, when she didn't elicit a response, 'It must be something in the Rutherford water.'

That caused me to look up. 'Sorry?'

'Haven't you heard?'

'Heard what?'

'Connie Watkins is with child.'

My heart sank. Watkins' son Noah was the estate steward in waiting, and though he and Connie hadn't yet moved into the hunting lodge, it was only a matter of time. I'd been at school with Connie, and she was a buxom, pretty girl with an insensitive, self-absorbed sort of personality. She wouldn't think to hold back about every step of her pregnancy to anyone polite enough to listen and, in all likelihood, moan about it. Given a chance, she'd be in Vivienne's face like a shot, both complaining and bragging. Even now I could hear her breathy voice. *'It'll be you next, Vivienne. At least, let's hope so. Rumour has it you've turned twenty-nine.'*

I was right about Viv's reaction to the news about Connie Watkins. She fell into the worst slump I had witnessed. She stayed in bed, and nothing I could say or do lifted her spirits.

I tried to persuade her to see a doctor, but she declined – the elderly family GP had been a friend of Henry Percy, and his discretion was far from guaranteed. She thought it better to continue with the dignified stance Theo and Honora were employing and ignore the problem.

Impotent and frustrated on her behalf, I mulled what to do. If the possible cause of the miscarriages from my library research was correct, both man and wife needed an appointment with a medic, so I gave up on that fight and instead prepared vitamin-loaded tinctures for Vivienne to drink and offered what comfort I could.

'A baby is the one thing,' she repeatedly said. 'It's the one hope that makes my existence here bearable.'

'I know, and you'll have one; you just need to hang in there.'

'Can you imagine what it'll be like when I visit Watkins or Noah at the Ridings? And suppose Connie's baby is female? You know how much having a little girl means to me. The pretty hairstyles and dresses, the clothes and shoes.' She covered her face. 'It doesn't bear thinking about.'

I pondered on how to proceed for days. Should I mention my theory to Vivienne and cause a great deal of upset? I might be wholly wrong; I may have put two and two together and reached ten. Speak to Honora or even the housekeeper? Well, both were a non-starter: I doubted Honora even knew I existed, and I'd rather have approached the Kray twins than my mother. In the end, I decided to deal with it myself. If I got the sack, well at least I had tried.

–

I found the master of the house in the study, his feet up on the desk and already on the booze at teatime.

'Please may I have a word, Mr Percy?' I asked.

He stared at me as though I'd appeared from Mars.

'It's about Mrs Percy. The younger Mrs Percy.'

'Well, I suppose so.' Fleeting concern replaced his flummoxed expression. 'Is she ill?'

The June sunshine shone in through the panelled window. 'Not as such.' I lifted my chin. There was no other way than to say it. 'I have reason to believe you may have gonorrhoea.'

He pulled down his legs at that. 'I beg your pardon?'

Theo wasn't the brightest button in the box, so I made myself plain. 'It's a venereal disease. I'm sorry to put it so bluntly, but I think you might have the clap.'

'What on earth—'

'It's a sexually transmitted—'

'I know what it is. I'm not a fool.' His face turned a livid red. 'And you are suggesting… How dare you? How dare you!' he shouted. 'Who the hell do you—'

As though she'd been listening at the keyhole, my mother strode in and all but dragged me away by my hair. But I persisted in getting my message across. 'If passed on to a woman – such as a wife…' I shouted as I was bundled towards the door, 'it can cause infertility or miscarriage.' I held onto the jamb and spat out my parting shot. 'If you want an heir, I suggest you see a doctor!'

I was, of course, summarily dismissed by the housekeeper. I was given all of two minutes to pack up my meagre possessions, then marched into the kitchen and pushed out of the back door.

Thank goodness I had Gran in Scawsby to go to. Her eyesight was near gone, but her ears almost wagged with intrigue. It would have been nice to get the whole story off my chest, but discretion and loyalty to my mistress were paramount, so I just said I'd addressed the master out of turn.

'Out of turn, eh? Well, you've gone and done it now,' she said with a chuckle. 'I don't know about the Percys, but Maggie will never forgive you.'

I didn't much care if I never set eyes on my mother again. My only hope was that one day Vivienne would understand why I'd done it, why I'd left without saying goodbye, and that she'd forgive me.

I didn't hear from Viv for three unbearable weeks, which gave me plenty of thinking time. The different permutations thrashed in my head every night. Was my amateur medical sleuthing and diagnosis even right? Had Theo heard what I said and understood the implications? Had he come clean with his wife? If he had, would she ever forgive him, or indeed me, as the messenger? Had either of them been to the doctor for treatment? Suppose it didn't work? How would Viv cope then? Why hadn't she been in touch? Gran didn't have a telephone, but she could have nipped a note around in the car. Did she hate me? And what about me and my future? Without Viv and Rutherford, I felt completely bereft. And I was twenty-four years old now; I could hardly go back into the education my mother had deprived me of.

My heart skipped a beat when I spied Vivienne's blonde bob at our gate from my bedroom on the Tuesday. Holding my breath, I tiptoed out and listened to the conversation from the top stair.

'May I come in?' I heard her asking Gran. 'I'd like a word with Millicent, please.'

'Why of course, madam,' I heard Gran reply in her very best voice. 'Could I tempt you to a cup of tea and a custard cream?'

'That would be lovely, thank you.'

When Gran finally left us to it, I looked at Viv carefully and let out the air trapped in my chest. 'You're not angry with me?'

'Why on earth would I be?' She nodded her acknowledgement. 'Sorry. It was a bit full-on with appointments, then the last week…'

Putting a finger to my lips, I crept to the door and quietly opened it to ensure Gran wasn't listening. When I peered through the window, she was at the front gate, chatting to a neighbour, so I returned to my guest.

I gripped Viv's hand. 'Let's quickly chat,' I said, 'before Gran comes back with an offer of Bourbons.'

–

Vivienne didn't ask me back to Rutherford that day but returned on the Thursday with a determined air about her.

'We've had a family meeting and Theo is amenable, but the housekeeper, who as you know has a huge influence on my mother-in-law, is very much digging in her heels.'

Her hair piled on her head Bardot-like, Vivienne looked simply glorious.

Her mouth twitched. 'But it's not up to either of them, is it? As mistress of the house, I'll decide!' The smile fell from her lips. 'But how do you feel about it, Milly? After the way Theo bawled you out, you might not be willing…'

Why she doubted I'd say anything other than yes, I had no idea, but it was agreed I'd return to Rutherford House within the week.

As for Mrs Shaw, the next time I set eyes on her, she was dead in her coffin.

Chapter 11

Christie

Wondering what we look like to the local residents, I tighten my wool scarf and stroll shoulder to shoulder with Lillian to the shops. Friends? Cousins, perhaps, even with such different colouring? Or maybe just inmate and jailer, as many people see the Devonshire. Whichever it is, I definitely like her, and though I want her to find a home and live a happy life soon, I will miss her too.

I resist the urge to slip my arm into hers. Getting too attached to a patient is unprofessional and smudges the edges of objectivity, which is vital to help them get better. But everything is fine; I'm simply a little lost at the moment, and empathy is a good thing. We're both only children; we've both lost a mother. In some ways, a father too. My dad even took the bloody dog.

'What are you thinking about?' Lillian says.

I turn in surprise. 'That's the sort of question I'm supposed to ask you.'

'You go first.'

'My... well, *our* dog, I suppose. On balance it wasn't fair to leave him home alone all day, so my dad took Sammy with him to Aberdeen, even though the poor thing is a Yorkshire terrier as opposed to a—'

'Scottie?'

I laugh. 'Precisely.'

'So why has your dad moved away?'

The honest answer is a step too close to self-disclosure, but I picture his baker friend Ruthie and a thought occurs. 'To get his end away, I suspect,' I say dryly. 'How about your dad? Did he meet anyone else after your mum died?'

'So you want to know about my father.' Lillian raises her pale eyebrows. 'Very smoothly slipped in.'

'And very smoothly avoided.'

'Nope,' she replies. 'I can't remember that much from when I was really little, but my mother never settled anywhere for long. She'd be at the Ridings one week, Rutherford the next, then God-knows-where.' She squints. 'She was like a wasp you can't bat away, and yet you can't quite work out where it is either.'

Though intrigued, I flinch at her analogy. A wasp. A buzzing insect that stings. My own mum was many miles away from that, and yet I can feel Lillian's hurt. We both had mothers who abandoned us.

'Dad tried to give me stability, but he worked long hours, so when Imo was on one of her hippy walk-abouts…' She blinks. 'Imogen. My beautiful and insubstantial mother even then. So, I'd go over to Rutherford and spend time with my grandmother.' As though picturing it, she chuckles. 'There were a million other rooms, but Granny liked – and still does, I assume – her first-floor sitting room. You should see it; an orange sofa and a leather swivel chair. Not to mention a whole bookcase of vinyls. It's pretty much a Sixties time warp.'

'You sound very fond of it.'

'I am,' she replies, her tone abruptly snappy. 'But I'm an adult, and I have no intention of living there again.

You can snigger all you like, but I know what I saw. The privations of boarding school were bad enough, but when I came home for the holidays and had to stay there… Well, I was afraid to go into my bedroom, then when I'd used up every excuse in the book to procrastinate and finally got into bed, I was desperate to sleep, yet fearful of it too. Because that's when I'd see her, or hear her, even smell her. It was horrible.'

Though the late February wind is already sharp against our cheeks, I feel a deeper shiver pass through me. The apparitions are, in all likelihood, childhood nightmares or even sensory hallucinations, but I'm both spooked and fascinated.

I pull Lillian to a bench and sit down. 'I'm not sniggering, Lillian. I wouldn't dream of that. Honestly.' I lift my hands. 'I have no idea if ghosts exist, but I guess it's subjective. If you see one, then they do to *you*, and that's what counts.'

She doesn't reply, so I take a breath. 'Did you tell anyone?'

'My grandmother, of course, but…' She frowns. 'But when I tried to explain, she was… well, dismissive, I suppose. She was lovely, but she'd hush it away by saying it was just a bad dream, that I should close my eyes and try again because all young ladies need their beauty sleep. And I couldn't be too specific. Imo was her daughter, and she'd been so devastated when it happened, I didn't want to add to her grief. So I just said I was spooked.'

'How about your dad?'

She fumbles to light a cigarette. 'I wanted to say something, but the subject of Mum was… Well, he had his own problems to cope with.'

Wondering what they were, I nod. Of course, his wife had died, yet I sense something more. When Lillian doesn't elaborate, I squeeze her hand. 'How did this make you feel? Suffering so much and not being able to share it with anyone?'

She shakes her head. 'Part of me was relieved.'

'Why?'

'I don't know. Genies and bottles, cans of worms, Pandora's box.'

'I'm not following.'

'Curses, Christie. Curses that lurk in the walls of Rutherford. That's what the locals said at school. As a small kid you don't pay much attention, but when death...' Despite the foreboding in her eyes, she looks at me solidly. 'Which is why I won't be returning to Granny.'

'Understood. Neither I nor anyone else will make you go anywhere you don't want to be, either for a short time or permanently. OK?'

'Good.' She roughly blows her nose. 'I do miss her, though.' She fleetingly smiles. 'My grandmother, that is, not Imogen. Well, not much these days.'

'Presumably, you'll see her on Sunday as usual?'

'Sunday?' She squints for a beat, then chuckles. 'Oh, that isn't my granny, that's Milly.' Her smile fades. 'I haven't seen Granny in person since I moved to London.'

I mentally do the maths – she must be talking about a period of around ten years – a huge shame when Lillian clearly thinks so lovingly of her.

'But we used to FaceTime and now we write letters, so...'

'Is your granny infirm, then?'

'God no. Both she and Milly are as fit as fiddles.' She sighs. 'Apparently Granny was due to sell up and buy somewhere more manageable, but when Mum didn't come home, she vowed she'd stay at Rutherford until she appeared. She hasn't left the house since.'

It sounds so familiar I hope the shudder which ricochets through my whole body doesn't show. 'You mean Imogen went missing?'

Lillian's eyes seem to flicker. 'No. At least not for long. She was in a car accident and she died.'

I find myself staring. Though I can't say what, something feels off about Lillian's story. There's an impulse to shake her and get the truth out, but I can hardly do that, so instead I go back to the woman who visits her each Sunday. 'So, who is Milly?'

'Oh, Milly is the housekeeper.' Her lips twitch. 'But for you and the general public, she's to be addressed as Mrs Shaw.'

Chapter 12

1968

Milly

Though Honora seemed to shrivel a little more each day without her formidable Mrs Shaw beside her, the New Year celebrations were particularly joyous in Rutherford House. A new baby was on the way! Five months had passed, and Vivienne's growing bump was clear for all to see, so it was considered safe enough to have a party and announce her pregnancy to the world.

It was unsettling to witness Connie Watkins hold on to Noah's arm and swan around the faded yet opulent front parlour like a celebrity, but I didn't mind watching from the wings with Cook and her kitchen maid. Honora's safe world had already been badly shaken by the housekeeper's death and 'modern times', so I was happy to respect her traditional ways and stay with the staff out of sight.

Vivienne's face and whole demeanour were a joy to see. Her happiness positively glowed as she moved from guest to guest, chatting for a few minutes before moving on. Though the thought of the '*discharge from the tip of the penis, which may be white, yellow or green*' and '*swelling of the foreskin*' extracts from the medical tomes I had read still revolted me, I had to concede that Theo seemed happy too. I didn't know the detail of the visits to a private doctor last year, but I suspect he'd been given a good talking-to about lifestyle choices – as well as antibiotics – as he was around Rutherford more and drinking less. Or perhaps the admonishment had come from his wife, as there was no doubt the balance of power in the household had changed.

With a nod of approval, I looked down to straighten my crisp apron, but when I glanced up again, my smile fell. With her annoyingly attractive post-pregnancy curves, Connie was waddling towards Viv. 'You're due in April, I believe?' she asked with a winsome smile.

'Yes, that's right.'

She inspected the mound of Vivienne's belly. 'A boy, mark my words.'

'Oh really?'

'It's a boy shape. Like I was with my Duncan.'

Though I knew Vivienne would prefer a baby girl, she donned a bright beam. 'Let's hope so! Theo will be delighted.'

'Ooh, just think! They'll be in the same year at school.'

'Yes, I suppose they will.'

'The lads'll be playmates, then. Even best friends.'

Catching Connie's pally nudge, I tutted and began to turn away, but her loud voice echoed through the old doorway. 'Maybe us too, eh? Now I'm all settled in at the Ridings, we're only a stone's throw away, so we can have toddler get-togethers, teas and the like.' She tittered. 'Or preferably a girl's night out down the pub.'

I straightened my shoulders and made for the stairs. Connie and Viv as best friends? Over my dead body.

The labour started unexpectedly early. Vivienne was at the Ridings, having a rest between her rounds of the estate with Noah Watkins, and fortunately there was a telephone to hand. Apparently, Connie had left with Duncan in his pram only minutes before, so at least that was something. She'd already become a little too familiar with Vivienne, trying to ingratiate herself with the Percy family, even though she'd always called them the stuck-up 'hoity-toity'. Once or twice she'd had the cheek to sashay up the Rutherford steps and ring the doorbell, even though she hadn't been invited. Mrs Shaw would have turned in her grave, but Viv politely stood on the veranda and listened to Connie spouting birth tips as though she was the flaming midwife rather than a tuppenny barmaid.

Ironic though it felt, my mother's tales of her midwifery days at Rutherford House flooded back that long night. I could almost see her standing at Vivienne's shoulder and handing out her calm and pragmatic commands: deeply breathe through the pain; don't push too early; wait until your body tells you; focus on the prize at the end.

I'd hardly been her 'prize', but I was excited for Vivienne to have hers after so many years of trying. More than anyone I knew, she deserved this baby, and I wanted to do all I could to ensure its safe arrival despite her frequent tears.

'I never knew it would be so very painful,' she repeatedly said.

I bit my lip to hold back my own emotion. 'Together, we can do this,' I replied.

Frederick Charles Rutherford Percy was born a month early, on the Ides of March, as it happened. If Vivienne was disappointed not to have a girl, she didn't show it. Instead, she finally smiled and kissed his downy head. 'He's beautiful, isn't he, Milly?'

Choked with tears, I nodded my reply. 'Shall we call in his daddy?' I eventually managed.

I suspected the whole household had hovered in the corridor and listened through the night, as Theo appeared only moments after being called. He shuffled in and peered at the tiny tot, now swaddled in a soft blanket.

After several moments, he cleared his throat. 'May I?' he asked his wife.

'Of course,' she replied, searching his face for approval.

Vivienne needn't have worried. His eyes already doting, he carefully scooped up his child and turned to Honora. 'We have a son, Mother. We have our heir.' Then, with a peck on Vivienne's forehead, 'Congratulations, darling.'

Everyone duly cooing and admiring, little Freddie was passed from pillar to post. When he reached my arms, I studied him properly. Vivienne had her newborn; I'd care for him and love him as much as I did her, but he was a scrawny little thing and as light as a feather. For my mistress's sake, I could only hope he wouldn't be yet another disappointing 'weak and witless' Percy.

Chapter 13

Present Day

Christie

I know I'm giving Lillian and her life too much thought every evening when I'm home alone. But given a choice between that, watching some inane TV or swiping through Hinge with the usual mix of hope and despondency, I guess it's not so bad. What feels more disingenuous – and weirdly dangerous – is my internet research. It took a little while to match the images Lillian showed me with various Yorkshire manors online, but I have unearthed photographs of Rutherford House, its hunting lodge and the Percy family members. In truth, it feels like stalking.

Though I quickly read an article about Honora and Henry Rutherford-Percy's tenure during and after the war and the gradual decline of the estate until Henry's death from pneumonia at the early age of fifty-three, it's the photographs of Lillian's relatives which draw me in. I study the sepia-toned portraits of fur-coated Honora and bearded Henry, then move on to the next generation, the handsome Theo and his undoubtedly beautiful wife Vivienne, Lillian's grandma. As expected, she's stylish and clad in Sixties garb, even during her evident pregnancy at a village fete, but other than a distant bundle in her arms, there are no snaps of her children.

I sit back, disappointed. Seeing Lillian's granny is interesting, but the person I'd wanted to closely inspect was Imogen, her wasp-like mum.

–

Last night I had a bizarre dream that I lived on the Rutherford-Percy estate. I have never ridden in my life, and the closest I have been to a pony is tentatively stroking a nose or a forehead on walks in the Sheffield countryside surrounding my home. Yet, behind my closed eyes, I was dressed in high boots and a nipped-in tweed jacket and strutting around some stables, looking immaculate. That was the first clue it was make-believe. The second was the huge glossy horse I effortlessly climbed onto, then galloped off on into the sunset.

My lips twitch as I beep into the Devonshire. It wouldn't take Doctor Finnegan long to work out what the fantasy meant, especially me mounting a handsome beast, but when I put my head around Lillian's door, a weird sense of déjà vu hits me. Her room is empty, but as if inviting me to look, her photo album is open on the desk. I glance over my shoulder, guiltily step over and peer at a sleepy-looking stone barn with slits for upper windows and a dusty yard surrounding it.

Though more forlorn-looking in Lillian's photograph, the outbuilding could have been the one from my dream, so I almost jump from my skin when I hear movement behind me.

'Morning!' I say, swivelling round and trying to recover myself. 'Sorry, I didn't mean to be nosy.' My nerves come out as laughter. 'Though perhaps that's not entirely true. I'm as snoopy as they come, which you might just have noticed.'

Lillian's taut expression seems to relent a touch. 'That's the old stable block and bothy.'

'Oh, right. So what's a bothy?' I ask, my heart finally slowing.

'Just a shelter.'

'Interesting. I've never heard of one before. A shelter for what?'

She seems loath to answer but eventually shrugs. 'Traditionally for gardeners, groundsmen and other outdoor workers, I suppose. You know, to have a rest, grab a drink between tasks...'

I turn to examine the image again, but Lillian beats me to it and flips over the page, so I'm greeted with the immensely more upmarket hunting lodge.

'Your home visit. How about there for a day or two?' I ask, my thoughts popping out as words. 'I understand why you're so reluctant about the main house, but—'

'It's empty. No one is there.' She looks at me as though I've lost the plot. 'My father is dead, and I'm supposed to have someone to keep an eye on me, remember?'

'Sorry, absolutely, but what about the lady who comes here on a Sunday? Milly, you said. Couldn't she go across to the Ridings and stay for a night?'

Oh God, I said 'the Ridings'. I almost cover my mouth. Did Lillian tell me the name of her father's place, or did I find it out from my internet snooping? And why the hell am I so intrigued? But she's shaking her head.

'Milly wouldn't leave Granny alone for that long. Certainly not for a whole night.'

I feel myself blushing. On some level, did I already know this would be her answer? I try to temper my excitement. 'Then how about me accompanying you? It would save a whole load of admin for the community care team. It isn't far to travel, so we can do it just for the day.'

Chapter 14

1969

Milly

Baby Freddie lifted the spirits of the whole household. Honora, in particular, seemed to have a new lease of life, emerging from her rooms in the west wing every morning, donning her fur coat and pushing her grandson around the grounds in a Silver Cross contraption that was as ancient as the walls.

I had scrubbed it as much as the old fabric would allow and lined it in soft blankets, but I could see Vivienne, with her love of all things modern, was appalled.

'Would you like me to say something?' I asked her.

'Apparently, it was Henry's and state-of-the-art at the time, so we'd better not,' she replied. 'And the poor little mite only has to suffer it once a day, so I'm sure he'll survive.'

'Right you are.'

I wasn't the housekeeper as such yet, but despite being only twenty-six years of age, everyone treated me like one these days. I would never have admitted it out loud, but I rather liked the respect and, if I was honest, the slight fear. It was a shame Connie Watkins didn't feel the same. Far more often than I liked, Viv and I would 'bump' into her when we took Freddie out for a walk in the grounds.

'Cooee!' she'd say, waving us over. Then, adopting a surprised expression even though she was within yards of the house, 'Fancy seeing you here.' Completely dismissing my presence, she'd take a big breath and launch into conversation with Vivienne.

As gracious as ever, my mistress would stay and chat, deftly dealing with questions I considered somewhat too personal. Was Vivienne still feeding the little 'un herself? Connie had finally stopped, but just look at her boobs, they were more ample than ever, and Noah couldn't keep his hands off them. And how was everything down below? Sometimes it took a while to recover. Duncan was such a huge baby that she'd had to give it a few weeks, but it never did to let your fella down, so she'd thought of other ways to keep a smile on his face. Not that she'd be having a baby again. Doing that once was quite enough, thank you.

This was all well and good, but on the last of our 'accidental' meetings, Connie delved into Freddie's pram and all but pulled him out.

'How's our Little Lord Whatsit doing today then?' she asked him, rather than us. 'You want an Auntie Connie cuddle, dontcha?'

Vivienne duly smiled her polite smile, so the poor mite was scooped into the woman's arms and jigged around.

'Goodness me,' she said. 'I know my Duncan is six months older and he's been a big, greedy lad from the moment he was born, but isn't this one tiny.' She peered at Freddie's face. 'What a very pale little thing, specially with all that red hair. And he's so very quiet.' She tossed him like a butcher weighing a hunk of meat. 'How heavy is he now?' she asked. Then lowering her voice, she looked at Vivienne with loaded sympathy. 'If you're feeding him yourself, maybe he's not getting enough.'

As it happened, he was already on some solids. He'd also been checked by the GP and was just a small baby. Though I could feel Vivienne stiffen, she was too nice to do or say anything, so I decided enough was enough. A plan was in order to keep the bloody busybody away from Rutherford House.

—

As the year drew on, little Freddie did grow, and when he shaped the word 'Dada', he very much became the apple of his father's eye. His first steps were most likely late as a result of spending so much time on his dada's shoulders, but when they finally came, Theo took the credit, just like he had the first smile and first tooth.

Of course, Vivienne looked on fondly and clapped with delight too, but I could sense her increased feelings of alienation. Honora and Theo pretty much claimed Freddie as theirs, and even at his tender age, they thought nothing of introducing him to 'Percy traditions', which included holding ancient pistols, watching a farmyard hen take its last breath before dispatch to Cook, and sitting atop one of Theo's glossy Arabians.

Viv still loved her music, make-up and clothes, but her attempts to dress her child in the fashion of the time were thwarted by Honora on the grounds of, 'A little too modern for a boy, don't you think, dear? Money might be tight, but we do still have our status to think of.'

It was clear to me that Vivienne needed her much-desired baby girl, and siblings were surely a good thing, so I took a big breath and broached the tricky subject. 'It's time,' I said. 'Time to do it all again.'

She knew exactly what I meant and immediately shook her head. 'No, Milly. I've been blessed once and have Freddie.'

'And you'll be blessed again. Why shouldn't you be?'

She smiled thinly. 'Conception to begin with…'

The whole venereal disease episode was something we never mentioned, but I was sure she had the same visuals as I had, not just of the clap itself but how Theo came to have it. Yet at the end of the day, repugnant though it might be, his part in the coupling was necessary.

'See it as a mere five-minute means to an end,' I replied.

'And the dreadful pain of childbirth. I never realised just how horrible it would be.'

'But soon forgotten.' I took her hand and squeezed. 'What did we say the last time? Focus on the prize! That's what makes the bad bits so very worthwhile.'

I could see excitement overcoming her trepidation. 'Just think, Viv,' I said. 'A new decade, a new baby. I just know it'll be a girl this time. And this baby will be all yours.'

Chapter 15

Present Day

Christie

Though I could drive the motorway route, I take the more scenic path along the Dearne Valley to Doncaster. It's longer and involves a million roundabouts, but I need time for my heart to settle. Which is all very silly. However nervous I am, my passenger must feel it tenfold. We're headed to the place where her father was found inexplicably dead in his bed at the young age of fifty-four. The thought sends a shiver down my spine. My own father is only a little older, and his leaving Sheffield still feels as though something has ruptured in my chest. God knows how I'd cope if he was taken from me forever.

I glance at Lillian, silently puffing away at a cigarette beside me. Would I have a complete meltdown like she did? Perhaps. But I hope it wouldn't be quite so dramatic or public. According to her records, she received the dreaded call from her grandmother at work, made her way up the tiers of her office building until she reached the top, then climbed over the bannister and screamed down to the busy lobby below. No one could quite hear what she was saying, but she was clearly ranting, deranged with shock and grief, and the emergency services were immediately called. Thank goodness some brave passer-by on the sixth floor had the gumption to grab her from behind and hold on; otherwise, there would have been another tragic ending.

'It's a tooth for a tooth,' she apparently repeated, wide-eyed and tearless, when security staff helped her colleague drag her back to safety.

God knows what that meant. She completely shut down after that, was sectioned for her own safety and brought back to Yorkshire at Granny's behest. Though the section was lifted, she's still with us on a voluntary basis, which is why, I have to remind myself, we are here.

–

The hunting lodge is as beautiful as it was in the photographs, but there's a forlornness about it. Perhaps it's the frosty side lawns which are in dire need of a trim or the overgrown bushes and privet hedges, but the shudder which shoots through me is similar to when I first saw a dead patient – the body is there, but the soul has gone.

I pull up the car by the pillared entrance and turn to my silent companion. 'Ready?' I ask.

She nods but doesn't move. I'm on the point of speaking again when she juts up her chin, flings open the door and climbs out. But instead of going to the front as I expect, she tromps across the driveway and disappears around the side of the house. I scramble out with my bag of goodies, finally catching up with her as she disappears into a wooden shed. When she emerges again, she's holding a key.

'Oh, I thought...' What had I assumed? That she'd made arrangements to open up with her grandma's housekeeper, I suppose. But she's already unlocked the back door and disappeared, so I follow her in.

Hearing the rattle of her footsteps up the stairs, I move towards them, but on second thoughts, I decide she's entitled to her privacy and to determine how the day should go, so I stay on the ground floor. Yet her calling the shots is the very problem; since agreeing to the visit, she's said little.

With a view to brewing up, I take out coffee and milk from the provisions I've brought, but to give Lillian a little time, I explore the downstairs, my awe, excitement and envy increasing with every step I take. How I'd love to live somewhere like this with its wooden ceiling beams, panelled sash windows and open fireplaces in every room. Yet there are feelings of sadness too; it looks as though the house is exactly how Lillian's father left it, fairly tidy but with the telltale signs of a man living alone – a single crystal tumbler beside a brandy decanter, a folded newspaper, a pile of glossy hardbacks on various sports.

I move to the hearth and inspect a line of framed photographs. From a shrinking violet in ballet shoes to a confident-looking graduate in a mortarboard, they're all of my patient at different stages of her life. Some have her father in them, and though there are more images adorning one recess, none of them include a woman who might be Imogen, which seems somewhat strange. In my home, there aren't as many snaps of me and my parents as I would like, yet they all line the wall of my staircase so I can say hello to my mum each time I climb them.

I peer more closely at Duncan Watkins. Tall, attractive and blond, yet somehow dead-eyed, he looks familiar. But then he would, as he's the spit of his daughter.

'Why none of Imo?' I quietly ask him. 'Was it too painful to look at her? Or perhaps you didn't love her?'

'Or maybe he was scared.'

I jerk around at the sound of Lillian's voice. My cheeks burning, I swallow. 'Sorry?'

'Maybe he knew she'd come for him one day. To punish him. Maybe she did.'

A shiver trickles down my spine. 'Why would she want to—'

But my sentence is cut off by the crunch of tyres on the driveway. We both turn to the window and watch a tall man around our age climb from an old Land Rover. Lillian tugs me away.

'Hide. Don't let him see us.'

We retreat to the kitchen, crouch down and listen to the sound of the doorbell, shortly followed by the knocker. 'Don't answer,' she hisses.

My heart is ridiculously thrashing. 'Why not?' I ask.

Wide-eyed, she stares at me. 'What's he doing here?'

I almost laugh at this ludicrous situation. 'I have no idea! Who is he?'

'No one,' she says eventually. 'Just someone from the village.'

Chapter 16

1988

Duncan

Although it's only Easter and still several months off, it feels as though Duncan and Jana talk about nothing other than their twelve-week tour of South East Asia beginning in June – the order of places they'll visit, the cost of the flights, the jabs, the currency, the kit they'll need.

The spring sunshine on their shoulders, they are walking off the Sunday roast they've just had at the Ridings. To Duncan's surprise, his mother turned up and even contributed a pudding. But that's Jana for you – with her usual charm and light touch, she called Connie during the week and persuaded her to 'join in the fun'. And the meal was indeed fun. Until his mum had too much to drink, at least.

'So, are we agreed on Thailand, Laos, Vietnam then Cambodia?' Jana now asks.

He stops for a kiss. 'Whatever you say. You know your wish is my command.'

'Behave! We need to be serious about this before we start shelling out money.'

He inhales the tang of manure. It'll be strange not being here and helping his dad for the summer months, but he's excited to explore places he's never been. 'Yes, agreed. Then island-hopping in Thailand at the end. Including Phuket.'

'Great. So, breaking it down further.' Jana counts on her slim fingers. 'Bangkok, five days, Chiang Mai, four, then Chiang Rai for—'

She stops and squints into the distance. 'Who's that ogling us from her horse? I've felt her eyes burning my back for the last five minutes.'

Duncan looks too. To his surprise, it's Imogen Percy, sitting straight-backed on one of her dad's old Arabians.

'It's a blast from the past. I haven't set eyes on her in years.'

'And she is?'

He lifts his arm in greeting but – not surprisingly – she doesn't wave back. 'She's Vivienne Percy's daughter.'

Her auburn hair flying behind her, he watches her gallop away. During the summers he worked for his dad, he came across her from time to time at the stables, and even as a girl she was an accomplished rider. 'Yeah, Imogen Percy. She went off to some posh finishing school, or whatever they call them, but I guess she must now be around eighteen and back home.'

'Shouldn't she be wearing a riding hat?'

'It would be wise, but she's on her own land, so...'

'Well, I'd call it pretty stupid. What was she like?'

He's not sure how to answer. As a very small girl, she'd constantly stare at him and give him the creeps. Then, when they were a little older, she acted as though he wasn't there, and on the occasions she had to speak to him for one reason or another, she made it clear what their respective rankings were. Not that he blamed her after what happened that last summer. 'A bit haughty and spoilt, I suppose.'

Jana takes his hand and tugs him away. 'As one would expect of the landed flaming gentry.' She chuckles. 'Connie doesn't have much time for the Percys, does she? Their housekeeper, too. What did she call the poor woman?'

'Freaky,' he mutters. He knows Jana is intrigued by the Percy clan, but he wishes she didn't encourage his mum by listening so intently to her alcohol-infused tales.

'And is she?'

'What?'

'Freaky?'

He pictures Mrs Shaw and thinks about that one. Neat, slim and perhaps a little stern, she's always looked pretty normal to him. 'No, not really. She's an old-fashioned spinster type, I guess, but very loyal to the family.' He snorts. 'An idea my mum clearly struggles with.'

'Oh, come on, Connie isn't that bad. She's always wanted what's best for her beloved boy.'

Duncan rolls his eyes. 'Who's that then?'

'Same as my beloved boy, as it happens.' Jana falls silent for a while, then gives him a sidelong glance. 'What she said about the brother. Is that true?'

The usual guilt spreading, he inwardly sighs. Even after all these years, he doesn't want to think about Freddie Percy, let alone talk about him. 'Put it this way,' he replies. 'Take what Mum says with a huge dose of salt.'

Chapter 17

1970

Milly

Fearful of being caught short again, Vivienne stayed housebound a month before the baby's due date. Yet even before she was born, Miss Imogen Bernardine Rutherford Percy was a proper little madam by doing things her way and arriving almost two weeks late. But in fairness to her, once she'd decided to greet the world, she did it very quickly, arriving twice as fast as her big brother. Twice as hardy and heavy too.

There was no need to call in Theo and Honora this time, as Imo immediately made her presence blaringly known.

As the family gathered around the bed to peer at the latest Percy, even Honora chuckled. 'Goodness me, look at that cross face! I think we've all disturbed her nine-and-a-half-month slumber.'

'Indeed,' Theo said. 'But what a beauty already.' He looked at his son, as ever in his arms. 'This is your little sister, Fredster. As her big brother, you'll be in charge, look after her and make sure she stays safe. What do you reckon? Thumbs up or thumbs down?'

Freddie covered his ears by way of an answer, which brought on another round of laughter.

'I'm with you, son. A rather loud little lady. Something tells me we'll not get much peace around these parts any more.'

He wasn't wrong.

–

As the months went by, Theo and Freddie continued to do their 'boy things' at the stables, in the fields or the farmyard, but the rest of the household were running around Imo. In truth, we were all smitten. She was indeed a noisy and demanding little miss, but just as my or Cook's patience grew dangerously thin, she'd turn on a sixpence, don her sweetest smile and reach out her arms for a cuddle. I suppose we knew she was playing us somehow, but her affection was frankly irresistible. As for Vivienne, her love for her daughter was set in stone the moment she was born, and I saw from her glowing eyes that nothing and no one would ever smash it.

But I wasn't jealous, not one jot. 'We're a team, you and I, Millicent Shaw,' she said after the birth. 'And now we have a new member.'

As the early Seventies rolled on, Freddie watched his little sister charge around the house and gardens in awe. She crawled, walked and talked far sooner than he had, and before long she was as tall as him. Though she bossed him around mercilessly, she'd endow him hugs, too, so he was happy to abandon his short-lived role of leader and become a loyal follower.

To my surprise, one or two of Theo's foreign invest-ments came good, and though he was loath to leave his happy family for long, he spent some periods away. As intuitive as ever, Imo took advantage of these breaks by asserting her authority over her brother even more.

'What on earth have you been doing, Frederick?' Honora would demand when he turned up covered in mud and sporting a new graze or bruise. 'Where have you been to get in that state?'

'With Imo,' he'd reply, gesturing to his sister. But Imogen would be right behind him, dirt-free and wide-eyed.

'We were racing and he tripped,' or 'We were playing hide and seek in the barn and he fell,' she'd say with a shrug. 'He isn't as strong as me.'

There was no doubt that Imo was stronger, fitter and faster than Freddie. She was smarter, too, and knew not to mention their climbing great oaks, balancing on the old attic beams like gymnasts, circumferencing the ancient well or riding the larger ponies when they were still far too small. And though she said to Vivienne, 'Me and Freddie do everything the same when we play. I don't make him do anything he doesn't want to do, Mummy,' I caught a goading look in her green eyes when she took her brother's hand, and I wondered if that was entirely true.

Chapter 18

Present Day

Christie

Still crouched in the Riding's kitchen, I feel Lillian start to shake beside me, but when she stands, she's laughing. I gaze in surprise, not only at her belly laugh but at her whole carefree demeanour. It's as though she's climbed from the outer shell of her body and revealed the ten-year-old inside. And that girl is so recognisable, it takes my breath because I also had to grow layers of skin on top of the vulnerable, grief-stricken child. But I have my dad, I remind myself; I had him then too.

She must sense I have a question as her smile abruptly falls. 'What?' she asks.

'If you don't mind my asking, when your mum died, why did you go to boarding school?' I gesture to yet another affectionate snap of her and Duncan on the kitchen dresser. 'You and your dad clearly had a special bond...'

'Granny decided it was best all round.'

'But your dad must have needed you as much as you needed him...'

'The police were here every two minutes, all right?' she says crisply. 'Or taking him into the station for questioning. It was horrible.'

I try not to show my shock at this new information. 'Oh, I see. I'm so sorry to hear—'

'And I was due to go to St Hilary's when I was eleven anyway, so after the summer, that was that.'

She moves away, but I can't let it go. 'I thought your mum's death was a car—'

'It was. But she was gone for longer than usual, so he reported her as missing.'

'And even so, the police...?'

'They always assume it's the husband, don't they?'

I think of my own missing mother. Sure, they questioned both me and my father extensively in our living room, but the officers were gentle, understanding and kind. Maybe that's because my dad was in a recording studio with witnesses during the relevant period, so had a firm alibi.

I take a breath to ask more, but Lillian sharply interrupts. 'They backed off eventually, so my dad didn't do anything wrong, OK?' She seems to deflate. 'I'm tired. I need a lie-down.'

'OK. Shall I bring you up a tea or coffee?'

'Sure, if you like.' She moves to the corridor, then looks back. 'Actually, I'd like to have a nap. If I manage to drop off, do go out and explore.' She gestures to the front door and thinly smiles. 'Dad loved the land as much as anyone. Even in early spring, it really is beautiful out there.'

My mind rattling with questions, I give it fifteen minutes before climbing the stairs. Though I peer into a room with pretty wooden letters spelling out Lillian's name, I find her in another bedroom, her father's, I assume from the contents. When I reach the bed and place the mug on the side table, there's one pill missing from a blister packet of Temazepam, and she's clearly drifted off.

Contemplating what to do now, I glance around the room. The wardrobes are open, and Lillian has clearly been rifling through boxes of photographs. I'm tempted to look through them, but it feels a step too far. Besides, it usually takes the sleeping pills thirty minutes to fully work, and after my earlier inquisitiveness, I'd hate to lose her trust if she caught me snooping.

I quietly step to the window, look out at the stunning countryside and nod to myself. The drug usually gives at least six hours of sleep, and Lillian invited me to have a recce… I might as well make good use of the time.

–

In case she wakes, I write Lillian a note, find a pair of walking boots and a thick coat in the scullery, then leave by the back door. Wondering whether I'm wearing a dead woman's attire, I walk past my car and head in the opposite direction from the way we arrived. I have no real plan in mind, but I'm acutely aware I'm on private property, so I avoid the main roadway which, I assume, leads to the big house, and I wend around the narrower paths.

After tramping for some time, a clump of tall pines seems to thin, and the building I recognise from Lillian's album comes into view. One half is clearly an old stable, and though I struggle to remember the name of the other, she described it as a shelter for outdoor workers, so I walk to the panelled window and peer in.

Though I can't say why, a spasm of discomfort passes through me as I take in the sofa and dated furnishings. I'm already feeling spooked when the sound of rustling from the woods unnerves me even further. Expecting to see some kind of apparition, I slowly turn around, but I'm greeted by a sleek and friendly black Labrador.

'Hello,' I say, crouching down to stroke him. I read his name tag. 'Hello, Casper. You're a handsome fella. Who do you belong to?'

'Me.' I look up to the deep voice. Bloody hell, it's the man from earlier, the giant who'd arrived in the battered Land Rover. He frowns from beneath his baker boy hat. 'And who do you belong to?' he asks.

Somewhat ungainly, I wobble to my feet. What should I say? Lillian didn't want to be seen at the Ridings, and it wouldn't do to give the game away, but then again, my car is parked in the driveway, so it is obvious that someone is here.

He seems to read the cogs of my thoughts. 'That was your red VW, I take it?'

'Yes.'

'And you are?' I hesitate again. 'A friend of Lillian's?' he asks. Then, 'It's fine. I wasn't going to come in. Since… well, for the last few months, I've been keeping an eye on the place at Vivienne Percy's behest. Is Lillian back, then?'

I take a moment to work out my speech, but a white grin breaks the guy's stony expression. 'I don't usually have this effect on women, especially if they have a beloved moggy called Tiddles.' He holds out his beefy hand. 'I'm OJ, the vet around these parts, but also a friend of the family, so I know about Lillian's current circumstances.'

'Ah.' I return his open, amber gaze. 'Then I'm Christie, Lillian's nurse, here from the Devonshire on a day visit.' I smile wryly and gesture around. 'She took a sleeping pill, so I came for a stroll to pass the time.'

'Temazepam?'

'Yup.'

'She'll be knocked out for a while yet.' He looks at his watch. 'The bothy's unlocked, but I'm not sure you'll find a clean cup.' He scratches beneath Casper's chin. 'We're headed for a shandy and a sandwich for lunch. You're very welcome to join us.' His eyes sparkle mischievously. 'It's a brisk ten-minute walk if you can take the pace.'

I don't know the man from Adam, but I do like his dog, and I might get more gen about the fascinating Percys. Even a snippet about the big house's curse. 'You're on,' I say, accepting the challenge with a chuckle. 'You and Casper lead; I'll follow and try my very best to keep up.'

Chapter 19

Milly

After the gonorrhoea fiasco, Theo never quite recovered his power over Vivienne or the household, but he was immoveable about his son following in his footsteps and attending Eton College at thirteen. Fortunately, Freddie was still only nine, and even Theo agreed that he wasn't yet ready for boarding school. The primary in the village had been decreed too lowly for a Percy heir, so from the age of five, Freddie was driven to a fee-paying prep school in Doncaster by his mother each morning.

'The others seem like nice boys,' she'd say on her return. 'Yet no one has ever asked him for tea or to play after school. Or even to a party. Is that normal?' She'd bite her lip. 'But I suppose it isn't surprising. None of them live near us, and it isn't as though they could easily turn up here and knock on the front door to go fishing or cycling anyway.'

This particular Friday was the last day of term. Vivienne said the usual and looked at me with an imploring gaze. 'Friends are so important, Milly. And someone *local* would be the icing on the cake...'

In truth, our Freddie wasn't quite 'normal'. He smiled his sunny smile and goofed around for us, but he was timid with outsiders. He was still very small, yet paradoxically his somewhat long chin made him look older than his years. Though he never complained, I suspected his peers teased or even bullied him, the bad days evidenced by his creeping into Vivienne's bedroom in the dead of night and curling beneath the rug on her orange velvet sofa.

I knew where Viv was going with her speech and I tried to fend it off. 'How about a party?' I suggested. 'The young'uns have them for everything these days. It doesn't have to be a birthday.'

'I'm not putting him through that again, Milly.'

Invitations for Freddie's ninth had been duly handed out by his class teacher, but those who'd actually bothered to reply had declined. I'd wanted to march there myself and give each little bugger a good talking-to, particularly because I knew as much as anyone how cruel kids could be.

Vivienne persisted with her plan. 'Come on, Milly, you know it makes sense. They're the same age and live a stone's throw apart. And it isn't as though we don't know his family...'

She was referring to young Duncan Watkins, of course. I had no objection to the lad, but my opinion of Connie and her vile gossip hadn't changed since I'd whispered some tittle-tattle of my own in her gullible ear.

Viv's blue eyes were beseeching. 'With Theo away, what else will Freddie do all the long summer holiday?'

'Play with me, of course.'

We snapped around to the voice coming from beneath the desk. Imo had taken to eavesdropping over the past few weeks – or at least we'd only recently discovered it – and though we tried to exercise caution, she still managed to take us by surprise.

'Imogen!' Viv exclaimed, her hand on her chest. 'You have to stop this. You know it's rude to listen to people's private conversations.'

Imo climbed out and straightened her dress. 'Freddie doesn't need friends; he has me,' she said, ignoring the rebuke.

'And he's very lucky to have you, but he also needs pals his own age.'

'Why?'

'Well, you do, don't you? You have lots.' Viv looked at her watch. 'In fact, I'm taking you to Tammy's house in ten minutes.'

I'd personally have called Tammy and the others *followers* rather than friends. Imo considered her retort for a moment or two, but in the absence of one, she flounced off.

'That child!' Vivienne said with a fond chuckle. But she was only momentarily distracted from the issue at hand. 'So, Freddie and Duncan. I could broach it with Noah or even nip over with a peace offering for Connie.'

'No, I'd best do it,' I quickly replied. I'd not disabused Viv's assumption that she'd done something to offend her. Now I'd have to see the bloody woman and water down my creative 'Rutherford curse' stories.

–

After hearing an account of Connie calling Freddie 'a right funny-looking thing', I couldn't bring myself to visit the Ridings. Instead, I adopted Viv's ploy of speaking to Noah when I spotted him on the land. I pointed out that, in all likelihood, the boys would be master and servant one day, so getting to know each other's ways could only be a good thing. Though 'I think you mean employer and employee, Mrs Shaw,' Noah replied, he agreed there'd be no harm in it, and he'd speak to his wife. I'd have liked to be a fly on that particular wall, but it seems a compromise was reached, as Noah came back suggesting the two lads use the bothy as a 'hangout' over the summer.

'I'll freshen it up,' he said. His cheeks pinked. 'Connie's after a new settee, so the old one can go in there for starters. The old portable, a few toys, and a supply of crisps and pop should sort it.'

A tiny part of me had to admire Connie's negotiating skills. Her 'old' sofa wasn't even that old. I wondered what else she'd managed to wangle from the deal.

–

Imo was beside herself when she learned it would be a boys-only gang, all the more so when she discovered the second participant was Duncan Watkins.

'It isn't fair! Girls are just as good as boys. That's what you always say! You said Daddy was wrong to prioritise Freddie just because he is male. Now you're just doing the same.'

'Prioritise' was a long word for a seven-year-old, but it was clearly a comment Imo had overheard. Though it momentarily stopped Vivienne in her tracks, she wanted her plan to work for Freddie.

'Maybe you can join in later,' she said. 'But I mean much later, Imogen. They need a chance to get to know each other first. So you're to leave them alone. Otherwise, there'll be consequences.'

Viv took her daughter by the shoulders and looked her in the eyes. 'Understood, Imogen? You won't go there until I say you can?'

Imo's thunderous expression was replaced by a smile. She slipped her arms around Vivienne's waist. 'Of course I won't, Mummy.'

Chapter 20

1988

Duncan

Down from Newcastle for another weekend, Duncan and Jana stayed at the bungalow last night, and they're now at the Ridings. It rained all day but the evening is balmy, so the sash windows are open, allowing the noises of the woods to filter through. The sounds of amorous foxes, rutting deer and screeching owls are usually comforting as he drifts into sleep, but his mum's usual gossip about Rutherford House has thrown him back to a time he tries hard to forget. Another sighting of Imo Percy in the distance too.

Jana stirs beside him. 'You're still awake.'

'Yeah. Sorry about that. Too many beers.'

The irony of the mating wildlife isn't lost on him. Jana was clearly up for making love when they came to bed, but he wasn't in the mood, so he feigned 'being too knackered'.

She hitches over and nestles her head in the dip of his shoulder. 'Better out than in,' she says. 'Then you'll stop dwelling on it.'

He wonders whether to pretend he doesn't understand what she's talking about, but she knows him pretty well, and this is Jana, for goodness' sake, the one person he can tell everything.

He takes a deep breath. 'When I was nine, my dad asked me to do him a favour.'

'Oh yeah?'

'He wanted me to hang out with Freddie Percy. I wasn't best pleased; I vaguely knew him, of course, but he went to a private school somewhere, and I doubt we'd ever had an actual conversation.' He clears his throat. 'And he was a bit, well, odd all around, especially his looks. It's hard to describe now, but at the time I thought he appeared like a tiny grown-up in boy's clothing. Anyhow, because it was my dad asking, I said yes. When Mum got wind of it, she was furious – she was my mother, Dad should have asked her first, me going to the big house would be over her dead body and so on. I don't think it helped that the request came from the housekeeper rather than the family. I couldn't be done with all the arguments, but at the end of the day, Dad persuaded, or maybe bribed Mum into agreeing we could meet on neutral ground.'

'Neutral ground?'

He faintly snorts. 'Yeah, like a war, which Dad said was entirely in her head.'

'So where was this neutral ground?'

'The bothy next to the stables. Over the years, it had been used for the groomsmen or outdoor workers to grab a drink or shelter, so that wasn't particularly enticing to me either. But in fairness to Dad, he made it nice by giving it a lick of paint, moving in our old sofa, a TV and some toys. When Vivienne inspected it, she added bean bags and comics and a tuck box of goodies, so from the point of view of comfort and treats, it wasn't so bad.'

'But?'

'But it was hard bloody work. I watched the clock until the agreed hour had passed, then hurried off on my bike to meet my mates from school.'

'Did you tell them where you'd been?'

Instead of answering the pertinent question, he continues with his story. 'Then something changed and Freddie came out of his shell.'

He pauses in thought. Was it really the day Imogen appeared at the bothy shortly after her brother arrived? Even though she was two or so years younger, she confidently opened the latch and stepped right in. 'I'm joining in today!' she said.

'Go away, Imo,' Freddie replied. 'I've already said no.'

'You don't mean that.' She wended her way around the room, and when she'd finished brushing every item with her fingertips, she settled down on the couch and smiled a sweet smile. 'So, what are we playing?'

But instead of just complying as Duncan had expected, Freddie repeated, 'No, Imo. He's my friend, and you're not wanted here,' yanked her up by the wrists and all but shoved her out.

He now comes back to the glint from Jana's eyes. 'Yeah, he opened up, and it turned out he was a fantastic mimic, a mini Mike Yarwood. Give him any name from TV or *Top of the Pops*, or even people we knew, and he could do an impression. But it wasn't just that, he was really, really funny and a bit naughty too. I wouldn't have dared to nick anything from Mum's kitchen, but over the summer weeks he'd turn up with various titbits of food I'd never tasted before – smoked salmon or caviar – as well as freshly baked delicacies. Even more daring, he stole a bottle of sweet trifle sherry, and one time, we tried a Cuban cigar.' Almost smelling it, he inhales. 'Meeting up with Freddie was no longer a chore but positively fun. I didn't see a weirdo but a friend.'

He falls silent then, and though Jana doesn't ask, he knows another 'but?' is on the tip of her tongue.

When he finally speaks, his voice is a croak. 'It was entirely my fault. Bragging, I suppose. Needing to show the older lads from the village I'd drunk alcohol too.'

'So you told them about Freddie and the bothy?'

Duncan nods. 'I didn't think for a moment they'd have the spunk to turn up on private land. There was only two of them, but at twelve or thirteen, they were so much bigger than us.'

Even now, he can picture their cruel guffawing, their spiteful 'mong' and 'spaz' prodding and jibes. And especially poor Freddie's hurt, crumpled face before Jonny Cullen took a swing and smacked it.

'I did nothing to defend him, Jana. Not a thing. Instead...' His throat dry, he swallows. 'So fearful of them hurting or turning on me, I was a coward and...' Tears burn the back of his eyes. 'I unforgivably took their side and laughed with them.'

Chapter 21

Present Day

Christie

The pub feels roasting hot after the energetic yet chilly walk here. I eye up my new friend over my half pint of shandy. Although bloody starving, I feel obliged to nibble my cheese and pickle sandwich politely in front of a stranger, but he isn't exercising the same restraint. He ordered two, and he's already on the second.

I lift an eyebrow. 'I gather being a veterinarian is hungry work?'

'Aye, that and being a "big lad", as my mum always puts it.'

I'm reasonably tall, but he must tower a good eight inches over me. And though he's broad, it's pure muscle, if his arms are anything to go by. I inwardly admonish myself for finding him attractive. He has a beard, and though not a yeard by any means, a decision has already been made that facial hair is a no-no, so I try to rein my lustful thoughts in.

'Do we pass?' he asks.

Embarrassed to be caught ogling, I pet the dog. 'Casper most certainly does.'

'And me?'

Though I feel myself flushing, I laugh. 'That depends on whether you still live with said mother.'

'So living with a spouse would be fine, but woe betide a man who lives with his old mum.'

'Something like that.' I like the twinkle in his eyes and his forthright manner. 'So do you live with one or the other?' I ask.

'I left one in Matlock and moved in with the other.'

'Ah,' I reply. 'Sorry to hear that.'

'Yup, a divorcee. What gave me away?'

'I have a good ear for accents. Yours is still pure York-shire, so you must have retreated over the border from Derbyshire and gone home to your *old mum*.' I want to know more, so I casually add, 'Any kids?'

'Nope.' His gaze seems to haze. 'Part of the problem.' He rubs the tabletop and adds, 'I did; she didn't.'

'That must be tough.'

'It was. Especially when she hadn't seen fit to mention it to me at any point up until then.'

We sip our drinks and fall silent for a while. Though I regret my own impulsive directness, I find myself chuck-ling. 'I have a confession to make.'

'Already?' he replies. 'A bit much for a first date.' He theatrically takes a deep breath. 'Right, I've steeled myself. Let it fly.'

'Until last year, I also lived with a parent, my dad. He's buggered off to Scotland now, though.'

My companion folds his arms. 'A low, low blow after all you've put me through.' Then cocking his head, 'You're just about passable, I'd say. How come you haven't been snapped up yet?'

'Passable? Cheeky bugger.' I know from his appraising gaze that he's teasing, but there's something guileless about him, too, a trustfulness that makes me want to share my tortured life history. Which is all very weird, as I *never* do that. 'It's a long story.'

He looks at his watch and scrapes back his stool.

Bloody hell, he's leaving! I'm actually offended. 'Boring you, am I?' I ask sarcastically.

He throws back the rest of his drink. 'Afternoon surgery starts at two, so I'd better head off.' He picks up my mobile and inputs a number which rings his own phone. 'But I'm already looking forward to being bored on our second date. How does Saturday sound?'

Stuck for words, I watch both him and Casper lithely make for the exit. 'Maybe,' I call as the door closes behind them. 'I'm a woman in demand, so I'll have to consult my extremely busy diary.'

I revert to my half-eaten sandwich, but a fizzing excitement in my belly has replaced my hunger. I stare at the blank screen of my phone. Damn. Why didn't I just say yes and pin him down to a time and a place? Did he even hear my sardonic reply? And will I ever find my way back to the stables, let alone the Ridings?

Trying to focus on why I'm actually in Sprotbrough today, I chew the bread absently. Bringing Lillian home to sleep wasn't quite the plan, but hopefully it's a start. And even if my interlude with the giant vet goes nowhere, it's nice to feel admired.

I snatch up my mobile at the sound of a beep.

So our second date, the text says. *I'm a great chef. How about I demonstrate my skills on Saturday? I'll sort the food and cooking. You provide the booze and kitchen.*

Chapter 22

1977

Milly

The 16th of August started so well. Theo was abroad again, but he'd brought a puppy back from one of his travels to 'keep Freddie company' whilst he was away, and Honora had taken to emerging from her rooms not long after dawn and taking it for a walk around the flower garden in lieu of a baby and pram. The rest of the household would be asleep, but of course I'd be up for the handover.

'Thunder is fed and raring to go, Mrs Percy,' I said that morning.

'Thank you. You are such a gem, Mrs Shaw. I have no idea how we'd cope without you.'

Wondering if the eager cocker spaniel – named by Freddie at Theo's behest – would pull the old lady over, I watched her depart with a fond smile. I wasn't sure whether she was mistaking me for my mother or whether I'd been silently upgraded, but I was pleased by her gratitude. After all, that's what my labour of love was about. Vivienne made sure I had as reasonable a salary as finances would allow, but I didn't need money. This house was my home, these people my family; I felt a warm, fuzzy feeling in my chest. One thing was for sure; I'd come a long way from that illegitimate, unwanted and unpopular young Millicent. I had been truly blessed.

–

Freddie was rarely volatile or bad-tempered anyway, but he'd positively blossomed over the past few weeks of the summer. If he wasn't actually taller or broader, he certainly acted it; he hadn't appeared on Vivienne's orange sofa even once, and today he was sauntering around Rutherford with a comical sense of self-importance. It made Viv and me laugh but in a loving, pleased way.

'Bless him,' I whispered. 'It's such a joy to see him happy.'

'So confident too. I think he'll be a changed boy when he goes back to school in September.'

Viv was too nice to say 'I told you so', but she'd been right about young Watkins. After a quiet start, it seemed the two lads rubbed along very well. Of course, I'd seen Freddie pilfer a thing or two from the kitchen, but I'd always turned a blind eye, much to Imo's annoyance. This lunchtime was no exception.

'You saw that, Milly!' she snapped when he hurried out with today's swag.

'Saw what, young lady? And it's Mrs Shaw to you.'

'You saw Freddie steal the cupcakes and didn't tell him off. Cook made them for me! Me and Tammy are decorating them later.'

I glanced at the stove over my shoulder. Cook always made a baker's dozen, and Freddie had had the good sense to leave an even number. 'Well, there are still ten left, which is five each—'

'That's so, so unfair.'

'What's so unfair?' I asked. She knew very well I'd cover for her too. Indeed, I'd regularly ignored her naughty behaviour when Viv would have taken her to task.

Changing tack, she adopted her wide and hurt eyes. 'Freddie's your favourite; that's what's unfair.'

Though far from true, I looked at her pointedly. 'Then you'd better look sharp and do something about it.'

'Then I will,' she retorted, sweeping away as only Miss Imogen Percy could.

–

I didn't see Freddie return from the bothy, but I found his Raleigh Chopper abandoned by the back door.

He usually stayed out until he appeared windswept, pink-cheeked and smiley at the dinner table. 'Is Freddie back already?' I asked Cook.

'Aye. He looked a bit out of sorts but said he was fine and that he'd fallen off his bike.' She tutted. 'I said those things were dangerous. Too heavy or something; it's been on the news. He was all in one piece, though, and Imo went after him.'

My heart heavy, I made my way up the stairs. Like a telepathy of sorts, I already knew from the ache in my chest that there'd been a rupture between Freddie and the Watkins lad. But that was the trouble with happiness for you; something bad always followed.

I knocked on Freddie's door, and when there was no answer, I quietly turned the handle and peered in. His face blotchy from tears, he was lying on the bed, but Imo was sitting, crossed-legged, by his side. For a moment or two, I quietly watched her animated face as she chatted to her brother. Perhaps she was a little too pleased to have him back onside, but I nodded and retreated. I was sad the boy had lost his new friend, but at the end of the day, family were the only people you could really rely on.

–

I was late finishing my chores that evening. As Theo was away, I locked up as usual and looked in on the children, fast asleep in their beds.

'Sleep that soothes away all our worries. Sleep that puts each day to rest. Sleep that relieves the weary labourer and heals hurt minds,' I quoted as I wearily shuffled along the corridor.

I stopped outside Viv's sitting room and took a steadying breath. Shakespeare was right; the innocent were sleeping; all would be well in the morning. But when I opened her door, I put a hand to my chest.

'What's happened, Viv?'

Though she was ready to retire, her face was crumpled and patchy; she'd clearly been crying.

She gestured to the blank television screen. 'Reginald Bosanquet...' Her sobs stifled her words. 'The *News at Ten*... At the very end...'

I struggled to imagine what had upset her so much, but she finally took a big gulp of air. 'He was only forty-two, Milly. Too young, far too young.'

'Who was?'

'Elvis, Milly. Elvis Presley has died in his bed at Graceland.'

It seemed a funny old thing, her grieving for someone she'd never met. But what did I know? Other than Gran, Viv and the kids, I'd never formed an attachment.

I usually peeped in on the children again, then retreated to my own chamber, but sometimes Viv asked me to stay. 'Shall I keep you company tonight?' I offered.

When she nodded, we made our way to her bedroom. As we lay in the dark, I tightly held her hand and tried to comfort her with gentle words, yet she still sobbed as though it was the end of the world.

But it wasn't, not by a long chalk. At dawn the next morning, I found her son dead.

Chapter 23

Present Day

Christie

I'm ridiculously buzzing when I finally leave the pub. It's funny how the best – and worst – things in life happen when one least expects it. Yet someone must have been smiling down on me today; I've apparently been on one date, and I'll be going on another in three days. Even better, the guy in question seems to be around my age, and although he has an ex-wife, he has no kid baggage and lives in South Yorkshire; he doesn't have three eyes, body odour or a worrying rash; he's tall and fit and pretty damned attractive.

And seeing as Saturday will be our *second* date… I feel myself blush at my explicit thoughts of a toned torso – and the rest – but another thought hits. Oh God, I'll have to change the bedding, let alone tame, trim and shave, just in case!

Two echoey chimes of a church bell bring me back to earth with a bump. I'm actually at 'work', and it's time to get a grip. A good two and a half hours have passed since I left Lillian asleep, and I need to find my way back.

Noting the mottled sky and the damp in the atmosphere, I lift up my collar and hurry back towards the woods. But when I reach the gate and peer at the dense greenery, I have second thoughts. In truth, I was so busy ogling my new friend and trying to keep up with his long strides, I didn't pay attention to the journey from the stables, let alone the path I ambled from the Ridings to there.

I open my phone and consult Maps. Though I have to turn it several times to get my bearings, I eventually work out a route through the village. Feeling a little calmer by having a plan, I take a deep breath and get my professional head into gear as I walk. Has today been a complete disaster in terms of my remit? My patient has simply slept, so possibly, probably. But at the end of the day, she's in the Devonshire voluntarily; this isn't a supervised visit as such; there's been no sign of self-harm since she has been in my care; Dr Finnegan has already decided she is not a danger to herself and wants her to stand on her own two feet. And if Lillian chooses to take a sleeping pill in the middle of the day, I have no authority to stop her.

And yet, and yet, I feel the nag of something I can't quite put my finger on. Is it nurse-patient concern, friendly worry or just nosiness on my part? Whatever it is, I feel a pull, even a need to find out more about Lillian, her past and the Percys. And what about Duncan Watkins? From the photographs, he seems an attractive, loving man, but there's no doubt Lillian is defensive about him, almost protesting his innocence too much. And what about his blue-eyed yet blank gaze? Did he do something wrong? The police undoubtedly focus on spouses to check for foul play, but repeatedly questioning the man at his home and the police station went further than that. Did he have a history of violence? Or maybe he and Imogen had been seen rowing...

Imo, Imogen, the wasp. An insubstantial buzzing insect, but one with a nasty sting. What did the woman do to make her own child dislike her? No, more than that. Lillian used to imagine seeing her ghost. That suggests trauma and fear, doesn't it?

The notion pulls me up short. I haven't given my own mother much thought over the past few weeks, let alone 'seen' her or had a 'Mum moment' of panic at the sight of a leopard print something or other. I smile a sad smile. I don't want to forget her, but not having her constantly haunting me is positive, I know. Perhaps getting stuck into someone else's life is a good thing, a distraction therapy of sorts. And yes, the realisation that a contemporary of mine, despite apparent wealth and good fortune, had it far, far tougher than me.

I blithely consult Maps again to check I'm on target, but my stomach does a little flip. Apparently, Village Vets is just ahead. Stupidly grinning, I look up and ogle a substantial bay-windowed, red-brick Edwardian-style house, which clearly doubles up as the practice, then I remember my 'date' has his two o'clock surgery in there, so I swiftly move on.

Spots of water hit my cheeks, so I dig in my bag in the hopes of an umbrella. I find a bucket hat but no brolly, so I squash it on my head, then glance up as a clock chimes again. Thankful only a half hour has passed, I cross over the road to inspect the ancient spire. Considering the clear sound of its bells, the church is a dark, sombre affair. I take in its black door, black windows and equally dour-looking old gravestones, but as I peer beyond the fir trees, I step back in surprise. If I did believe in ghosts, there'd be one in my very eyeline, but I don't believe in phantoms, which means...

I look at my watch to double-check the time. Would Temazepam really wear off in less than three hours? Did I simply make assumptions, or have I been duped? Either speaking to someone or muttering to herself, Lillian Watkins is stood by a boxy granite tower. As though she's just registered the rain shower, she abruptly opens her umbrella, a gash of bright red against the sea of grey.

I stare for a few seconds. Should I interrupt the private moment or leave her alone? But the downpour has become persistent, and wild horses wouldn't stop me from seeing who or what she's talking to.

'Lillian,' I call, waving to let her know I'm there. Yet as I weave through the clumps of thistles, a horrible shiver passes through me. Suppose she is right; suppose spirits show themselves; what better place than their burial? As a mental health nurse, I've had many challenging – and frightening – moments in my career, but they've been with the living and not the dead.

By the time I reach her side, my heart is pumping so furiously that I ignore her questioning expression and force my eyes to the mossy structure. Though a six-foot-by-two iron covering cleaves the erratic grass, I can clearly picture the eroded stone steps that lead down to the door to the crypt.

I blink the surreal image away. For the first time I fully understand Lillian's terror, how she must have suffered as a girl at night in her Rutherford bedroom.

'The family vault, I assume?' I finally manage to say.

She nods. 'Can you imagine what it looks like inside? There's no way I'm going in there.' She rubs the top of her left arm. 'When the day comes, I want to be with my dad.'

Considering her grim expression, I wonder who she was talking to. But she seems to read my mind as she gestures to a marble plaque, a more modern addition at the base of the structure. 'I was telling her to leave me alone.'

The inscription to '*a dearly beloved daughter, wife and mother*' brings tears to my eyes. This is what I've so badly missed. Not only a final resting place to visit and chat to my mum but the closure that goes with it.

'Imogen Bernadine,' I eventually say. I work out her age. 'She was only twenty-nine; that's too soon.'

'Yes. Dying young seems to be a Percy thing.'

I step to the tiered monument and squint at the dedications from the bottom up. The lowest one is hard to decipher, but the next is '*in affectionate memory*' of Henry, then later Honora, Lillian's great-grandparents. Expecting to see the name of her grandfather, I move to the next layer, but it's in memory of two men, Frederick first, then Theodore.

'Brothers?' I ask, turning to her.

She shakes her head. 'Look again.'

With a frown of concentration, I quickly do the maths. Theodore was young indeed, but Frederick...

I spin around in surprise. 'He was only nine.'

'Yes, he'd have been my uncle Freddie, my mother's older brother.'

'Gosh, how tragic. What happened to him?' I ask.

'I don't know.' Though Lillian shrugs, the tension shows in her jaw. 'But Imo once told me Dad killed him.'

Chapter 24

1988

Duncan

God knows how Duncan slept after his confession, but in the morning he wakes to Jana's chestnut eyes, which observe him from the adjacent pillow.

The memory of Freddie's wounded countenance scuttles back. 'You hate me for my cowardice,' he says.

'No I don't!'

Barely hearing her words, he covers his face. Even if she does, she can never hate him as much as he hated himself and still does at moments like this.

'Duncan.' She peels his hands away. 'You were nine years old and scared.'

'But much bigger than Freddie. He was my friend; he deserved my protection, not my betrayal.'

Jana sighs. 'Look, I get it. I understand all those feelings of remorse, but all kids do mean things, the lads who bullied you included. Name me a person who didn't do something rotten as a child. I certainly did to my little sis.'

Freddie's expression flashes in again. The fear was bad, but the look of hurt was so much worse. And it was deeper than just hurt, wasn't it? His pal's heart was ripped out by his treachery.

He takes a huge, shuddery breath. 'He died that night, Jana.'

'God, really?'

'Then Mum packed a suitcase and moved me and her out. She was tight-lipped all day, so I knew something really bad had happened, but it wasn't until we were at Gran's...' He swallows. 'She came up before bed and told me. She had no time for the Percys, but even she was crying. It was horrible; my emotions were everywhere. Shock, sorrow, but mostly guilt. I wanted to spit it out and confess, but I was too afraid to. So instead, I played it out in my head every night before sleep. Then I'd dream I did everything differently, that I'd defended my friend and fought the others off. That Freddie was still alive and making me laugh.' He spreads his hands and sighs. 'He wasn't. He was dead, and I was still the complete chicken who'd—'

'It was a horrible, terrible coincidence.'

'Was it?'

'Yes, absolutely.'

'Suppose he killed himself because of me?'

'He didn't commit suicide, Duncan. Your mum says it was a tragic accident.'

Duncan falls silent. Jana didn't see Freddie's final glance, so there's no point trying to explain. But she rubs his arm after a while. 'Let's take a walk and visit the bothy before heading back. Facing demons is a good way to expel them...'

Right now, he'll try anything to feel marginally better. 'OK, let's give it a go.'

Jana lifts the bothy's old latch. 'Have you been here since?' she asks, stepping in.

Duncan follows her and glances around. Maybe it's because he's a grown man these days, but it's far smaller than he remembers. 'No, not actually inside,' he says. 'Mum whisked me off to the bungalow, so save for the wake, I didn't come back to the estate for a few years, but at thirteen or so I started the summer work for my dad.' He gestures towards the stables. 'It included mucking out, grooming and feeding the horses, but no, I never came in here, not even for a drink of water.'

'It's a bit dated and dusty but still pretty nice for a kid's den.' Jana chuckles. 'My mum's house isn't much bigger than this.' She turns to him. 'So how do you feel now you're here?'

'OK, actually.' He takes her hand and absorbs her warm strength. It's true; he feels fine; there are no ghosts, no sense of anything bad; it's simply an old, homely building. Remembering the laughter and fun for the first time in twelve years, he says a silent goodbye to his friend, then reverts to the love of his life. 'You always… I don't know, ground me, make me feel safe. What would I do without you?'

She slips her arms around his neck and kisses him softly. 'Well, fortunately, that isn't something you have to worry about.'

He feels himself stir. 'How about we explore the upstairs?'

'OK…'

With a grin, he tugs her towards the narrow staircase but stops as a memory rushes back.

'What is it?' Jana asks.

'I did come inside, just the once. Mum was hurrying me away to Gran's, but I needed some stuff I'd left here, so I came back before I knew what had happened to Freddie. It was strange. The two village boys had pretty much trashed the place, but when I looked in, it had been cleaned and was tidy.'

Chapter 25

1977

Milly

I found Freddie's broken body towards one side of the staircase, and though I knew without a doubt he'd passed, I immediately called for an ambulance. By the time it arrived, his bloody little head was in Vivienne's lap. Up until then, she'd been dumb from shock, but perhaps uniformed paramedics and police officers made it real because she suddenly started a dreadful keening which brought Imo to the landing outside her bedroom above. She stared, white-faced, over the ornate balustrade for several beats, then her bare feet were smacking down the stairs, and it was all I could do to catch her before she launched herself on her brother.

'What's happened to Freddie?' she screamed. 'Why is he on the floor? Why is his hair all matted and sticky? Why isn't he moving?'

They were the very things we all wanted to know, and everybody seemed to look up to the first and second bannisters, then down to the marbled floor we were standing on. The great hallway, high archways and tiered, open landings had been designed this way many years ago to show off the Italian-style fresco at the very top, but it was a death trap, a misadventure just waiting to happen.

The memory of Freddie's tear-strewn face from last night edged in, but I firmly pushed it away. This was an accident, a tragic, tragic accident. I knew the pain would come, but for now I had to be strong, a leader. Still holding Imo by the shoulders, I cleared my throat and spoke to the chief police officer.

'Freddie was told many times not to mess about on the landing and certainly not to play on or climb over the handrails for any reason at all. But it wasn't unknown for him to... to be a daredevil.' I reached for Vivienne's hand and tightly squeezed. 'Lads will be lads, I'm terribly sorry to say.'

A loud sob from the doorway made us turn. I didn't know how long Honora had been listening and watching, so I sharply inhaled and waited for her to speak. As she edged towards the body, the officials respectfully lowered their heads and stepped back.

'My boy,' she said, her voice barely a whisper. She groped towards me and held on to my arm. Her eyes were like two empty black holes. 'My boy, Mrs Shaw,' she said. 'How on earth will we tell him?'

–

Noah Watkins was a tower of quiet strength over the following days. He dealt with the administration, the paperwork, the hospital and the police, but even he couldn't track down Theo. The master of the house was apparently in Nigeria dealing with something related to his investments in oil, but Noah hadn't yet had a reply to his urgent messages to get in touch.

The three women of the house stayed huddled in the drawing room, and when I brought them their first dinner on trays, Honora looked at me absently and said, 'You must eat with us, Mrs Shaw. Do sit.'

It was the first time I'd been invited to dine with the family, and quite honestly the kind gesture almost broke me. But I had to blow away the urgent need to sob and be the tenacious, efficient housekeeper for them. And yet none of them cried either. It was as though Honora, Vivienne and Imogen were frozen effigies, incapable of speech or emotion. There was shock, of course, but also a sense of trapped air; they couldn't respire, relax or even think until the master came home. Until the poor man found out his beloved son and heir had died in his absence.

I continued with my chores, sweeping, dusting and cleaning, feeding and walking the confused puppy, fetching and removing cloche-covered plates from the drawing room. Each time I returned to the kitchen with a barely touched meal, Cook would look at me with red, raw eyes, but neither of us had any words. We were holding our breath too.

–

Noah finally heard from Theo after two weeks had passed, and he offered to collect his employer from the airport and break the news to him in person. It was considerate of the man to lift that particular responsibility from Vivienne's shoulders, but I'd have liked to know what he said.

The last day of August was particularly humid. All wearing black, we lined up by the steps to greet Mr Percy. It was too, too similar to the day he'd brought his bride home, but his mother had insisted we do it, and though Viv had muttered 'Really, Honora?', I'd sensed the old lady was hanging onto her dignity by a thread, so I'd quickly intervened with 'Right you are, Mrs Percy' and duly organised the staff.

As Noah's vehicle approached, I tried to catch little Imogen's eye and give her a small smile of reassurance, but she clutched her mother's hand and kept her pale, impassive face forward. When the car finally pulled up, a communal shudder seemed to pass through us all, despite the warmth.

Drawn yet tanned and handsome, Theo stepped to his mother, then his wife and daughter, kissing each on the cheek. He shook hands with the staff, then he turned away and viewed his domain without speaking for some time. Just as the silence felt oppressive, he straightened himself, spun around and took a deep breath.

'Thank you all for your loyalty and support. If you'll excuse me, various arrangements need to be made.' His voice breaking, he looked up to the heavens. 'But firstly, I want to see him; I want to see my son.'

Chapter 26

Christie

On Saturday, I clean the house like a woman possessed. I had no idea it was so dirty, but I suppose that's what happens when one has been as slothful as I have since Dad left. I chuckle to myself. Even if OJ stands me up, the day hasn't been wasted. Who knew a bathroom could gleam like that, or a kitchen floor be so bit-free! But in truth, I'll be pissed off if there's a no-show by my friendly giant man. Having something to look forward to, and give the weekend shape, has been great. And besides, I'm hungry. It feels as though I haven't eaten proper food for a decade.

Squashed beneath her red umbrella, Lillian and I had ambled back to the Ridings on Wednesday.

'Do you want to go into the house again?' I asked when we arrived.

'Nope,' she said, stopping at my VW. Her lips twitched. 'It wouldn't do to miss whatever delicacy is on offer at the Devonshire.'

She always complained about the disgusting cuisine there, so I looked at her curiously. 'How was it today?' I asked. 'The first time back home must have been a challenge.'

'It was…' Her brow creased in thought. 'It was OK.'

The answer didn't tell me a great deal. 'That's good.' I noticed a mobile peeking out of her handbag. 'Oh, I didn't know you have a phone.'

'I do now.' She shrugged. 'It's Dad's. Was Dad's.'

As though someone was watching, I felt a cold flutter brush the nape of my neck. A mobile phone was so personal, I wasn't sure I'd want to look at a dead person's. But then again, we might have known more about my mother's disappearance if she'd had one.

Lillian seemed to read my mind. 'Yeah, a bit surreal. But I left mine in London, so it'll be useful for texting and making calls. I'll give you the number if you like.'

'I would like,' I said, climbing into the car. 'Thanks.'

'So what about you?'

'Me?'

'Yes. You seem… Sort of on a high?'

Light and carefree, a *high* pretty much summed up how I felt. I laughed and turned on the ignition. 'That's fresh air for you. I'd better take it easy, though; wouldn't want to overdose on my first outing.'

I now chuckle a little unsteadily. Bloody hell, it was bad if my giddiness was so obvious even then. I need to rein it in as excitement ne'er ends well. And besides, suppose I don't fancy my date when he turns up? Suppose I get the ick before we've even started? I spray some product on the glass hob, rub furiously and smile at my reflection. There's clearly only one way to find out.

–

I needn't have worried. When OJ arrives at my front door with two bags stuffed with goodies, he kisses me on the cheek as though we've been friends for years and says, 'Cookhouse this way, I take it?'

'It is,' I say, following him in. And yes, even from the back, he's as broad, loose-limbed and attractive as I remember. With a tight bum too.

He turns and grins. 'You can watch if you like.'

I dumbly gape. Bloody hell, is the man telepathic?

'Watch me making your dinner?' he adds.

I nervously guffaw. 'Oh, I see. Good, right.' I perch on a high stool at my tiny kitchen island and gesture around. 'Oven, fridge, cutlery drawer, whisk. Not mentioning the Tellier cherry and olive stoner.'

'Thank the Lord for that.'

'And I'm happy to help. You know, with the peeling and chopping...' I nod to the wine on the side. 'And drinking.'

'A very generous offer.'

Having no idea what he likes – or if he even imbibes anything other than shandy – I went for a red, rosé and white at the supermarket, each costing a tenner. 'Would you like to join me?'

He cocks an eyebrow. 'Some might consider that a bit fresh so early in the evening, but if you insist...'

'Join me in a glass of wine.'

'I would indeed. Whatever you're having...' He pulls out various items from his carriers. 'Does fish sound OK?'

I fetch the Pinot Grigio from the fridge and snap it open. 'Fish sounds divine.'

–

The cooking takes a good hour, and by the time we sit down at the table, I'm a tiny bit pissed. We've humorously fenced about favourite bands, books and films, but we haven't exchanged more personal information.

'So...' I say.

'You're going to ask me what OJ stands for. Or whether I've been on trial for allegedly murdering my wife.'

'Ha ha. Is that the first question your dates usually ask?'

'Pretty much.'

'How many are we talking about?' I snigger at his bemused expression. 'Sorry. I'm a tad nosy at the best of times, but vino exacerbates it, so apologies.'

'Not at all. I like a straight-talking woman.' He spoons in his last mouthful of mackerel risotto. 'Go for it.'

'OK. So you live with your mum—'

'Belinda. But as it happens, not for long.'

'Really?'

'Yup, someone in the pub told me I was a freak for still living with her.'

'Very funny.'

'And I suppose it is about time I stopped sharing a bedroom with my brother...'

'Do you really?'

'Nope. We work together, though.'

'He's a vet too?'

'Pete is. A couple of years older than me.'

'Wow, clever family.'

'Mum especially. She set up the practice.'

'She's still working, then?'

He laughs. 'How ancient do you think I am?'

'Well, it was you who mentioned your *old* mum.'

'She'll be sixty in five weeks, and after months of denial, she's decided to embrace it with a "fuck-off" party, as she puts it. Vol-au-vents, fizz and dancing. You should come.'

Out of nowhere a thump of sadness hits me. My mum always loved a bop. She would be – or is – fifty-five years old now.

'Hey.' OJ dips his head. 'Are you OK?'

'Sorry.' I try for a sardonic tone. 'I should have warned you that booze makes me a bit… wacko too.'

'Nosy *and* wacko.' He strokes an escaped curl behind my ear. 'You're a bit of an all-round disaster, then?'

'That's me.'

'A very endearing one, though.' I struggle to meet his gaze, but his voice is gentle. 'You lost your mum?'

Lost. Not dead or alive but lost. The word feels so apt, it brings tears to my eyes.

I nod.

'And your dad buggered off to Scotland, leaving you feeling lost too?'

I nod again.

'Do you want to talk about it?'

'Yes, but not right now,' I manage. I smile a wobbly smile. 'I might cry, and streaky mascara on a second date isn't a good look.'

He reaches for my hand. 'Let's go to bed, then.'

Chapter 27

1988

Duncan

Preening his hair in the mirror, Duncan belts out 'Everyday Is Like Sunday' with Morrissey. His exams finished later than everyone else's in the house, but he sat the final one this morning, so he's finally free to join his mates in the pub. The plan is to have an all-afternoon session, go somewhere for a curry, then have a lads' bender for the rest of the night.

The timing has worked out pretty well. Jana handed in her dissertation a couple of days ago, so she's gone home to Leeds, which gives him a week to hang out and get trashed with his housemates before his travels begin.

Stiggy and the others have been ribbing him, saying the end is nigh, that Jana'll get up the duff or push him into marital bliss when they return from their trip, and that they'll never see him again. But in all honesty, if anyone is *pushing*, it's him. Sure, he's only twenty-one, but his parents were pretty young when they got married, and though he wouldn't want kids for a while, the prospect of playing house with Jana in September feels good. They've touched on it briefly and have agreed a small terrace with a yard would be better than a flat, but everything depends on getting employment. Jana's psychology degree should qualify her for a wide range of options, but they haven't talked properly about what he will do. She hasn't said anything, but he senses she's not keen on him working on the Rutherford estate. At least not yet.

'I know you've helped out and been paid by your dad in the past, but you'd need a proper full-time job to fund rent or a mortgage. Is there one available there?' she asked at some point. 'And if there is, presumably you'd be hired by the Percys?'

'Yeah, I guess so…' In truth, he hadn't really thought it through. The steward role had passed from his grandfather to his dad, so the expectation – at least in his own head – was there. But his dad is still only in his forties, fit and healthy and devoted to the estate.

'Would working for the Percys be a bad thing?' he asked.

'No, of course not,' she replied. But her eyes were definitely flickering.

He now blows that particular worry away. He has a week-long boozing session with the lads, then three months of blissful travel with Jana to look forward to. She's been unbelievably efficient booking flights and some accommodation, but not all of it.

'Suppose we can't find somewhere to stay? Are you sure we shouldn't sort all the hostels up front?' he asked.

'Nope. It'll be fun to decide when we're there. Then we can be flexible, see where life takes us.' She pecked his lips. 'You know, be romantically impetuous?'

Shaking his head, he laughs at the thought of all those evenings he spent yearning for Jana, slowly making his way across a bar or a club, desperate to chat her up yet never quite doing it. Romantically impetuous, he's not. But he is bloody lucky that everything came good.

He feels his pockets for cash, snatches up his keys and strides to the front door. But just as he opens it, the telephone beside it springs into action. He stares at the damned thing. Should he answer or leave it? Yup, leave it. Though there might be a change of pub venue…

He scoops up the receiver. 'Hello?'

'It's me, love.'

Only his mother could achieve such perfect timing. He feels bad being rude, but if he lets her start speaking, he won't fit a word in edgeways for a good fifteen minutes. 'Can't talk right now, Mum. I'm off out.'

'This is important, love.'

She's said similar in the past when she's called a bit pissed, and it's usually something his dad's done to offend her.

'It's about Dad,' she says, confirming his suspicions.

He rolls his eyes. 'Mum, I haven't got—'

'He's been in an accident. He was on the roof of the new livery stables they're building, and he somehow fell off.'

'What?'

'No one realised until he was due to meet Vivienne. When she found him, she called an ambulance.'

Fell off a bloody roof? Words emerge through the shock. 'He's alive, though, right?'

'Yes, love, he is. But he's in hospital; that's where I'm calling from.'

Duncan's stomach somersaults. This apparently calm woman is his highly strung, excitable mother. Whatever has happened must be very bad.

'What's wrong with him, Mum? What are his injuries?'

'He's in surgery now.' The waver in her voice chills him. 'I'm afraid it's serious, love. He's broken his back.'

Chapter 28

1977

Milly

Freddie's death was a dreadful blow for us all, but I watched Theo carefully. From my own dealings with him, I knew this tragic accident would either make or break him. He was still very much a boy inside his grown-up body, and I willed him to grow into the man he could be.

It felt as if my wishes were working at first. Grim-faced, he arranged and attended his son's funeral with great dignity. He read out a long, beautiful eulogy and shook the hand of each and every villager who attended the solemn service. Though a vigil took place at the big house, he arranged and briefly spoke at a wake in the church hall so the locals could raise a glass to a 'fine young man'.

Much to my disgust, Theo invited the children and their parents from Freddie's class to the private affair at Rutherford. There were precious few accolades, and those clearly coached by their teacher, yet he listened intently to each one. Only one boy saw my Freddie as I did, and that was the young Watkins lad. Of course, I'd kept an eye on him too, trying to discern what had happened at the bothy, but the poison in my heart was diluted by his face, pallid and etched with sheer grief as he headed doggedly for Theo.

'Mr Percy?' he said hesitantly.

'Hello, Duncan. How are you?'

'I just wanted to say...'

I was stood next to Imo, and we both watched with bated breath to see what tortured words would come out of the lad's mouth.

'I wanted to say he was funny. Freddie was really funny. He did brilliant impressions. He made me laugh more than anyone I know.'

To my surprise, Theo kissed the top of his head. 'Thank you, young man. Thank you. That means more than you'll ever know.'

It felt like a sea change somehow, but once the last mourner had left, Theo cleared his throat, announced he was exhausted and would go to his chamber for a lie-down. Days passed without him emerging, and despite becoming headachy and feverish, he declined Vivienne and Honora's pleas to see a doctor, even when his skin turned yellow. Four weeks later, he died, and though no one could change his mother's insistence that her son expired from a broken heart, the post-mortem diagnosed malaria. It also concluded his condition would have been treatable had he allowed it, so perhaps Honora had a point. Or maybe his death in bed was a nod to Elvis. Both men were aged forty-two, and in many ways, Rutherford House had been Theo's Graceland.

–

Honora had lost a husband, a son and a grandson, so I don't know how the poor woman coped. I half expected her to 'expire' from grief too, but the old stalwart was made of sterner stuff, and though she mostly stayed in her wing and ate her meals there, she still saw it her duty to rise each morning and walk Thunder.

It was heart-warming to feel her increasing dependence and affection for me. I realised that dementia was edging in and had been for some while, but it was nice to play rummy or whist over high tea and listen to her chatter about the 1940s, who went to war and when, the staff she slowly lost, and of course the young women 'we' tended, and all those chubby babies that were born.

'And we didn't lose one, did we, Mrs Shaw,' she said with a beam. 'Not one.'

I sniffed away a tear at that comment. Her face was a picture of pride at having given those newborns life, yet she'd suffered so much heartbreak herself.

'Were they really all girls? I can't remember one boy.' Her frown cleared. 'Well, it's hardly surprising. Us women always have been the strong ones, haven't we, dear Maggie.' She grasped my hand. 'It wasn't always our choice, was it, but we did what we had to do.'

Chapter 29

Present Day

Christie

The March sunshine shining through the window, we stay in bed on Sunday until noon, nuzzling, exploring and, when my stomach loudly rumbles, deciding on the menu for brunch and our evening meal.

'I thought cod for dinner,' OJ says. 'In fact, there happens to be a couple of nice fillets waiting in your fridge.'

'You brought food for today!' I playfully thump him. 'A bit bloody presumptuous.'

He pulls me in for another kiss. 'Second date and all that...'

I can hardly protest after my own carnal thoughts, so I change the subject. 'Fish... I'm guessing you're a pescatarian.'

'Yup. I consume pretty much anything, but I give meat and poultry a wide berth.'

'From tending to animals?'

'Yeah. It was mostly farm work in Derbyshire and a few riding stables.'

'You like horses?'

'Oh yes.' He smiles ruefully. 'Pepper was my first baby, but the ex got custody.'

'Custody?'

'Not really. I let her have him along with everything else. Though good old Casper insisted on coming with me. Now my working day is a mix of everything.'

'Ponies, sheep, old ladies and their Tiddles?'

'Precisely.'

I take a breath. 'I miss my little dog. Sammy. Dad took him.'

'When he buggered off to Scotland?'

Nodding in lieu of an answer, I fall silent. OJ pulls me to his shoulder and waits for me to speak. When I do, my story pours out in a rush. 'When I was eight, my mum walked me to school and waved goodbye from the gate as usual. I never saw her again. At least not for real. I spot women around my age wearing her scarf all the time, but of course it isn't her.' I swallow and strive for humour. 'A bugger she was wearing a pattern that never goes out of style.'

He peers down at me quizzically.

'It was in leopard print.'

'Ah. She was never found?'

'Nope.' I picture Lillian at her family monument on Wednesday. 'So I've never even had a grave to visit. No one to shout at for leaving me.'

'And you're the only child?'

I nod.

'So, your father's moving on feels like—'

'Yes, more abandonment. And a betrayal of Mum, if I'm honest.'

He pecks my forehead. 'I'm so sorry, Christie. I can't begin to imagine how tough all the unanswered questions must be.'

'Yeah. So there you have it. Christie Morfett, the all-round disaster.'

Yet it isn't so bad right now; a tiny weight has lifted from my shoulders. Second date or not, I've never confided in someone so soon. Indeed, considering my history of attachment and commitment issues, whatever *this* is, it has become intense pretty damned quickly. I lean in and kiss OJ softly.

'What's that for?' he asks.

I want to thank him for being so lovely – and loveable – but that *is* a step too far, so I reach for humour instead. 'The amazing fishy brunch you're about to make and serve me on a silver platter.' I suddenly twig he's never mentioned his own father. 'So what about your dad?'

His brow creasing, he thinks for a moment. 'Sort of the opposite to you. He kept coming back.'

It reminds me of Imo, the wasp. But presumably, this parent is for real and not in OJ's head. 'So he left the family?'

'Yeah, several times. He was the village bad lad Mum fell in love with and thought she could tame. She couldn't, we couldn't. At least not until—' He abruptly stops speaking.

Goosebumps prick my arms. 'Until, what?' I eventually ask quietly.

'Until me and my brother were big enough to... to persuade him to get lost for good. We thought we were doing the right thing for Mum, but it took her a long time to forgive us.' He frowns more deeply. 'I guess you can't help who you love.'

'That's true.'

The image of my own mother at her mirror filters in. Did she run off with a 'bad lad'? For the last two decades, I've been convinced she left me and Dad for a new life, a new relationship, a new home. That one day I'd find her and see her again. I can't pinpoint what has changed, but now I'm no longer sure.

Chapter 30

1988

Duncan

Duncan stirs in his bed at the Ridings and, as he has for the past three weeks, he immediately thinks of Jana and her sister, where they'll be waking and touring, eating, socialising and sleeping today.

It's the socialising and sleeping parts which bother him the most. The backpacking community form tight bonds, he knows. Will Jana stray? Will she find someone new and dump him completely? Both thoughts are unbearable. He knows in theory he's an attractive catch on the outside, but he isn't smart and confident and savvy like she is, he isn't the full package like her.

And yet he insisted she fly to Thailand as planned. He kicks himself regularly, but he's sort of proud of himself too.

'I'm not going,' she said when she learned the news about his dad. 'I'll come with you to the Ridings and help out with whatever is required.'

As if he was a frightened kid, he wanted to accept her offer. He needed her to stay, look after him and tell him what to do. His dependable, fit and active dad could be paralysed forever; he was bloody, bloody scared of the sudden and huge responsibility which had been placed on his shoulders. And yes, of growing up. But he found his love for Jana was stronger than his own selfish needs. He knew her little sister would jump at the chance of travelling to South East Asia; he didn't want to deprive Jana of something she'd so meticulously arranged and was hugely looking forward to.

'Everything is booked; you can't miss this opportunity. I'll be fine here; you have to go.'

'But it won't be the same without you.'

'It will. Have a blast. I'll be here when you're back.'

He now flicks his head to the adjacent, empty pillow. For most of the past year in the student house, he had Jana beside him like a hot-water bottle each morning. God, he misses her. Her smile, her curves and her smell. How he longs for the easy, fun sex he took for granted. And it's so silent without the noise and bustle and high jinks of Stiggy and his flatmates beyond the door, in the kitchen, the bathroom and lounge. But he has to look on the bright side. He's doing a huge favour for his dad; he'll be paid for a job he enjoys; he can put his earnings towards a deposit on a house with Jana. Which is all the more reason not to stay in the sack feeling sorry for himself. He yanks back the duvet and nods. It's six-thirty; time to get his arse into gear and grab a shower.

–

Ruffling his damp hair, Duncan strides into another sunny morning and thanks God his dad's injury isn't as bad as the medics first feared. Though Noah sustained a severe fracture and other damage to his spine, he isn't paralysed. He is, however, bedridden and will be for up to six months, which is driving him nuts. He was transferred from the hospital to the bungalow, but he's now subjected to Connie's questionable care, which has totally swung from concern to annoyance. Why the hell was Noah on a roof in the first place? He's the estate steward, not a flaming carpenter. Why wasn't he taking more care? The Percys don't pay him enough for working all God's hours, never mind danger money. He should sue them for damages. And why drag in poor Duncan? Couldn't the family have used some agency or other and found someone to cover until Noah mended?

In fairness, his dad feels bad about that. 'I'm sorry, lad,' he said to Duncan in private. 'You and I know it's far more complicated than your mother makes out. The Ridings is ours and worth a fair few bob these days, so the salary is nominal and anyone worth their salt wouldn't go for it.' He gestured to his prone body. 'I hope this is temporary, but—'

'It's fine, Dad,' Duncan interrupted, conscious of Noah's frustration, embarrassment and fears. The doctors had warned about the long-term complications of his injuries and the likely rehabilitation and therapies involved. Whatever the future, Noah Watkins wouldn't be riding, fixing or climbing, let alone walking, any time soon.

'I'm more than happy to do it,' he added. He smiled a wonky smile. 'Except for the accounts. Who knew being a *glorified gardener* involved so much maths.'

Mathematics is the very thing on Duncan's mind this morning. Thankfully his dad is at the end of a telephone to advise, but he's due his first monthly meeting with Vivienne Percy later today. He had an inkling – not least from his university studies – but he didn't realise quite how extensive his father's 'estate' duties are. He knew they'd include overseeing the agricultural aspects of the land, personally carrying out or subcontracting maintenance, fixing, mending and so on, but the bookkeeping started by his grandfather has surprised him. It includes the blasted accounts, but there are also logs of work done, repairs to buildings, fences and roads, as well as records of the parkland, livestock and crops, not to mention managing the employment and wages of the temporary workmen.

He stretches and takes a huge breath. To top it all, there's today's consultation, financial update and tour of the grounds with the mistress of the house. He knows that Vivienne is actually just his employer – and a very pleasant lady to boot – but he still feels inordinately nervous, like he's attending a job interview he's bound to fail.

Then finally, there's Freddie... Jana helped him put his guilt about the bothy into context, but he hasn't looked Mrs Percy in the eye since the dreadful day of his friend's funeral. Did she know then what he did to her son? That he stood by and did nothing to help him? Will she look into his soul and somehow know, even now?

Chapter 31

1978

Milly

After the devastating double death, I stayed strong for Vivienne. At times it felt as though she might dip into her old malaise, but she found solace by attending the local church each day for prayer, and I'd chivvy her along and remind her there was Imo to think of.

'As though I'd be able to do anything else,' she'd reply.

But it was said with a wry smile and a heart full of love. We adored and admired Imo as much as ever, but that didn't stop us finding her a challenge.

Freddie's death had knocked the poor girl, too, and for a time she fell worryingly quiet, appearing from nowhere with a pink nose and red-rimmed eyes. It was hard to pull her up on her usual hiding right then, as none of us blamed her. After all, we hid and cried to ourselves one way or another. Then her father died and she changed again. Fury replaced sorrow, and though she didn't say it, I knew what she thought, and it wasn't helped by her eavesdropping on the adults, be it her mother or grandmother or the staff: Theo Percy had two children, but he only loved one. Why else would he have refused medical treatment and 'allowed himself' to die?

Sometimes I'd spot her in the library, consoling herself by leafing through books, but when I realised her reading matter was wholly inappropriate for a child her age, I felt obliged to shoo her out and lock the door. Then she began disappearing for longer periods out of the house. More than once, Noah found her roaming the rooms at the Ridings and had to bring her back.

He spoke to me in confidence. 'I've no idea how she found her way in, Mrs Shaw, as I keep everything locked. I wouldn't mind the poor lass making herself comfortable in Duncan's bedroom if a woman was around, but as you know, Connie decided somewhere closer to school would work better for the lad.' He flushed. 'Anyhow, I'm living alone at the Ridings during the week, so I fear it isn't appropriate to have her popping in...'

'Understood, Mr Watkins.' He shuffled his feet, and his cheeks coloured more. 'Was there something else?' I asked.

'She likes riding, as you know, and she's sticking to her pony for now, but...'

I nodded, understanding his concern; I'd also seen Imo size up and stroke her father's two Arabians.

'And she isn't always wearing her helmet. It wouldn't take much for another...' He paused. 'Well, horses are unpredictable animals at the end of the day.'

They were indeed, much like Imogen. Both Vivienne and I tried to tackle the problem clothed in love, but flouncing and slamming doors became ever more prominent, smiling and charm increasingly rare.

'At least she's happy at school,' we muttered between us. 'That's something.'

–

Mrs Wimpeney, the head of St Anthony's School for Girls, didn't broach Imo's 'precocious' behaviour until parents' evening when the academic year was almost over. I suspect she rather hoped Viv would quietly take it on the chin and find a new school for September. But Vivienne, from her animated account when she returned to Rutherford, was furious.

'Imogen's brother has died, shortly followed by her father. I'd have thought that would allow for a little leeway,' she apparently said to the ruddy-faced headmistress.

'Which is precisely why I have left it until now, Mrs Percy. Going forward, we can't have… language content like that. I've spoken to her about it myself several times, but sadly nothing has changed.'

'Doesn't her happiness count for anything? She's popular here; she has friends.'

Mrs Wimpeney's flush became a shade deeper. 'For all the wrong reasons, I'm afraid. None of the pupils have said anything to me or the staff, but they've clearly shared what they've heard from Imogen within earshot of their parents. Which is why the complaint has come from them. The girls are eight and nine years of age, but Imogen is clearly… advanced for her age.'

'Only her vocabulary, Mrs Wimpeney.'

'Agreed, but—'

'And that's because she's extremely bright. She listens and observes and reads. Surely you should be applauding that, not making her feel that she's, she's…'

I stopped Vivienne there. I didn't want to dwell on what Imogen had seen, read or heard and described to her school friends. 'So, what was the outcome?' I asked.

'She suggested I consider another "educational establishment", as she put it. The gall of the woman!'

I took Viv's hand. It seemed to me that Mrs Wimpeney, head of St Anthony's School for Girls, was trying to do Vivienne a kindness by *suggesting* rather than expelling. And of all things, Vivienne Percy abhorred washing her dirty linen in public. 'Maybe she's right,' I said. 'Perhaps it's for the best. A fresh start might be just what our Imo needs.'

Chapter 32

Present Day

Christie

After my long weekend off, I take a steadying breath before tapping on Lillian's door and peering in.

She turns from her task at the desk, but her expression is relaxed rather than sulky or accusing. 'Did you have a good weekend?' she asks. 'A date with the bearded man?'

I picture the neatly trimmed beard in question and laugh. I must be going soft as I can't wait to see it in person again very soon. 'Yes, I did as it happens. How about you?'

She gestures to her bedside table. 'Milly brought me that.'

It's a very chocolatey cake with a candle in the middle.

'Oh God, of course. I'm so sorry for forgetting. It's your birthday. Happy birthday!'

'Thank you. "All the threes", as Milly put it, once she'd finished telling me off.'

'For...?'

'She wasn't best pleased with me for not mentioning last week's visit.'

'Oh right. How did she find out?'

Despite following him through the woods under the guise of extracting Percy gossip, I'd clean forgotten OJ's appearance at the Ridings and his mentioning he knew the Percys. Presumably, the information came from him.

Lillian shrugs. 'No idea. She always knows what's going on, so I wouldn't be surprised if she's psychic. But she's never cross for long, and she marked the occasion of my birth with the usual account of her part in it.'

'It sounds as though there's a good story in there.'

She chuckles. 'Milly thinks so.'

'How about I do my rounds then return with a cuppa to go with that mouth-watering cake?'

'OK, let's do it.' She lifts her pale eyebrows. 'But you might not find it quite so delicious when you taste it.'

–

When I return with the drinks and two plates an hour later, Lillian's mood seems to have changed.

'Help yourself,' she says dismissively from the bed. 'But it'll be revolting. Cook used to do all the baking.'

'Wow, you had a cook?'

'Yes, pretty much until she died. She seemed ancient when I was small, so she was probably in her nineties, same as my great-grandmother, who held on for years even though she was completely batty. All the women in Rutherford have longevity.' She smiles thinly. 'Except Imogen, of course.'

The image of the Percy monument, and those fictitious stone steps, hits me again. 'Did telling her to leave you alone help? You know, at her grave?'

She lifts her shoulders and falls silent, so I remind her about the birth story. 'You promised me the *account* of your coming into the world...'

'It isn't that interesting.' She looks at me and relents. 'Apparently, my mother went into labour on the fourteenth of March, today. My grandma was freaking out, worried I'd be born on the fifteenth, so Millie rolled up her sleeves and used her previous experience as a midwife to "help the labour along" as she puts it. I arrived at ten to midnight, before the proper midwife arrived, so I was the first person she saw and all that malarkey.'

'So why was your granny freaking—'

'Not Granny. My other grandma, the one in Spain.'

'Oh, right.' I don't know why I didn't twig she has two sets of grandparents. 'Your dad's mum?'

'Yes, Connie. Apparently, she was mega-superstitious about the fifteenth being the Ides of March. You know, Julius Caesar and misfortune? I guess Milly wanted to shut her up. Or maybe stop the bad omens.' She sighs. 'But they came anyway.'

I rub Lillian's shoulder. 'I'm so sorry for your loss. Losing one parent is devastating, but two...'

'My parents...' To my surprise, she stands up, steps to her desk and turns a column of photographs face up, like a pack of cards. 'I've been thinking about them. How can one go from this to, to...?'

I glance at the blond, handsome man I know to be Duncan Watkins, but I study the woman more closely. Finally, a snap of Imogen Percy, the wasp! But she seems far from that in the first. Like a sprite, her long red hair flows behind her as she joyfully dances in a meadow. The next is of them both, and though Duncan is facing the camera, she's gazing at him intently, a young person clearly in love. I work my way along the line, inspecting the same couple standing apart but with Lillian in the middle, a birthday girl from a baby to a toddler to an infant. A few are of Duncan alone with that same dead-eyed expression, then a final one of the inscription on Imogen's grave.

Goosebumps spreading, I turn to look at Lillian. 'From this to what?' I ask.

'To getting rid of her,' she replies.

'You think your father had something to do with your mother's death?'

'Yes, maybe.'

'Why do you think so?' I ask.

My mind rushes as I wait for her answer. Imogen died in a car crash. Did Duncan tamper with the brakes, drive her off the road or do something else to make it look like an accident? But Lillian was only ten. How on earth would she know?

Hesitation and debate seem to pass through her eyes. I brace myself for something momentous, but after a few seconds, she withdraws into herself with a shrug. 'I don't know. Why else would Imo come back to haunt us?'

Chapter 33

1988

Duncan

Invigorated from the July sunshine, physical exertion and the jobs he's ticked off today's list, Duncan returns to the Ridings for lunch. He's too agitated about his meeting with Vivienne Percy to rustle up anything more substantial, so he heats a tin of soup and absently eats it as he goes through his mental checklist before she arrives. He's already walked the route he plans to take her around the grounds, the paperwork is in neat piles on the study desk, and the Earl Grey tea she apparently prefers is ready on the kitchen side.

'You can do this,' he mutters, giving a mental nod to Jana. 'You're as good as the next woman or man. Colour, class, gender and race don't matter; we're all the same inside.'

By the time the knocker raps, he's almost convinced himself that it's true, but when he opens the door, he finds himself gaping in confusion. His visitor is *Miss* Percy, and though she has physically changed from the girl he remembers, the attitude is still here. He takes in her smart riding attire, lifted chin and tight bun, and almost chuckles at his thoughts of *class* difference. Jana might think there should be none, but this girl clearly considers there is.

She sweeps in and glances around the hallway. 'I haven't been in here for yonks, but it's exactly the same,' she says, as though it's a bad thing.

He takes a breath to point out the house and its land belongs to the Watkins, and that it's no business of hers, but she turns and rests her superior gaze on him.

'I've come in place of Mummy. She has a headache.'

Thankful he didn't give her a mouthful after all, Duncan looks at his shoes. 'Right.'

She looks too. 'Unusual footwear for labouring,' she says.

It's difficult not to bridle at the word labouring, and though he knows he should bite his tongue, he can't help his reply. 'I changed my *footwear* when I came home after working solidly all morning since seven. Feel free to inspect my work boots in the scullery.'

'Thank you. I think I shall.'

Gobsmacked, he watches the infuriating woman saunter away. But when she doesn't reappear after a minute to two, he strides to the kitchen and finds her inspecting the framed photograph of him and Jana in Paris. She replaces it and gestures to the kettle. 'I believe we start our meeting with tea.' She peers at the Earl Grey packet. 'Oh dear, can't stand the stuff. I hope you do green?'

–

The meeting in the study goes from bad to worse. Clearly super-intelligent, Imogen fires out a series of questions about the accounts and finances Duncan doesn't know how to answer.

She eventually tuts. 'I think you need to get up to speed with the books, Duncan.'

It's all he can do not to shout in her face. Instead, he takes a deep breath. 'I've only been here a few weeks, but I assure you I will. And it's Mr Watkins to you.'

Her face transformed, she suddenly laughs. 'You are too, too easy to tease.'

That pisses him off even more. 'The purpose of this meeting is to talk about business, so if we can please remain professional. What else would you like to discuss?'

She pulls a dour face. 'OK, Mr Watkins, if you say so.' She leans forward and taps a page of the ledger, so Duncan does the same to see what she's looking at.

As she sucks in air to speak, he mentally prepares himself for another swipe. 'I used to have a huge crush on you,' she says in a whisper. 'So huge I stole a photograph and slept with it under my pillow.'

He sits back and frowns. What the hell?

'Then, when everyone in the dorm was asleep,' she adds with raised eyebrows, 'I'd pull it out, catch a glimpse of those sharp cheekbones, those eyes and stunning lips, and I'd masturbate.'

He stares, disbelieving, but she stands and straightens her jacket. 'I'm off now,' she says. She graciously offers her hand. 'Thank you, Mr Watkins. Until next time.'

Chapter 34

1981

Milly

When Imo turned eleven and was ready for high school, both me and Viv wanted to keep her close. Unfortunately, the South Yorkshire options were limited. She'd already left another school 'under a cloud', and though Viv had agreed with the headmistress that the word 'expulsion' wouldn't be used, Imogen Percy was getting something of a reputation for being disruptive and a bad influence on her peers.

As ever, Vivienne struggled to see any wrong. 'She doesn't steal or get into fights, Milly. She's simply a clever girl who gets easily bored when she doesn't have a challenge. You'd think they could do something after all the fees we've struggled to pay. What about putting her in the year above, giving her harder homework or a mission of some sort? Perhaps even responsibility would help. Do they have school prefects these days?'

It was true about the money, and it wasn't as though there were coffers stashed away in the attic. Theo's investment in oil had come good, but Noah Watkins warned it wouldn't last, that a recession in Nigeria was inevitable and that the cost of maintaining the house and grounds increased disproportionately as every year passed.

Viv wasn't quite correct about the theft, though. I'd seen Imo's stash of goodies in her wardrobe drawer for myself, and I suspected it was more a case of getting others to do her dirty work or perhaps being too smart to be caught. But I wasn't about to dob her in, not even to Vivienne. I was the only person Imo really opened up to, and it was important to maintain that trust.

'You know how Granny is completely batty these days…' she'd said when we were alone a few days ago.

'I'm not sure batty's a nice word, but yes, she can be forgetful.'

'Can stuff like that be inherited? You know, craziness?'

'It's simply old age,' I replied. 'It happens to some pensioners, so it's just one of those things you don't need to worry about for a very long time.'

'And what about the peculiar things she sometimes says?'

Busy with my chores, I kept my eyes averted. 'Like what, for instance?'

'Oh, I don't know. About the old days when she lived in the main house with Grandfather.'

'Oh yes?'

'Yeah. Sometimes she asks if I'd like to hear a fairy tale.'

Despite my thrashing heart, I smiled reassuringly. 'Well, you know fairy stories aren't always nice, and they're not true anyway, so it's best to ignore them.'

When she didn't reply, I couldn't help but ask. 'What sort of things are they about?'

At that point, Imo shrugged and said she hadn't been really listening, so I let it go. But I'd heard Honora's 'fairy tales' too, and they weren't at all suitable for young ears or indeed nice.

By the summer we were all out of ideas for Imo's schooling, but she was clearly still up to her old eavesdropping tricks as she piped up one dinner.

'Why don't you send me to boarding school?'

'Why would we do that, darling?' Viv answered. 'We want you here at home with us.'

'Well, I have to go somewhere, and I believe education is mandatory unless you plan to home tutor me.'

So, she had been listening. Vivienne looked crestfallen. 'Would you want to go? Wouldn't you miss us?'

She gave her mother a sidelong glance. 'It's the fees, I suppose.'

'No, not at all, it's just—'

'You planned to find the money for Freddie and Eton.'

It was the first time her brother's name had passed Imo's lips since he'd died, so in all likelihood, Viv and me just gaped. Imo rolled her eyes. 'But he was a boy, of course, so far more important than a mere girl.'

'Do you want to go away to boarding school, Imogen?' Vivienne finally managed.

'Yes, actually, I do.'

So that was that.

Chapter 35

Christie

Feeling a little guilty for reverting to a baked potato after my healthy weekend meals, I pour on the baked beans and flop down at the kitchen table. I'm shattered this evening. My shift was long and demanding, and though I'd have loved to stay with Lillian, study those photographs intently and shake the truth out of her, I had other patients to attend to, patients who turned out to be in far greater need.

During lunch in the canteen, a guy called Lenny with autistic spectrum disorder complained he'd been given 'something green'. The chef came to look, and when she pointed out there was not an iota of such on his plate, Lenny became agitated, pulled the poor woman to his chest and put his knife to her throat. Though the blade wasn't sharp, the situation was alarming for everyone, especially the other residents sat at their tables, some of whom became particularly distressed. Above the maelstrom of yelling and crying, Lenny was eventually persuaded to stand back and hand over his weapon. The chef tried to put on a brave face, bless her, but the shock reverberated throughout the rest of the day; patients had to be calmed, made to feel secure again and fed in their rooms. Then there were the necessary staff consultations, reports and paperwork to do afterwards.

The commotion kept me focused until it was time to leave, but once I was sitting in my car and blowing out a huge breath of relief, thoughts of Lillian's half disclosure about her dad scuttled back, and I've been mulling on them ever since. I had already gleaned her suspicions from her defensive stance, so I wasn't entirely surprised. However...

I shovel in my food and picture her flickering, tormented eyes. There's definitely more to the story, but what?

—

I fill the washing machine, take a long, relaxing shower and decide on an early night, but when I look at my phone, I've missed a FaceTime from OJ from nearly an hour ago. Feeling the usual flip of excitement, I settle myself against the pillow and call him back.

He lifts his eyebrows and looks pointedly at his watch.

I laugh. 'You should be honoured I've called, it was a tough one, but I chose you over the *News at Ten*.'

'Then I am indeed honoured. And you look so sweet. New jim-jams?'

'Not new but actually clean. I happen to have a selection of them. These are the "it's nearly April but it's still bloody cold" pair.'

'Bring on Saturday. I guarantee you won't need to wear any.'

'Hot-blooded, eh?'

He grins. 'Something like that. So how was your day?'

'Before or after the knife incident at work?'

His smile falls. 'You're joking. Are you OK?'

'It wasn't as bad as it sounds. The blade wasn't sharp, and it was over pretty quickly, but settling some of the patients and making them feel safe was a challenge.'

I picture Lillian at the canteen door, watching the action unfold with an unfazed expression. Maybe she'd seen similar before. Perhaps she'd witnessed domestic abuse growing up…

I clear my throat. 'Actually, that's something I meant to ask you.'

'Go for it.'

From his background on my screen, he's clearly at a desk. 'Are you still at work?'

'I am. Evening surgery, then paperwork. Was that the question?'

'No, no it wasn't.'

I can't say why, but I feel stupidly nervous or apprehensive asking about the Percy family. Because I owe a duty of confidentiality to Lillian? Or maybe because it's simply none of my business. But nosiness prevails.

'When you were being very stern with me for trespassing at Rutherford's old stables…' I begin.

'Stern like this?' He pulls a cross face. 'I know, it's irresistible. Was that why you insisted on taking me to the pub?'

'I didn't… Anyway. You said you were a friend of Lillian Watkins or something similar.'

'No, not at all; I barely know her. Mum inherited the Percys' veterinary needs from the other village practice when the old vet retired. Vivienne doesn't like to leave the house, so Mum's always gone there to see to the dogs and have a women-only natter. But more recently…' He cocks an eyebrow. 'It seems men do have their uses when it comes to keeping an eye on empty properties. You know, giving trespassers a good hiding when required.'

'I got off lucky then.' I take a breath. 'So, your mum – Belinda – she must have known Duncan and Imogen Watkins, I guess? Back in the day before Imogen died?'

He rubs his cropped hair. 'I suppose she must.'

He doesn't elaborate, so I press on. 'It was tragic for Lillian to lose her mum so young.' I know I'm being clumsy, but I can't help myself. 'I wonder if the police suspected foul play. They always have it in for the husband in *Midsomer Murders*.'

OJ turns some paperwork on his desk. 'Murder at Rutherford House? I doubt it,' he says absently.

'Because…' He seems to have lost interest, so I pull him back on track. 'Well, Lillian hasn't said it in plain terms, but I think it's something she worries about,' I say, trying to tiptoe around any breach of confidence. 'You know, that her dad had something to do with her mother's death.'

'Does she?'

'I'm only reading between the lines.'

'Nah. Imogen died in a car accident, so Barnaby is safe to hook a duck at the county fair. Or preferably get shackled in the stocks.' He grins, his focus back. 'If you play your cards right, you can be my date at the Sprotbrough village gala in June. In the meantime, let's talk about our plans for Saturday. What were we saying about jim-jams?'

Chapter 36

1988

Duncan

Duncan jerks awake and sits up to get his bearings. That's right, it's still the middle of the night, he's alone in his bedroom at the Ridings, and *that* was just a dream. Though he can still feel its pulsing insistence, he looks down at his hard-on as if it doesn't belong and mutters: 'It was a dream, that's all.'

Gritting his teeth, he flops back against the mattress. That bloody girl or woman or whatever she is! He stomped around fuming once she'd left the house yesterday. Her haughtiness, her arrogance, her rudeness. The way she'd put him down so easily, made him feel so inadequate and insignificant and then… Did she really utter that? His mind was still processing what the hell she was saying when she stood and held out her hand like bloody royalty. And the worst of it was that he found himself taking it, almost doffing an invisible cap and saying 'OK'.

Thank God he had fencing repairs to attend to, so instead of taking the Land Rover, he made his way on foot with his tool bag. He inhaled the balmy air and the nutty tang of the woods, and his heart finally slowed. Imogen had been testing him, that was all, trying to provoke a reaction. His lack of response was a good thing because surely that's what his dad would do? Yeah, calmly ignore it and carry on with business as usual. And it was a bloody funny story to share with Stiggy and the others.

But by the evening his mind had cranked up again. Who the fuck did Imogen Percy think she was? She was an eighteen-year-old girl who surely didn't have any authority around here. He could speak to Vivienne Percy on the telephone. Or just talk to his dad and ask him to say something. But he could hardly mention the word *masturbation*. Sure, him and his mates wanked and made jokes about it, but they didn't touch on the female version. He knew they did it – he wasn't a complete caveman, and he was keen for Jana to enjoy all aspects of sex as much as he did – but *saying* the word felt so out there, so obvious, so carnal. And it wasn't just that Imogen Percy had admitted aloud to masturbating; it was wrapped up in a parcel with him, a guy who apparently had sharp cheekbones and stunning lips... It was all too bloody confusing!

He now tests the severity of his rattling skull. He knew he wouldn't sleep, so he anaesthetised himself with several large measures of his dad's best brandy. It had the desired effect by midnight, but if this headache is anything to go by, he'll feel like shit in the morning, and he has a long day of physical labour ahead. More sleep is the thing, fend off the hangover.

He closes his eyes and tries to drift. Concentrating on work tasks is the thing, sorting out the order and what equipment he'll need, whether he'll have to subcontract the bigger jobs. But on the cusp of rest, the erotic fantasy slides back into his consciousness, and his penis immediately responds. Oh God, did she really do that? Did they?

Pulling upright, he groans loudly and shouts at the silent walls. 'No she didn't, and nor did I. It was just a bloody dream!'

Chapter 37

1984

Milly

We missed Imo horribly, but it was a relief to go about our business in the house without worrying about her snooping and listening. I had become something of a curator, reading, rearranging, recording and indexing the hundreds of old tomes in the Rutherford library, so I was happy to visit my gran once a week and stay within the grounds for the remainder. However, Vivienne became bored without Imo to worry about, so she upped her association with the church and resurrected the ladies' social events she'd attended before we lost Freddie. Still beautiful and stylish in her forties, she positively shone, and I was glad for her happiness and second wind. Besides, I had no concerns she'd meet some fella and introduce a new master to the house. Both she and Honora agreed those days were long gone 'and good riddance'.

Honora still insisted on her daily stroll around the walled garden with Thunder, often chatting to the mutt as though he was Theo or Freddie, but when Noah Watkins found her wandering dangerously close to a field of pregnant cows, I decided to walk alongside her. Though now in her eighties, she could set a good pace and was perfectly lucid mostly, but sometimes she'd go back to those 'fairy tale' stories. In fairness, her courtship with Henry had started as such: beautiful, well-bred girl met handsome, aristocratic and wealthy boy on holiday in Italy; they fell in love, married and had a child. But once his son and heir came into the world, it seemed Henry wasn't quite the 'weak and witless' Percy I'd heard about, and the romance became very dark. It was bleak listening, and I really didn't want to contemplate it, but it was better she let out her trauma and confusion to me rather than Vivienne. Viv was already aware her own husband had a sexual appetite outside their marriage; there was no need for her to know the rest.

–

Perhaps it was the many rules and extra discipline, but boarding school clearly suited Imogen. Vivienne eagerly consumed her daughter's weekly news, gave a little sniff of sadness, then handed the letter to me. But I'd take my time, pocketing it for later so I could take in every word about her 'fabulous' new friends, her eager learning and adventures. Then I'd write back on Vivienne's behalf, recounting her exploits at church and in the village, embellishing and humourising, as any epistler should.

As things had turned out, the only school which could take Imo at short notice was Ivor College, 250 miles away in Bournemouth, so even our initial visits in the Citroën or on the train were rare. By the time Imogen was fourteen, she was happy to 'do her own thing' and stay with Sienna or Flora or Camilla for exeats and half term, so we only saw her during the longer holidays, and even then she got itchy feet. Vivienne duly wrote polite thank-you notes to the parents via Imo and begged her to return their hospitality by inviting the young ladies to stay at Rutherford, but Imo rolled her eyes and said, 'Really?'

She was referring to the condition of the house, of course. Sadly, the interior needed more than just a lick of paint; wallpaper was furling, dados and picture rails yellowing, damp patches from leaky pipes creeping through the ornate ceilings. Furniture and furnishings were no longer as plush as they once were; the spectacular old drapes had weathered, and the fabric on the grand settees had worn. What Imo didn't know about was the gradual sale of family heirlooms. The extortionate cost of her school uniform, the equipment and general lifestyle, let alone the fees, had to come from somewhere. Noah did his best to squeeze what he could from the books, but he considered his primary duty was to the estate. So, me and Vivienne had toured the house and opened up the east wing, discovering elegant rooms we hadn't even known existed. We were sad to pinpoint antique chattels worth selling, but as ever, Imo's happiness was what counted, so it had to be done for her – discreetly of course.

Chapter 38

Present Day

Christie

The doorbell rings at eight on Saturday. Expecting the postman, I slip on my dressing gown, scuttle down the stairs and open up. To my surprise, it's OJ.

I glance at my watch. 'I know you said *early*, but...'

'A rare, whole weekend off.' He pecks my lips. 'Unless there's an emergency and Pete needs an extra pair of hands. Mum's away tonight too. Romance must be in the air.' He stands back and takes me in. 'Talking of which, I'm liking the skin-coloured Friday night jim-jams...'

I tighten my belt decorously. 'It's common practice to take them off before one's morning shower.'

'I could help scrub your back if you like.'

I gesture to his shorts. 'I thought we were starting our tromp bright and early.'

'Tromp? Is that what town girls call it?'

'Pretty much.'

He pulls me in for a kiss. 'Then I'm sure the tromp can wait.'

Despite a protracted breakfast, I'm still tingling and jelly-legged by the time we set off. I take OJ's proffered hand.

'Sex after our walk and not before, the next time, methinks,' I say.

He cocks an eyebrow. 'So there'll be another next time?'

We're heading for the Derbyshire peaks this morning, Win Hill Pike in particular. I gesture to the countryside ahead. 'Hmm, I'll see how you perform at this. You might not manage three whole hours of—'

'Tromping?'

'Precisely.'

I glance at him from time to time as we stroll. His receding hair is cropped short, but his dark eyebrows and trimmed beard shape his handsome face. This is actually our fourth date in person, and we speak all the time in between, but I sense insecurity behind his quips. Maybe the divorce from his wife? Or perhaps he can tell I'm a woman who gets the ick far sooner than is normal… Still, that hasn't happened yet, not by a long chalk. The sex is fantastic, and I like his company; he's attractive, intelligent, he has a great job and clearly wants kids. And even though it has only been three or so weeks, I feel I know him pretty well. In truth, I'd like to introduce him to my dad.

Shocked by my train of thought, I tune into what he's saying. 'Win Hill Pike is locally known as the Pimple, but sometimes it's called the Old Witches Knoll.'

'Ew, pimple. I think I prefer the latter.' I laugh. 'You seem very well informed. I guess *country* boys must know a lot about witchcraft. A lot of it goes on in Sprotbrough, does it?'

'A vet hears all sorts of myths and superstitions relating to animals. Cats, of course – if one wandered into a

Cornwall mine, the workers would put down their tools until it was found and killed. As for horses, even now some folk have various charms to protect them. And did you know it's considered bad luck to see a white mare?'

'Really?'

'Yes, but never fear. To offset the bad luck, you simply cross your fingers until you see a dog.'

'Well, that's a relief. Casper apart, there's plenty of those around.'

'And apparently a cure for whooping cough involved inhaling the breath of a sheep. If that didn't work, you'd find a piebald pony and do the same.'

'Oh, so I just get up and close to said pony and hope for the best that I don't get bitten for my troubles?'

'Yup.'

'Now you're making it up.'

'Nope. As for local rumours about people, I don't know about *witchcraft* but...' He seems to change his mind. 'Offal was used to remove a witch's curse – first take the heart of a sheep, stick pins into it, then roast it at midnight, and the curse will be gone.'

'So, we're all sorted for Win Hill Pike,' I reply with a chuckle. But I look at him curiously. A Sprotbrough rumour about the occult. He was definitely on the edge of spilling the beans about something. What on earth was he intending to say?

Chapter 39

1988

Duncan

During his lie-in on Saturday, Duncan gives himself a good talking-to and recovers his equilibrium. He just needs to chill out and not take things so seriously. His current job as estate steward is temporary; Vivienne Percy will know he's only just graduated and that he's simply standing in his dad's boots until he's mended. Sure, his dad is still lying flat for much of the day, and full phys-ical strength could take a year, but he'll be able to do the paperwork much sooner. As for Vivienne's weirdo daughter... well, he'll just shrug it off and avoid her. Besides, forward girls aren't anything new; before uni he was used to being challenged and chased; back then, he took it in his stride.

So what changed? he thinks as he shaves. Jana, of course. She wasn't an easy catch from the village; she was − and is − a whole head and shoulders above the rest. Beautiful, mature, funny and smart, she was worth waiting for and savouring. And when he went to collect this morning's mail, he received not one but two missives in her tiny scrawl, two postcards packed with news.

Wish you were here! Love and miss you so much, they both ended.

He smiles at his pink-chinned reflection. All those feelings of insecurity over the last week were misplaced, thank God. His love hasn't forgotten or abandoned him; the Thai postal service is to blame.

His mum phoned him yesterday and invited him for tea. Not in the mood – or indeed having the time – he took a breath to turn her down, but she spoke first.

'You'll get used to the loneliness if you're not careful, Duncan. You're only twenty-one, and you should be out having fun. What do they say? All work and no play makes Jack a dull boy.' She tittered. 'And none of us ladies like dull boys, I can tell you that for nothing!'

It was a rare moment of insight by his mum, but she was absolutely right. Though he talked to his dad every day, he'd been so focused on work, he hadn't gone out, seen his old village mates or even called Stiggy and the other uni lads for a chat. He *was* bloody, bloody lonely and hadn't even recognised it as that.

He now stretches his stiff limbs and heads for the wardrobe. A whole day off is the thing. A bit of retail therapy in town, his mum's for tea, then the Clothiers Inn. There's sure to be a face or two he recognises from the old days.

–

'So, show us what you've bought,' his mum says the moment he puts his foot in her front door.

'How about letting the lad in first?' he hears from the back bedroom.

Connie pulls her duck face. 'Your dad might be a cripple, but there's nothing wrong with his hearing. Eyes in the back of his head too.' She divests Duncan of his shopping bags. 'Course, he has me to thank for coming back here at all. If I hadn't kept this bungalow, he'd still be in that smelly hospital ward.'

'With nurses who are nice and don't call their patient *cripples*,' echoes back.

Duncan chuckles. Despite the bickering, he senses his parents are enjoying each other's company. Even during his daily consultations with his dad, his mum has inter-jected from the background, and he recognises her inter-ference as a sort of love for them both. And after so long alone at the Ridings, a little sniping here and there is actually better than silence.

He makes his way to his dad's orthopaedic bed. 'How's it going?' he asks.

Instead of complaining, his dad lifts his eyebrows. 'Not all bad, son. Pressure sores and ulcers can be a problem, but...' He lifts a palm before Duncan can express his concern. 'But the doc advised... How did he put it? "Daily comprehensive visual and tactile skin inspections."' He laughs. 'She might not be medically trained, but it turns out your mum is a dab hand at that. Hydrating the skin too.'

The Imogen dream flashes in, but he pushes it away. 'Too much information, thanks, Dad. I never thought I'd say I'd prefer to talk about ledgers, but in this case...'

Noah shakes his head. 'Mum's banned me from work talk. She says you need a day off.'

Connie puts her head around the door. 'And so you do.' She lifts the black jacket Duncan treated himself to. 'Very smart, though are you sure about a T-shirt rather than a shirt underneath it?'

'It's a Levi's. That's the look, Mum.'

'If you say so. Are you wearing it to the pub tonight?'

'No, it's a bit—'

'Oh, come on. What's the point of having nice clothes and not wearing them?' She slips it on and gives a twirl. 'If you don't, I will.'

—

Although Duncan enters the Clothiers feeling a touch nervous, he's immediately greeted by the rumble of easy chatter and the familiar smell of hops and tobacco. He relaxes even further when he spies Andy Maher at the bar.

'Bloody hell, blast from the past,' Andy says when he approaches. 'I heard you were back, though. Sorry to hear about your dad. How's he doing?'

'So far so good.'

'Great. A pint?'

Duncan accepts his old schoolmate's offer, and they sit at a table. 'Only on the halves?' he asks. 'It's Saturday night; what's going on?'

Andy taps the side of his nose. 'Places to go, people to see.'

'Bloody hell, don't tell me you've got a woman?'

'Maybe. And there's footie tomorrow so...'

'Ah. Glad you've mentioned that. I don't suppose there's room for a brilliant left foot?'

'Join the queue, mate.'

Duncan takes a gulp of his beer. Back in the day, the Sunday team begged him to play, so it isn't the answer he expected to hear. He tries again. 'Come on, man. This is a guy who had trials for Donny. Played for uni too, so I've still got what it takes.'

Andy finishes his ale, stands and pats Duncan's shoulder. 'There's a list. Get your name down, and maybe if a defender gets crocked... I'm off, so I'll see you.'

Feeling stupidly offended, Duncan sullenly stares at his lager for a couple of minutes, then he shakes himself down, throws back the liquid and makes his way through the crowd to the bar. He orders another pint and glances around while he waits. Finally clocking someone he knows, he moves to say hello, but Leroy has his arm around a girl he once had a thing with, so he has second thoughts and turns back for his drink.

He looks at the counter in confusion. 'He's taken it over for you,' the landlord says, nodding to the table he was sitting at before.

'Oh, right.'

Duncan's stomach automatically clenches. Over the years, he's given Jonny Cullen a wide berth, crossing roads and leaving pubs if necessary, but he's a grown man now, and it's stupid to be scared of him. And rumour has it that Jonny's a changed person with a wife and a kid. Yet what does he want today?

As huge as ever, Jonny stands when he approaches. He flicks Duncan's lapel. 'What the fuck is this? Didn't have you down as a poofter.' He gives him a sniff. 'You smell like one too.'

Hoping his fear doesn't show, Duncan sits. 'It's called fashion, Jonny.'

Jonny grins. 'Or perhaps I should have guessed, eh? A gay boy.' He makes a gesture with his fist. 'Maybe that's what was going on at the stables, eh?'

A blend of anger and agitation shoots to Duncan's face. He still feels deeply ashamed about his role in what happened to Freddie, but at the end of the day, this is the bastard who roughed up a helpless boy. 'What do you want, Jonny?'

'Not a lot, as it happens. Some casual work here and there for my beer money. Seems your old man was willing to take on every sod in the village except me. But now you're in charge, things can change. A bit of protection goes a long way.' He pats Duncan's cheek. 'Maybe think about it, eh?'

His heart beating furiously, he watches Jonny saunter away. Was that some sort of threat? He'd like to bolt, but instead, he sips his lager and tries to calm himself. Everything is really OK. After all, what can Jonny actually do? He's already treading a fine line with the law, and perhaps it's just bravado masking a desperate plea for employment. Not that he'll have him anywhere near Rutherford land.

After enough time has passed to make a dignified escape, he pulls back his chair and makes to stand. But his legs feel insubstantial, so he wobbles back to his seat. What the fuck? He's only had two pints and he's completely pissed. Though he had a couple of cans at his mum's to calm his nerves, and he isn't used to drinking these days. Bloody hell, he's so tired he can't even sit up. If he just rests his head on his arms for a few moments, he'll be as right as rain.

A flash of auburn hair and the dream slithers in.

Yup, if he naps for two minutes, he'll be fine.

Chapter 40

Present Day

Christie

After such an energetic, romantic and fun weekend, I go into work for Monday's early shift bright-eyed and bushy-tailed. Though I know curiosity killed the cat, I'm keen to casually ask Lillian about rumours of witchcraft around Sprotbrough. I even consider mentioning OJ to see what she knows about his family, but the moment I've let myself into the foyer, Sunia puts her head around the staff room door.

'Madam has finally gone,' she says.

I immediately know who she means. 'What? When?'

'Yesterday. Her granny came as usual, and Lillian left with her.'

'But—'

'She'd already packed up all her stuff, and as her granny pointed out, she was here on a voluntary basis. We checked with Doctor Finnegan and she said Lillian was good to go, so...'

'Right. Granny as in...?'

'Yeah, the little woman with the dyed hair who visits each week. Who else?'

I can't help but feel Sunia is enjoying my surprise. And yes, my obvious dismay. With an effort, I rearrange my expression. 'Well, she's had a rough time so I'm pleased for her.' I pat Sunia's arm. 'We've clearly done a good job. Want a cuppa while I'm making one?'

Once I've completed my usual round and dispensed the morning meds to my patients, I take a breath at Lillian's door. It's wholly wrong to have a favourite or become emotionally involved, but with the best will in the world it's bound to happen. Like teachers, nurses are simply people at the end of the day, and they'll click with some personalities more than others. But right now it feels more than that. I'm upset, offended that Lillian should scurry off behind my back. I thought we had a connection, a friendship; I'm frankly astonished that she's left without telling me.

I look into the room. If I'd had some semblance of hope that Sunia was winding me up with an April fool's joke, the emptiness puts paid to that. The bed, the desk and chair are there, but the few personal effects Lillian had have vanished. Similarly with the en suite; shampoo, conditioner, toothbrush and toothpaste are all gone.

Wondering what changed her mind, I perch on the stripped mattress and think back to our last conversation. Nothing sticks out, so I idly open her bedside drawer. It has been cleared, too, but when I reach in, my fingers catch something at the back.

I peer at my find, a blister pack of Camcolit with a Post-it note attached. Lillian's mood stabilisers and a smiley face... What does that mean? That she's happy to leave them behind or...? After the weird episode with the sleeping pills, I suspect I'm being played, but the pull is irresistible, so I fetch my phone from the staff room and nip to the toilets. I scroll through my 'L' contacts to search for the mobile number Lillian gave me, but when I find nothing, I try 'W'. Spooked that I'd unconsciously listed her under the name 'Duncan Watkins', I compose a text.

> It's Christie here. Great to hear you're back home!

The moment I send it, I'm worried. Is this going beyond the bounds of professionalism? And the Ridings isn't her home. The last place she resided was in Fulham. Maybe the Post-it and pills were a message that me and the Devonshire were now in the past. But the phone rings whilst it's still in my hand. Duncan Watkins is calling.

'Hello?' I say cautiously.

'I didn't have your number, so I needed you to call me.'

'OK...'

'And I thought you might get in trouble if I left you a note. So I sort of left one anyway.'

I take a breath to make some sardonic comment, but Lillian speaks again. 'After that butter knife fiasco, I thought it was time to get away from the loonies.'

'It's as good a reason as any.'

'And Milly was coming on Sunday, so I just decided to do it.'

'It's fine; you don't need to explain.'

'Of course I do. We're friends, aren't we?'

'I guess we are.'

'Then I'd like you to do me a favour. It's sort of urgent. At least it is in my mind. When are you next free to drive over here?'

Though an alarm bell shrills in my head, I look at my watch. 'My shift finishes at two,' I find myself saying. 'So, I can be there some time before three.'

Chapter 41

1988

Duncan

Duncan tries to peel back his eyelids. It feels as though he's been dancing on the cusp of consciousness all night, images flitting in and out as though they are real. He thought he'd got rid of Imogen Percy, but the bloody woman came back to haunt his sleep, sashaying around his bedroom and touching things like she did all those years ago at the bothy. And wearing his new jacket? No, no, that was his mum.

He sighs the bizarre scene away, but when he turns, an expensive scent seems to hover like a cloud. Bloody hell, what's wrong with him? Another image flashes in. Red hair splayed against the pillow, soft breath on his cheek, gentle fingers stroking the hair from his forehead. What the…? Nope, that isn't real; it's just his imagination, memories seeping through from his dreams.

He endeavours to focus on last night. His mum's, then the pub… But the rest is a blank, and he's too tired to crank up his mind. And he really doesn't feel at all well; sleep, he needs more sleep.

Duncan stirs at the undeniable smell of toast.

'Finally,' a voice says from the bottom of the ocean.

He struggles to swim to the surface, and when he does, it's daylight so it must be morning, but his legs are so leaden and his head stuffed with sand, it feels like a ten-ton truck has hit him. Bloody hell, he's never had a hangover like this before. And the breakfast aroma… Did he sleep at his mum's?

He pulls himself up and opens an eye. Sitting cross-legged on the bedroom couch, Imogen Percy looks back. She gestures to her plate. 'Want some?'

Gobsmacked, he stares. What the hell is she doing here? And no, he couldn't eat if he tried. And what the heck is she doing in his robe? But he can't speak right now; if he does, there's a danger he might puke, so instead he gingerly returns to the mattress.

He hears her pad over and climb onto the bed. As she inches towards him, her floral scent hits his nostrils. Christ, that memory was real, wasn't it? Her gentle touch and soft whispers in the early hours. Despite feeling like shit, he feels himself stir. He's starkers, but he can't remember a thing. What the fuck happened last night?

As if reading his mind, Imogen props her head on her hand and smiles with her neat, even teeth. 'Much as I'd have liked to, no we didn't. It was fun taking off your clothes, though. What a bod.' She squints like a satisfied cat. 'Even better than I imagined before sleep in my narrow school bed; much bigger too, and I mean all over…'

Oh God, she stripped him. Did he do the same to her? Is that why she's wearing his… He eyes his blue dressing gown, then quickly looks away. Bloody hell, it's gaping at the front, revealing the mound of a small breast. A thump of guilt hits his chest. Whatever occurred, they're both naked. That's appalling behaviour on his part; he has Jana, and though he isn't actually engaged to her, it feels that way. But instead of shrivelling through remorse, his erection hardens.

He tries to focus through the mist of uncertainty, panic and – yes – hot desire. 'Look, I'm sorry. I have no idea what happened... I must have drunk too much. I guess I'm not used to it these days...' He stumbles over his words, trying to find an explanation for clearly blacking out and doing... Well, whatever they did. 'So, yeah, I'm really...'

But Imogen is dragging her finger from his forehead, down his nose to his lips. She softly strokes them. 'This mouth. So very kissable...'

'I have a girlfriend,' he blurts.

'So very kissable...' she repeats. Then she laughs. 'At least it would be if you didn't stink of vomit, darling.'

She jumps from the bed and drops the robe to the floor. Her breasts are as perfect and pert as he imagined, but she's wearing knickers, thank God. But then she speaks again. 'You owe me a new frock.'

His mind sticky with confusion, he tries not to gape. Oh God, did he tear it? Did he rake off her clothes like he did in the dreams? 'A dress?' he manages.

'You were sick, Duncan. You puked on yourself, and much to my dismay, on me too.' She shrugs. 'Still, I suppose that teaches me not to act out of character.'

He finds his voice. 'I'm not following.'

'Me being a saint. You know, the Good Samaritan. I've never done that before, and it actually felt quite empowering…' She tilts her head. 'Don't you remember anything?'

'No. No, I don't.'

She rustles in her bag and lobs over a packet of paracetamol. 'Take those, and I'll reveal all after a long, soapy shower. Do we have clean towels?'

'Yeah. In the airing cupboard next to the main bathroom.' He watches her blithely remove her panties at the door. 'So we definitely didn't…'

She turns, apparently unabashed by her complete nudity. 'No, we didn't, darling.' She strokes those slim fingers over her shock of pubic hair. 'Not yet.'

Chapter 42

Present Day

Christie

By the time I pull up in the driveway of the Ridings, I'm kicking myself for being... Being what exactly? Too eager to please? Too involved? But I'm also undoubtedly intrigued. On the phone, I asked Lillian what she wanted me for, and she replied that it would be easier to explain in person.

She opens the front door before I can knock and pulls me into a quick hug. 'I know it's a bit strange, but who else would I ask?' She smiles a wobbly smile. 'And we're friends, aren't we?'

I pause before answering even though I've already said yes to that question. Nurses have a duty under our code of conduct to maintain professional boundaries with patients at all times, and any form of sexualised behaviour is unacceptable. But this isn't a romance, and Lillian isn't my patient any more. Besides, I've already crossed a line. Perhaps I did the moment I read her clinical notes and saw she'd lost a mother too. 'Yes, we are.'

'Good.' She seems distracted. 'Shall we get a hot drink?'

'Sounds good as I'm parched.'

I follow her into the kitchen, sit at the table and wait for her to explain what's going on. Whilst she watches the kettle, I notice her frequent glances at the framed photograph of her and Duncan.

Still turned away, she finally speaks in a low voice. 'I missed the funeral, his funeral.'

'That's understandable. You weren't in a fit state. I'm sure your dad would have understood.'

'My grandma tried to ban Granny and Milly, apparently.'

'Your grandma in Spain?'

'Yes. Connie.'

'Why would she do that?'

Lillian shrugs. 'Gramps usually goes for the easy life and lets Connie get her own way, but he put down his foot about that.' She rotates and takes a big breath. 'He did the same about my dad's ashes.'

Wondering where this is going, I accept the proffered mug. 'Oh yes?'

'She wanted to take them with her to Alicante. He said no.' A shudder seems to pass through her. 'Dad left instructions about where he wanted them scattered.' She moves to a drawer and pulls out an envelope. 'The letter is in here.'

'Have you read it?'

'Gramps asked me if I wanted to look a while back, but I wasn't ready, and I didn't want to face it. But now I'm back, I need to, don't I?' She glances around the lofty room with huge, fearful eyes. 'I had another bad dream... Dad wouldn't do the same, I know he wouldn't, but I can't take that risk, can I?'

I rub the goosebumps from my arms. I don't believe in life after death, let alone spirits or ghosts, yet I feel that weird sense of being watched by someone or something again.

'But I can't do it alone,' she continues, 'so that's why I asked you over.'

'OK, fair enough.'

As though it has life, we both stare at the white envelope marked '*Letter of Wishes*', but when Lillian inhales deeply and slips out the contents, there isn't the long, legal-type document I expected, but a short, hand-written paragraph.

Lillian scoops it up to read, but her already pallid face seems to turn a shade paler. 'I don't get it.'

She pushes the sheet towards me, so I peer. 'I see what you mean,' I say. 'It's marked "2" at the bottom, so it must be the second page.'

'No, not that.'

I look at her enquiringly, then go back to the two sentences which simply convey Duncan Watkins' wishes for cremation and the scattering of his ashes.

Lillian stares for a beat, but then her gaze falters. 'The bothy garden,' she whispers. 'Why would he choose there?'

—

Making comments intermittently, we take the path I accidentally found on my last visit here. It's warmer today, though, the burgeoning spring sunshine peeking through the woods. I glance at my companion from time to time. Though I sensed Lillian had to work hard to mask her agitation at the kitchen table, we talked about what she wanted to do next about scattering Duncan's ashes. On the one hand, she clearly wanted to get the job done before another night passed, yet on the other, she clearly wasn't ready.

'I haven't got my head around it,' she said.

'Around...?'

'The whole thing. You know, finally saying goodbye to Dad.'

I was sure there was more to it. 'His chosen place as well?'

She nodded.

'Then why don't we take it a step at a time?' Something had clearly spooked her about the bothy or its garden. Maybe associations it evoked from childhood or even a horrible experience. 'Looking at things as an adult and in the light of day sometimes makes all the difference. Why don't we walk there now and see how you feel after that?'

'OK.' Lillian lifted her chin. 'Let's do it.'

She now takes a sudden turn through a bowed row of dark trees. 'This way,' she calls over her shoulder. 'It's a shortcut.'

Inhaling the dank, mossy smell of the vegetation, which seems to reach out and stroke my shoulders, I follow her along a rough track. When we pop out into daylight, I realise this was the way OJ and Casper must have come the last time I was here. No wonder their sudden appearance made me jump. But today the sensation in my stomach isn't alarm or even fear; it's excitement at the thought of my new boyfriend, a man in my life I fancy the pants off and actually still like. Who seems to like me too.

'You know what?' he asked before leaving me yesterday.

'No, what?' I replied.

'I might just be falling in love with you, Christie Morfett.'

I covered my pleasure with a sardonic 'Oh yeah?'

His eyes shone. 'Only this much.' He measured an inch with his fingers. 'So don't go getting ideas.'

Lillian breaks my reverie. 'You're grinning,' she says, lifting the latch of the old building.

'Am I?' I reply. 'It must be a good sign.'

'OK, let's do this.'

She steps over the threshold and I follow. But as I look around the room, my smile falls and a horrible iciness jolts through my body. I saw it the last time through the window, but it was such a fleeting glance I didn't fully register it that day.

'What is it?' Lillian asks, peering at me intently.

It's my turn to be secretive. 'Nothing. Nothing at all,' I manage to say.

Chapter 43

Duncan

Too exhausted to work everything out right now, Duncan throws back the pills and closes his eyes for ten or twenty minutes, but as the painkillers kick in, so does his sense of self-awareness. Christ, Imogen was right; his breath and his body stink. Carefully lifting his head, he looks around. His jacket seems unscathed on the back of a chair, but his soiled T-shirt and jeans are in a heap on the floor.

He pictures his mum's appalled face. Much as he'd like to go back to sleep and pretend *this* isn't happening, he needs to get up, open a window and sort himself out. He throws back the duvet, pads to the door and listens for sound; it's silent, thank God. Hopefully, the bloody woman has gone.

Holding the dirty clothes at arm's length, he makes his way to the en suite, chucks them in the bath and drowns the stench in cold water. Then he turns to himself, scrubbing his whole mouth for five minutes, then showering for a good ten. When his hair finally feels clean, he turns off the faucet, opens the screen and almost collides with Imogen, cleaning her teeth at the sink. Wearing a towel and a turban, she spits out the toothpaste and rinses the brush, his bloody toothbrush. Christ, how long has she been there?

As though answering his question, she arches her eyebrows. 'There's nothing as arousing as watching a man soap himself all over.' Her gaze slides to his penis. 'I was tempted to join you. Give you a helping hand.'

He searches for something to stop her looking at his increasingly insistent erection.

'I thought you'd gone,' he says, willing her away. 'I expect you have things to do.'

'Walking home wearing this attire? Hmm, that would set tongues wagging.' She leans so close he can smell spearmint. 'That wouldn't do when we haven't even done the dirty deed.'

She softly pecks his lips, and it's all he can do to breathe.

'Especially as I'm abstaining.' She chuckles. 'So, you're off the hook, Mr Watkins. For now.'

Unsure whether he's disappointed or relieved, he watches her move away. At the door, she turns. 'May I borrow a shirt and a belt?'

Thrown by the mundanity of her question, he nods. 'Sure, help yourself.'

'Coffee, then riding and lunch.'

Unsure what she means, he simply says, 'OK.'

'You do still know how to ride, don't you?' Closing her eyes, she inhales deeply. 'One thing's for sure, I need to mount something today.'

–

Due to lack of time and equipment to hand, Duncan follows Imogen's lead at the stables and clambers onto one of the remaining two Arabians without wearing a hat. He tries to block out Jana's disapproving grimace and replace it with an image of her on a sandy beach. It's fine; it's a Sunday, a day off. He's only going for a trot around the estate with someone he's known since childhood, whereas his girlfriend is on holiday doing God knows what with whom.

And besides, he isn't going to do anything he shouldn't. Apart from the fact he wouldn't betray Jana, Imogen is 'abstaining', whatever that means.

The warm breeze ruffles his hair as he adjusts the saddlebag. He can't help but smile at this bizarre position he's found himself in. Looking cute in his belted shirt and her high boots, Imo eventually appeared in the Riding's kitchen. 'How old is that bloody hairdryer?' she asked.

It must have been his mum's from many moons ago. God knows where she found it.

'Have you made up the sandwiches?' she added without waiting for an answer. She gave him a withering look. 'We can't have a picnic without them, can we?' Her lips twitched. 'Don't ask me to do it. I've been to finishing school, so I've no idea how.'

Reminding him of the Imogen in this very spot five or so years ago, she now peers at him scornfully again. 'Are you sure you're up for this? I won't repeat my Good Samaritan act if you take a tumble. Once in a weekend is plenty.'

The last couple of hours have been so arousing and surreal, he's completely forgotten her promise to 'reveal all'. He takes a breath to remind her, but she's already set off, her swathe of auburn hair flying behind her.

–

Breathless, exhilarated and very glad he made the food, Duncan flops on the picnic blanket. He eventually rolls over to Imo's green gaze.

'I knew you'd be starving,' she says.

'Telepathic too, I see. Is there anything you don't know?' he asks.

Fully dressed, he feels more confident – and safer – with her. And he's bloody pleased that he showed off his horsemanship to good effect.

'Here's something I know.' She snaps the tab of the Coke can and slugs the liquid back. 'You're trying to fight it, but you want to fuck me.'

Bloody hell, he relaxed too soon. But it isn't as though she'll seduce him at the edge of a Yorkshire meadow with two horses looking on. 'Ah, so you don't know everything,' he replies. He tucks into a sandwich. 'I don't go for girls who...'

It's on the tip of his tongue to let his thoughts out, to mention girls who are manipulative, spoilt, posh and condescending, but a shadow of hurt seems to pass through her eyes.

'For girls who what?' she asks.

'Girls who don't know how to make butties.'

She lifts a shoulder. 'Why would one bother to learn when one will marry well and have a cook to do it?'

'I guess.' He senses a sadness behind her bravado. 'So what did you do that was out of character last night?'

'I saved you. I found you slumped at your table in the Clothiers, barely able to speak, let alone walk. So, I bundled you into a taxi and brought you home.'

'OK...' He still can't remember a thing after speaking to Andy. 'So what did you save me from?'

'Maybe humiliation, a warning shot, but my guess is robbery.'

'I don't follow.'

'Oh Duncan, you're such an innocent numpty. I'd better keep a closer eye on you.'

'Why?'

'Fine one minute, then literally legless the next? Seems you have an enemy.' She kisses his nose. 'It's obvious, isn't it? Someone in the pub spiked your drink.'

Chapter 44

1986

Milly

We were proud of our Imogen during her tenure at Ivor College. She never missed even one weekly letter. She worked hard and played hard, regularly came top in various subjects and was on course to pass all her O levels with flying colours.

Viv and I continued to miss her, but it made the time we spent with her all the more precious, which is why we had mixed feelings when she telephoned to say that the Maddox family had invited her to holiday with them at Easter. Camilla was still Imo's inseparable best friend, so the suggestion wasn't unusual for a few days at their second home in Wales, but this jaunt was to Italy.

'Apparently, their apartment has the most beautiful view in all of Venice!' Imo gushed to Vivienne. 'I've seen photos, and from the bedroom, the dining room and the lounge, there's a view over the Canal della Giudecca and at the same time over San Marco and the Doge's Palace, over the church of Santa Maria della Salute and the end of the Canal Grande. Camilla says there is no other place in Venice that offers such an overwhelming panorama.'

Imo knew how to sell it, and poor Vivienne was torn. She had very fond memories of going there at around the same age, but this trip was for eighteen days abroad, which seemed a huge jump from a week in Abersoch.

'Romantic gondola rides along Canal Grande,' she said dreamily to me in private. 'St Mark's Square, the Rialto Bridge, St Mark's Basilica, the Bridge of Sighs…' She did a fair few sighs of her own. 'The exquisite sounds from La Fenice Opera House. It would be the adventure of a lifetime, but we'd have to pay for her meals, and Imo would need pocket money for days out. Can we even afford the cost of the flights?'

We probably couldn't, but Imogen was persuasive. She'd be home for the first ten days of the holiday, then fly from Manchester so Mummy could drive her there in the Citroën and wave her off. Then she'd return directly from Venice to school with Camilla for the summer term. That alone would save the cost of train travel and taxis from Doncaster to Bournemouth. As for money, Camilla's family were loaded. They were delighted to invite Imo and pleased their daughter would have a companion to keep her entertained; in all likelihood, any offer to contribute would be met with derision. However, she did understand Mummy's concerns, so she'd ask Camilla to speak to her parents and request one of them make contact.

After a week or so, I answered the phone and was greeted by a deep, eloquent voice. 'Is that Mrs Percy?'

'It's Mrs Shaw, the housekeeper,' I duly replied. 'I'll see if she's free. Whom might I say is calling?'

'Camilla's father, Robert Maddox.'

He sounded a touch older than I had expected, but it was probably a second marriage with the usual younger wife. I passed the receiver to Viv, and though I could only hear one side of the conversation, Mr Maddox assuaged

Vivienne of all her fears and charmed her into submission within minutes: of course all the costs would be covered. He, his wife and Camilla would meet Imogen at Marco Polo Airport and not move an inch until she was safely in their care. He would supply the address and other contact information required and ensure Imogen kept regularly in touch.

I wasn't sure that I'd be such a pushover, but it wasn't my call, and when I saw Imo's glowing eyes at Easter, I knew very well that neither Viv nor I would have said anything other than yes.

Chapter 45

Christie

I'm tremulous and jumpy as I drive home from the Ridings. I know it's silly; I've been here before. An animal-patterned scarf in the bothy does not a mother make. Indeed, when I stopped for petrol, I spotted a flash of leopard in a departing old Mini. The car seats, a coat or a jumper in all probability; it was too quick to tell.

And yet my mind needles. Who did or does the item belong to? 'Do you think this was your mum's?' I asked Lillian after a few minutes of looking around had passed.

She turned to the old coat stand and frowned. 'What was Imo's?' she asked.

It was a good point; the structure was cluttered with several items of outerwear, from a high-vis jacket to various cagoules and a duffel coat. Only I would have spotted the silk fabric peeking out from beneath. I gingerly tugged it to show her.

'God no.' She looked down at her jeans and Barbour jacket as if to compare herself with her mother. 'No, she was more floaty dresses with bell sleeves or crochet frocks. Sixties hippy retro, I suppose, even though she wasn't born until 1970. No idea why… To match her itinerant lifestyle,

I guess.' She snorted. 'Peace and love. Well, that was a joke.'

I was thrown from my own worries. 'Did they row much? Your parents?'

Turning away, she squinted at the square of garden and the woods beyond through the panelled window for several seconds. Then she shrugged. 'Doesn't everyone's?'

–

When I'm settled on my sofa with a large glass of wine, I call my dad.

'Christie!' he says as though it's a surprise to hear from his own daughter.

I immediately bristle. 'Sorry, have I interrupted something?'

'Just dinner but no worries.'

I look at my watch. Seven o'clock; I should have known; my dad is a creature of habit. But instead of offering to call him later, I find myself saying. 'With Ruthie?'

'Yes, she's done the honours tonight, actually.'

Though I want to cry, I try for humour. 'I hope she's cooked you meat and two veg, or she'll be out on her ear.'

'A rather splendid lasagne. We're following it with rhubarb crumble, but it isn't rhubarb as we know it, as she adds in blackcurrants and does something clever with the crust.'

She's clearly listening, so I relent. 'I'll let you enjoy it. Say hi to Ruthie.'

'Will do.' Then, 'Any particular reason why you've phoned?'

Because I still miss my mum, I yearn to shout. *Because another reminder felled me from nowhere today and brought on the old palpitations. Because I still need answers.*

'No, it's fine,' I reply.

'And you're OK?'

No! I want to yell. *You've clearly moved on with your fucking rhubarb crumble, which my mum would never have baked, clever crust or not.* But instead, I reply, 'Yes. Speak another time,' and end the call.

Yet still I stare at the screen, willing my dad to call me back. He's the only person in the world who understands the deep sensations of loss and abandonment and rejection that I constantly carry around with me. Feelings which have probably screwed up my life – staying on the periphery of relationships; not getting in too deep or becoming too attached; leaving people and men and friends before they do it to me.

My mobile finally vibrates, but by then I'm sobbing into my fists. When it rings for the third time, I take a big breath, ready to answer. It's not Dad but OJ.

'Hi,' I say, trying to keep the wobble from my voice.

'Third time lucky,' he says. 'Should I be worried you've got the ick?'

We exchanged romantic histories on our Derbyshire tromp, competing for the worst disaster. He trumped everything with his 'messy divorce', so I resorted to explaining my tendency towards knee-jerk dumping, which I sometimes regretted. Right now, I regret telling him about it.

'No,' I manage. 'Not at all.'

His tone is immediately concerned. 'Hey, you're upset. What's up?'

'Nothing. I'm just pathetically feeling sorry for myself.'

'That's allowed,' he replies. 'Want to talk about it? Some exceptionally pretty nurse told me that these things are better out than in.'

Feeling a glimmer of the happiness and hope this man gives me, I blow my nose. 'I had a Mum moment today. Then, when I called my dad to talk about it… He was busy, so I felt, well, discarded, I suppose.' I try for a smile. 'I told you it was pathetic.'

'Shall I come over and give you a hug?'

'It's Monday. We're both on—'

'Then we can set the alarm and have an early night. How does that sound?'

'It sounds perfect.'

'Good. Then I'll see you in half an hour.'

Chapter 46

Duncan

Duncan sits at the kitchen table and spoons cornflakes into his mouth. He usually has something more substantial to start the day, but he just can't get himself going either mentally or physically this week. Perhaps it's the after-effect of the 'spiking' on Saturday night, or maybe it's because he's confused. Yes, lady bloody muck. Imogen Percy. Imo. For whatever reason, he can't stop thinking about her, his mind roaming a whole spectrum between annoyance, indignation, danger, flattery and desire. And it's the last he ends on before falling asleep. It's still bloody there when he wakes, so he rushes to the shower to relieve himself. He imagines her 'helping hand' and he comes within seconds.

When they arrived back at the stables on Sunday, she'd changed again, retreating into the snooty girl with the impenetrable gaze. She wrapped her hair into a tight bun and held out her hand. 'Thank you for the sandwiches,' she said crisply. 'And for the loan of the shirt. I'll arrange for it to be laundered and returned to you.'

She hasn't brought it back. Though he's scanned every garden, every meadow, every field as he's passed, there hasn't been any sign of her. And why would there be? It's not as though he regularly saw her in the grounds anyway. She'll be ensconced in the big house, and he hasn't gone anywhere near it as yet; the need hasn't arisen.

'Will he have to go into Rutherford?' his mum demanded when his dad was still wired up in his hospital bed.

'Mum! Dad's in pain. He doesn't need to worry about that stuff yet.'

'Well, you're not to, son. Do you hear me?' she added with a set jaw. 'They can come to you.'

Connie always did have a thing about the big house, and after Freddie's death, he got it. He still felt dreadfully guilty, of course, but as he stood in the domed hallway for the wake, he sensed movement, even sound from the landing above. When he looked up, only dark shadows lurked behind the wooden balustrades, yet it gave him the spooks, and he was mightily relieved when his mum took his palm and tightly squeezed it. He'd usually be embarrassed by her public display of affection, but that day he was glad of it.

He now stretches and sighs. Today he's missing a hand of reassurance, Jana's in particular. Though it's Friday, there hasn't been a postcard this week yet, nor the phone call she promised. He knows it's expensive all the way from Bangkok and would last all of two minutes, but he'd like to hear her voice. It's bloody lonely in this house with only the TV or his cassette tapes to keep him company every night. His confidence in her love for him is slipping a little more each day; he needs her to tell him they're still a team.

The telephone peals halfway through Duncan's lunch. He strides from the kitchen table to snatch it up, but he pauses a moment, caught short by his own conflicted emotions. Who does he want at the other end of the line? Jana or Imogen? They are both frustratingly elusive, and yet Imo dominates his thoughts, which he knows on some level is exactly what she wants, what he must resist for his own wellbeing.

When he finally answers, it isn't a woman, it's his old mate Andy. 'Lorna's out with the girls, so I've been granted parole for one lucky night. See you in the Clothiers at eight for a pint or ten?'

It's exactly what Duncan needs. 'Yup, absolutely.'

'Then onwards to a club? You can wear that black jacket, and you won't look like a complete twat there.'

'Hilarious. It's called fashion, Andrew.'

They banter for a few more minutes, but it isn't until the call ends that Duncan's own words and a flash of memory filter back. Jonny Cullen spoke to him in the pub on Saturday, didn't he? He can't remember what was said, but after a fifteen-year intermission, he doubts it was for a friendly chat. Feeling a shiver pass through him, he glances at his glass of lemonade. Was his drink really spiked? Did Jonny plan to rob him? Bloody hell; will he be safe tonight or any other night in the Clothiers? He pictures the man's swagger, but another image sparks in from the other side of the bar. Yes, a girl with flowing red hair, intently watching them both like a sentinel.

Chapter 47

Present Day

Christie

After Monday's blip, I have a great week. I pretend to myself it's fulfilment at work, the new spring-summer outfits I added to my Zara basket and found myself buying on a whim, the comical postcard I received in the mail from my dad. But in truth, it's OJ. His company is so easy, warm and relaxed. He's great in bed, prepares tasty food and makes me feel secure and loved. So much so that I briefly called him back when he left my front door at six-thirty on Tuesday morning.

I kissed him softly, then measured an inch with my fingers. 'Only this much,' I said. 'So don't go getting ideas.'

'Love you more,' he replied.

Turning my mind to today's mission, I climb in the car. Lillian phoned me on Wednesday and said she was ready to fulfil her dad's ash-scattering wishes. Would I mind doing the honours with her when I was next free? Though I pictured the scarf on the bothy coat stand and paused for a beat, I quickly got a grip. Talking through my latest 'Mum moment' with OJ really helped me put it in perspective and reminded me to deep-breathe through those seconds of sheer panic and rationalise them.

I smile at the thought of his gentle coaxing and thoughtful responses to my tumble of angst. Perhaps my own adage of 'better out than in' is working for the person who uses it the least. So, after saying 'yes, of course,' to Lillian's request, we agreed I'd drive over on the next shower-free day.

I now peer at the sky through the windscreen. Though dry at the moment, it's mottled with clouds, so the weather may well take a dive for the worse. But it's Friday, and I won't have another available few hours for a while, so I'm happy to trundle across to the Ridings and see where the afternoon takes us.

—

It's inevitably raining by the time I reach Lillian's front door, but she doesn't seem overly bothered.

'It might dry off later,' she says after her usual quick hug. 'I promised myself I'd tidy the house today but I started baking instead. Anything to help me quit smoking.'

'Well done you! So, you've been to the shops? That's good. How did it go?' I ask automatically before realising that I'm still in nurse mode.

Lillian doesn't seem to notice as she heads for the kitchen. 'No, it was an online delivery. Walking into the village is fine, but carrying everything back is the problem. I guess I need to buy a runaround.' She smiles. 'Or one of those old lady shopping trollies.'

I wonder if that means she's staying in Yorkshire. 'Presumably, you didn't need a car in London? Do you still have the flat? Fulham, wasn't it?'

Focused on her chores at the counter, she replies over her shoulder. 'No, Gramps sorted all that.'

'Your grandad in Spain?'

So focused on the Percys, I'd almost forgotten the other half of Lillian's family again, Gramps and Grandma Watkins, the parents of the man who is gazing down from the frame on the dresser. Duncan's smile makes me feel uncomfortable. Did he really do something dreadful to his wife, the mother of his much beloved daughter?

I drag my eyes away. 'Gramps sounds very helpful.'

'He is, my Noah. He's efficient and kind and measured. Calmly takes everything in his stride, you know? A bit like you do.' She pulls a rueful face. 'I wish he lived over here, but...'

Sensing her tears, I gesture to the bowls on the work surface and change the subject. 'So what are you making?'

'Scones and a Victoria sponge. I thought a cream tea in the front parlour at three. How does that sound?'

'Bloody perfect.' I glance at the somewhat erratic baking mess. When I passed the lounge, it was in a bit of a state too. Though I'm here strictly as a friend, I remind myself that Lillian will still be adjusting to life on the outside, so to speak, and that a little subtle help might be in order. 'I'm not the best cook in the world, and I have a tendency to drop things on the floor, so I hate being watched. Cleaning isn't my forte either, but I'm wicked with a feather duster. Shall I make myself useful?'

Lillian sweeps back her hair with the back of her floury hand. 'Go for it,' she says. 'Whatever rocks your boat.' And though she does look somewhat tired, it's heart-warming to see her laugh.

Chapter 48

1988

Duncan

Duncan finishes tweaking his hair, sprays a blast of after-shave on his upper chest, then steps back from the mirror to get a better view of his torso. Though he says it himself, he's looking pretty damn good. He must have lost a fair bit of weight since the excesses of university, but he doesn't look scrawny as the pounds have been replaced by muscle. It isn't surprising with all the hefting, lifting and shovelling he's done over the past five weeks, but it's a sort of win-win. Despite the loneliness, he loves his job and the land, and getting fit is 'the icing', as his mum would say.

He nods to himself. Yeah, if Jonny Cullen tries it on, he'll be a pretty good match. And as for any 'spiking', he'll simply have an eye on his beer glass and keep his distance.

He moves to the wardrobe and considers his options for the pub and the club. July has been hot, and if the tan on his arms is anything to go by, the temperature went up a notch in the fields today. He pulls out a couple of shirts, his jacket and a new T-shirt, then turns to his hi-fi and waits for the next track on the compilation cassette Jana made him before flying to Bangkok. 'So you don't forget me,' she said with a tender kiss when she presented it. And in truth, it has worked. He wouldn't give the likes of Robert Palmer, Paul Young or any of her 'pretty boy' musicians the time of day usually, but singing along to this tape makes those kisses feel more tangible.

He gives the Levi's T-shirt a sniff. Can he really still smell puke, or is it just his imagination? Picturing Imo's withering look when she told him he stank, he bundles it into a ball and lobs it towards the laundry basket. It misses. Berating himself for letting the bloody woman into his thoughts, he bends to pick it up, but the crunch of tyres on the driveway stops him short. He moves to the sash window and peers out. Christ, it's Vivienne Percy's battered old Citroën SM. What does she want at this time on a Friday?

All fingers and thumbs, he pulls on his jeans and a shirt, then clatters down the stairs, but when he opens the front door, he gapes in confusion. It isn't Vivienne, but her daughter wearing a simple summer frock and holding a dish with oven mitts.

'I hope you haven't eaten,' she says, stepping in. 'I'll take it through. It's still piping hot.'

What the fuck? Trying to shake his disbelief away, Duncan follows her to the kitchen and watches her pull plates and glasses from the cupboards and cutlery from the drawer. Stuck for words, he stares at the lidded pot. What's going on? He's due to leave for the pub in fifteen minutes, and this is the young woman who's too flaming educated to peel a carrot.

He thinks of something suitably sarcastic to say along those lines, but she gestures to his seat. 'Please sit.' Her cheeks turn a deeper shade of pink. 'It's my third attempt. Mummy and Milly are pretty sick of it, but I think I nailed it this time.'

There's such an air of vulnerability about her that he does as he's told. 'What is it?' he asks. 'It smells good.'

'Bœuf à la Bourguignonne with—' She claps a hand to her mouth. 'The French stick is still in the car. I'll get it.'

'OK. Thanks.'

Once she's scuttled out, Duncan shakes himself from the spell and searches for ways to get out of this predicament. Just tell her straight that he has to be elsewhere? Bolt the food down, then hurry her out? Suggest it could be reheated another day? Even ask her to the pub?

But this sweet and uncertain person isn't someone he's met before. The girl who doesn't cook has cooked for him. It feels a huge thing, and he doesn't want to hurt her feelings. And, right now, he wants her to stay.

—

The smooching begins on the sofa, and though he doesn't want to compare her to Jana, he does. Their kisses are both lovely, addictive and delicious, but with Jana they feel like a partnership, a mutual coming together, whereas today it's as though he's in charge. But perhaps that isn't surprising. Imo is two or three years younger than him, she's been at a girl's boarding school for years, and despite her sexual bravado and talk, maybe she's inexperienced, even a virgin.

Oh Christ. If it's even remotely possible, that thought turns him on more. Of all the people Imogen Percy could choose to have sex with, she wants him. She's always wanted him. She had a photograph of him under her pillow. She sweetly cooked him a meal. It makes him feel like an invincible god. But he won't rush her into anything; that wouldn't be right. For now, he's happy to explore her trim body outside her clothes, then perhaps inch down the thin strap of her dress and see whether she'll allow him to caress her breasts, even pull down her panties and slide his fingers inside her.

Miraculously, she does and she does. And when she moves her slim hand to his crotch, he finds himself saying, 'Shall we go upstairs?'

'Yes.'

Her eyes huge and trusting, she takes his proffered arm and follows him into his bedroom. All fingers and thumbs, he yanks off his jeans and almost rips the buttons from his shirt. It's too soon in the friendship or relationship – or whatever this is – to have full sex, but he wants to cover her body with kisses; he longs for her to do the same, but quite frankly he's fucking desperate for her to reach down that hand again and jerk him off.

'Could you…?' she says softly, turning her back to him.

Too aroused to even speak, he unzips her dress and watches the delicate material slither to the floor. When she finally tugs off her knickers and rotates, it's all he can do not to crush the innocent loveliness from her. Instead, he lies on the bed and offers an arm for her to rest against his shoulder. She climbs on the mattress, but instead of nestling by his side, she spreads her knees and straddles his body.

'I didn't mean… we don't have to…' he starts to say, but she's already pressing herself down on his burning erection.

Fearful of hurting her, he momentarily freezes, but when she smiles and begins to move, he can't stop himself doing the same. Seconds later he's in heaven, then he's exploding inside her.

Chapter 49

Milly

It was nice to have Imo home from Ivor's for the Easter break. The Sunday itself was early that year, so after Vivienne returned from church, we were able to make an occasion of the day and a fuss over our girl. Cook had declared a 'banquet' was in order, so Honora and Vivienne sat either end of the grand dining table like in the old times, with Imo sitting in the middle. I ate with the family these days, but it was usually in the kitchen, so I felt quite splendid surrounded by the best crockery, crystal and a plethora of Sheffield cutlery. Who'd have guessed it?

No doubt my mother would think invisible little Millicent had risen above her station and duly turn in her grave, but in a way, Maggie was still here as I was the respected *Mrs Shaw*, and Honora continued to think I was her. I didn't mind; it clearly gave the old lady a great deal of comfort to talk and exorcise the past – at least for her.

Our festive dinner was a real treat. Goodness knows how Cook had managed it from her meagre budget, but she presented us with broccoli and stilton soup accompanied by freshly baked soda bread, a smoked salmon, dill and cucumber salad. Then there was roast lamb studded with rosemary and garlic, served with dauphinoise potatoes, spring vegetables and baby carrots for the main. Dessert comprised hot cross bun and butter pudding for Imo, and because Honora insisted on them with every meal, a prune and chocolate torte for her.

To top it off nicely, Vivienne suggested champagne. After all, what was the point of the Percy wine stash if nobody drank it?

'May I join?' Imo asked.

'Seeing as you're sixteen, you may,' Vivienne replied. 'Half measures, though!'

We all got a bit tipsy, even Cook. It was a lovely way to send Imo off on what Honora called her 'Grand Tour'.

–

We were blissfully ignorant about Imo until a late telephone call on the first Monday of her new term. I answered as usual.

'Rutherford House.'

'Is that Imogen's mother? Imogen Percy's mother?'

My belly summersaulted. 'Who is speaking please?'

'It's Mrs Fleming, Imogen's housemistress.'

I took a breath to say I'd put Vivienne on the line, but the clearly distraught woman continued to speak. 'I don't quite know how to say this,' she rushed. 'We can't find Imogen. There's no record of a message from you, but perhaps it has been mislaid by Matron or someone else? Please tell me she's ill and still with you.'

Not finding Imo sounded too, too familiar from the past, but she was reliable these days; she assured us she'd be returning to Ivor College direct from Italy.

'The summer term started today, Mrs Fleming. She should have been back in her dorm yesterday morning, and you're only just telling us now?' I demanded. I knew it wasn't my place, but I couldn't help myself.

'She's always so dependable. I just assumed she was, well, somewhere. But when they took the registers in today's lessons, we eventually realised...'

Despite my fury at the school's clear incompetence, I tried to keep calm. 'Have you seen her at all?'

'Well, no. Nor, it seems, have any of the girls...'

Vivienne was on her feet, her eyes wide with questions, but deep dread was creeping through my bones. I knew I should hand over the call to her, but my fist was stuck to the receiver.

'Is Camilla back?' I asked the housemistress.

'Camilla?'

'Camilla Maddox, Imogen's friend. Have you seen or spoken to her?'

'Oh...' The woman seemed thrown by the question. 'Camilla moved houses. She's in Powys House now, so I'm not sure she'd...' Then a shuddery breath. 'Oh dear. You do know the two girls fell out?'

'How long ago was this?'

'Oh, I don't know, time flies, but I'd say at least two years ago.'

Putting the phone to my chest, I turned to Vivienne. 'It's Imo,' I said. 'She hasn't returned to Ivor's. It seems she—'

But the loud rap of the door knocker interrupted my sentence. Abandoning the telephone, I hurried to the door, Vivienne close behind. It had to be Imogen, please Lord, it had to be. Tentatively relieved and ready with both admonishments and hugs, I took a deep breath and opened the locks. When we peered out to the black night, it wasn't our girl but Noah Watkins.

He stepped in, his expression grave. 'Imogen just telephoned, so I came over straight away.'

I gripped Vivienne's hand. I was sure she'd had the same thought as me in those few seconds before Noah spoke, but thank God Imo was still with us; she wasn't dead.

'She *telephoned*… Where is she?' I asked.

Noah cleared his throat. 'They allowed her a call.'

Viv's voice was tremulous behind me. '*Allowed* her? Who did?'

He peered at the note he'd written. 'The Polizia Locale Sezione San Marco, located in the Biblioteca Nazionale Marciana.' He paused and looked at Vivienne. 'I'm afraid she's in a Venetian police cell.'

Chapter 50

Christie

It doesn't take me long to dust, scoop up abandoned magazines and books and bash cushions into shape in the lounge, so I go through the downstairs with my pink tickling stick, finding a dining room, a cluttered study and what Lillian called the 'parlour', an old-fashioned, wood-panelled suite with huge French windows and a plethora of exquisite period furniture. Out of nowhere, I find myself willing the blessing of children on my friend. Lillian doesn't even have a guy in her life, so it is a huge leap, but it feels important to pass on all *this* to progeny who'd value it rather than it be cleared then snapped up for next to nothing by some sharp-eyed antique dealer one day.

My own 'inheritance' is substantially smaller than this, but I hope to do the same. Even before Mum went missing, I longed for a sibling, so I definitely want more than one kid, preferably three to share the load of all the good things – and bad – life spits out.

Yes, too many *bad* in my case. I picture the pine chest my mum once used for bedding. Her worldly goods are in there, and when I was fifteen, I overheard Dad ask my auntie Marsha if she or the family wanted to go through it for keepsakes. I stood behind the door, aghast at his offer, but Auntie Marsha sounded as offended as me.

'Why on earth would you say that?'

'Seven years are up, Marsha. The declaration of presumed death has come through.'

'Alistair! I can't believe you applied for it.'

'I know it sounds harsh, but it's needed to sort out her estate – property, money, assets…'

'Well, whatever there is belongs to Christie.'

'Absolutely; I agree.'

A thought occurs to me. Perhaps Dad already had *closure* many years before he left. Would seeing the official certificate help me acknowledge that my mother has gone forever? It's unlikely, but I resolve to do it anyway, a further step towards putting things into perspective and finally dealing with my grief.

I return to the kitchen and pop my head in. 'How's it going?' I ask.

Lillian glances at a pile of crustless bread. 'On course, I think,' she replies. But she does look fatigued, one drawback of her medication.

'The downstairs is pretty tidy and dust-free so far,' I say. 'Should I help clear up in here?'

'You haven't seen upstairs.'

'Righto, I'm on it. See you in a bit.'

I sashay up the handsome staircase to the landing above, but when I peer into each bedroom, only Duncan's is in disarray. Indeed, it's in the same state as the last time I saw it. Feeling somewhat invasive but intrigued too, I step to the wardrobes and crouch down to the photographs Lillian discarded on the carpet. Both the Percys and the Watkins gaze back at me, so I move to my knees and begin to go through them.

At first, I study each image with captivated eyes, almost laughing to myself as I identify each person – Honora and Vivienne Percy, Mrs Shaw, Noah and Connie Watkins. There's several of flame-haired Imogen reclining in a field or straight-backed on a horse, and a whole swathe of Lillian from baby to university graduate. Yet after a while it becomes repetitive, and when I realise the majority are dated on the reverse, it makes my task much quicker. I find boxes duly labelled – *Wedding Jan 1990, Christmas 1990, Imogen's 21st 1991, Easter Day 1992, Dad's 50th 1995, Vivienne's 60th 1998* and so on – so I pile everything in. But when I stack them back, I notice a container to one side marked *Newcastle University 1986–89*.

Intrigued by the connection, I open it up, take out a handful of snaps and spread them out on the carpet. I doubt Duncan studied music with my dad, but they might have been in the same halls of residence, football team or the like…

I still guiltily at a creaking sound from the landing or stairs. I'm supposed to be helping, not nosying at a dead man's personal stuff, so I quickly sweep them into a pile. But as I make to replace them, a familiar face takes my breath. Oh my God, it can't be. I peer more closely. Yes, it's Mum, my mum, squashed in the middle of four grinning lads. Palpitations hitting, I rock back against my heels, but after a few moments I slowly breathe through the panic. Mum went to Newcastle Uni too. It's certainly a surprise but not completely out there. And yet, and yet… My hand trembling, I look again. The tall guy with his arm around her shoulder… Yes, it is undoubtedly Duncan Watkins.

I endeavour to be the calm person Lillian described. Like the scarf, it could simply be another freaky coincidence, I reason. Yet a deep pain in my chest tells me it isn't. I go back to the carton, tip out the contents and frantically search through each image, but there's nothing to link my mother with here. Deflated and frustrated, I pick up the lid. A single photograph is stuck in a corner.

My heart thrashing, I tug it out and stare. The shot of the Ridings is similar to the one Lillian had in her album, but my mum's shadowy face isn't staring from an upper window as I had imagined that day; it's centring the portrait, happy and smiling and alive.

With a sharp breath, I flip it over.

Jana. Easter 1988, it says.

Chapter 51

1988

Duncan

The August sunshine beats down on Duncan's naked chest as he fixes the brackets to rehang an old gate. He's getting used to make-do-and-mend, as his mum would put it. He's always rolled his eyes at her plethora of sayings, but for the past two weeks he's found himself thinking them: floating on cloud nine, over the moon, as happy as Larry. Whoever bloody Larry is! Because that's how he feels, how Imo has made him feel. Fucking joyous and high and excited. Knowing she'll appear at the Ridings after he finishes work each evening and that they'll have sex which ends with a bloody mind-blowing orgasm that sucks the life out and devastates him until they do it all again.

Flexing his arm muscles, he grins. He knows it's ridiculous to feel smug, but he can't help himself. Imogen's sexual progress has been like a bud opening, petals *he's* unfurled. They've explored and discovered what she likes and, quite frankly, she can't get enough, which is more than fine with him.

He'd like to tell Stiggy or Andy: 'Guess who I fuck two or three times a day?' But he knows not to breathe a word to anybody about the relationship. His mum, in particular, would go apeshit if she knew. Besides, it isn't 'fucking'; it's more meaningful than that. He doesn't know if he loves Imo, but she's buzzing in his thoughts all the time. He needs to capture each moment with her, so he has his camera to hand, snapping that alluring smile, which is especially for him.

Of course, Jana and the guilt creep in when he lets it.

'How's your lovely lady doing on her travels?' his dad occasionally asks on the phone. 'She'll be back soon, won't she?'

'Yeah, September,' he replies evasively.

But Duncan doesn't know what September will bring. There hasn't been a postcard for three weeks now, and though on some level it hurts, perhaps it's meant to be, maybe it's a good thing.

–

Waking to the blare of the telephone, Duncan flicks his head to the next pillow. Why he does that every morning, he doesn't know. Jana has clearly deserted him, and Imo returns to the big house every night.

Should he bother answering? He feels listless, exhausted and flat today. But it could be his dad, and there's always the concern that there might be complications with his spine.

He decides to pick up. 'Hello?'

'I was about to give up. You sound groggy. Are you only just awake?'

It's Andy Maher.

'Why, what time is it?'

'Half eleven on a sunny Saturday.'

'Right.'

How the hell did that happen? Well, Duncan knows the answer to that. Imo. They soon got down to it last night, but at some point, she said, 'Open your mouth.' He did, and she popped in a small tablet. 'Swallow,' she said. 'You'll like it.'

In fairness, he did like it very much. He felt euphoric, his energy levels heightened, the whole experience enhanced. But Imogen later woke him and said, 'Shall we go again?'

He was frankly too knackered. 'That was so nice. Let's leave it there and have a cuddle.'

She stroked him with silky fingers. 'Oh, come on, big boy.'

'Maybe later. I'm really sleepy.'

With a chuckle, she presented another pill. 'That's what these are for...'

He now tries to focus on what Andy is saying. 'Some skirt is my guess...'

'Sorry? What skirt?'

'The reason for your elusiveness.'

'Nah, just busy. Standing in for my dad is full-on.'

'Well, tomorrow is the Lord's day of rest, and our centre half is crocked. Eleven o'clock kick off, then a long session at the pub. Are you up for it?'

'Yeah, absolutely. I'll dig out my boots and give them a polish. Thanks, mate.'

Feeling a little more buoyant, Duncan makes for the shower. He scrubs the weariness from his limbs and the sleep from his head, but when he greets himself in the mirror, he twigs what he's agreed to. Tomorrow is a Sunday, his usual whole day with Imo, which includes a long ride into the Yorkshire countryside, a picnic and outdoor sex. The thought normally arouses him, but in truth, the idea of footie with the lads appeals more. The last three weeks have been exhilarating, amazing, a whirlwind of excitement, but they've been physically and mentally exhausting too. A rest for a few hours will do him good.

He stares at his reflection. Question is, how will he break it to Imogen?

Chapter 52

1986

Milly

Though Vivienne strode up and down the drawing room and pelted out questions, I kept my counsel and watched Noah.

'I don't understand, Noah. She's still in Venice? Why didn't she catch the flight with the Maddox family? With her friend Camilla? And I spoke to the father, didn't I, Milly? Everything was organised to a tee. The girls should be back in Piggot House; she promised they'd travel straight from the airport to school on Sunday; yesterday. A problem with the aeroplane? But then why on earth would the police be involved?' She clapped a hand to her mouth. 'Not a hijacking? Oh Lord, was the aeroplane hijacked?'

'No. No, it wasn't. Imogen missed her flight.'

'Then why wasn't she there? What did she say on the telephone? Please tell me she hasn't been in an accident or injured?'

'She's fine. Shaken by her surroundings, obviously. But—'

'A police cell, you said. They're used for criminals, aren't they? Not young girls on a holiday. Was she mugged? I've heard about the plethora of pickpockets in Venice, so perhaps Imo gave chase and got hurt. Did you speak to an officer? What did they—' She frowned at him then. 'And why on earth did Imogen call you and not us?'

I stood and guided her to the sofa. 'Come and sit down. I'm sure Mr Watkins will explain what he knows.'

I liked Noah Watkins. God knows why the poor man had ended up with Connie and her dramas, but maybe that's why he was so thoughtful and steady. He was kind too, and that's what I saw in his face. He wanted to be honest but discreet; he didn't want Vivienne to suffer more than was necessary.

He perched on the armchair and rolled his cap in his hands for a moment or two. Making a decision was my guess.

'Imogen is fine. Anxious to come home, but well in herself.' He cleared his throat and addressed Viv. 'She called me because she didn't want to worry you. Yes, I did speak to a... a *commissario*, but of course a different language is always a barrier, so I haven't yet gleaned the full story. However, the good news is that I was able to make it clear Imogen is a minor, a juvenile, and he agreed to let the matter rest and allow her home.'

I waited for Viv to ask what 'the matter' was, but she was clearly focusing on the positives right now. 'Thank the Lord.' She stood and took his hand. 'Thank you, Noah. Thank goodness we have you to look after us all. So how do we get her back?' She glanced at the carriage clock. 'Can we even book a flight at this hour?'

I caught that look of pity in Noah's eyes again. 'Best I go and fetch her, eh? She's in a foreign land and has had a bad fright. I'll see to everything first thing in the morning and keep you posted.'

'You are so good to us, Noah. But what about the…
the finances…'

'Don't worry about that for now; one way or another,
we'll find it.'

–

Goodness knows how Vivienne slept, but I was wide-eyed
with internal questions all night. Imogen obviously hadn't
been holidaying with Camilla and her parents, and not just
this time either. She hadn't been friends with the girl for
the past two years, and the break-up was so severe that
Camilla had moved from Imo's school house to another.
And why had she ended up in a police cell? She must have
done something criminal to be detained or even arrested,
something so bad that the police had clearly asked Noah
to escort her home. And who the hell was the eloquent
man on the phone who'd claimed to be Robert Maddox?

But I had no intention of speculating 'the matter' with
Viv. It seemed to me the less she knew right now, the
better. I'd winkle the truth out of Noah or Imogen herself
and then decide how much to share with Vivienne. The
important thing was to get Imo home. And work out a
plan for how to pay for it.

Chapter 53

1988

Duncan

Duncan hunkers down against a huge oak tree, pulls out his lunch butty, takes a hungry bite and chews contemplatively. Thoughts of Imo, of course.

She took the news about the football game surprisingly well. He was nervous about saying it, so got it out there the moment she arrived on Saturday evening.

'That's fine. I'll drive Mummy out and treat her to Sunday lunch somewhere.' She studied him for a beat. 'No little white enhancers tonight then?'

The uppers had been an interesting but knackering experience, and he honestly didn't know why 'enhancers' were needed. 'Another time, maybe?'

'OK,' she said lightly. But she didn't stay long or instigate sex. 'See you when I see you,' she said when she left.

Though a little thrown by her indifference, it was good to watch some inane TV and get an early night. He worried that his aching limbs would affect his sporting performance, so he rose early on Sunday, did ten minutes stretching and ran for three-quarters of an hour. On the way back, he saw Imogen on her horse and lifted a hand in greeting, but she didn't wave back.

She'd clearly seen him, but he soon shrugged it off. He had the footie to look forward to, and when he got there, it was great to banter with the lads and get stuck into the match. Even better, he played bloody well, making a great block at one end and setting up a goal from a corner at the other. And once he was three pints in at the pub near the ground, he wondered if it was a good time to cool things with Imo. But it's now Tuesday, and he's missing the buzz.

Like a flaming mind-reader, Imogen's shadow makes him start.

'Bloody hell, Imo, you made me jump. Where did you come from?'

She shrugs and kneels down by his side.

He offers his crisp packet. 'I'd have made you a sand-wich if I'd known, but you're welcome to these if you're hungry.'

She doesn't reply. Instead, she unbuckles his belt and slips her hand into his shorts. When he's hard, she pulls away. 'Take them off.'

They've had outdoor sex before, but away from the estate and hidden from sight. 'We're in a field, Imo. I can see Rutherford's roof from here.'

'Part of the fun, *n'est-ce pas*?' Gracefully rising to her feet, she stands over him. She's wearing no knickers beneath her floaty dress. 'Don't you want to?'

His body does, it most definitely does, but his mind tries to rebel. Sure, they're beneath the branches of a large tree, but if anyone crossed the meadow, they would be seen. And he doesn't want people to know about him and Imo. It's private and inexplicable, and other folk might not understand. Indeed, he was asked in the pub what it was like working for the Percy family.

'*The Munsters*, you mean,' someone said.

'Yeah, Mrs Shaw the vampire housekeeper.'

'And the freaky daughter.'

But right now the freak is smiling that smile and saying, 'No one will see us if we're quick.' She laughs. 'And if Granny does, she's as mad as a hatter. She'll just think I'm sitting on your lap.'

His throbbing penis decides it for him. She sits on his 'lap' and rocks for a while, but when she strips off her dress and gyrates, from a mixture of alarm and desire, he is indeed 'quick'.

—

Duncan ends the week with a can of cold larger in his back garden. He glances around and takes in the long grass, the unkempt shrubs and arid bedding plants. Bloody hell, he's been so busy attending to the Percys' land, he's neglected his own. Same with him and Imo's needs. Though he's found himself half hiding, she's located him in the grounds every day and wheedled him into having sex in the open. He's managed to come each time, but it's more release and relief than pleasure. He knows Imo loves the danger, but he doesn't get it. He's a regular guy; he doesn't need that high nor the pills she pops on her tongue. Thank God she's stopped pressing them on him each evening, but she seems to disappear into another world while he keeps pumping away until she climaxes. He doesn't know how or why everything has changed, but it has. The whole thing with Imogen is no longer enjoyable but a chore.

The sound of the door knocker filters through to the rear. Imo usually comes around this way and walks right on in, but it isn't unusual for her to surprise him and change tack, like the Jekyll and Hyde character she can be. Not that she's done anything bad – that comparison isn't fair – but she is definitely 'mercurial', as Jana would describe it.

Jana, his Jana. He tries not to dwell on why she's deserted him. Of course, he's been far from an innocent, but she has simply dropped him. Deep down, he knew she would. Not because she has a mean bone in her body, but because she's too good for him; too smart, too attractive, too savvy, too nice. She was always going to find someone better.

The knocker raps again, so he makes his way through the house. Glimpsing the Citroën through the glass, he sighs and opens up. But it isn't Imo after all.

'Hello, Duncan.' Vivienne Percy self-consciously pats her blonde hair. 'I'm sorry to drop in like this. I'm sure you're having a nice sit down after an arduous day in this heat.'

He finds his manners. 'No problem at all. Would you like to come inside?'

'Thank you, but no. I was just passing, so I thought I'd drop these in. I rather fear our postman is losing the plot. Or perhaps it was someone new who didn't realise we weren't one and the same. Whichever it was, I'm so sorry they were delivered to us.' She hands over an envelope. 'I'll leave you to your evening.'

'Thank you. You too.'

He watches her gracefully climb into the old car, circle the driveway and roar away. Expecting invoices or demands, he ambles to the study and tips the contents out. It takes several moments for his mind to process what he's looking at. They are postcards. Not one or even two, but seven colourful postcards from Jana.

Chapter 54

1986

Milly

Vivienne was mightily relieved when Noah brought Imo safely home from Italy, but instead of throwing questions at him this time, she simply thanked him, retreated to her sitting room and stayed immobile on the sofa. She was clearly struggling with her 'nerves' again, and I was glad of her hiding as it allowed the dust to quietly settle whilst we all adjusted to the unexpected shock.

But Imogen's schooling was something which had to be addressed. After a terse chat with Noah, the two of us agreed it would be unsafe to allow her back to Ivor College, even if they were willing to have her. Thankfully the fees hadn't yet been paid, so that was something, and there were other options for Imo still taking her O levels locally if, of course, she agreed. When I broached Vivienne to discuss it, she put a hand to her forehead. 'Whatever you think, Milly. I'm afraid my head is too fuzzy to think these things through. But I absolutely trust you'll do whatever is best.'

Viv's malaise turned from days into weeks, but we all adopted her blinkered approach to some extent. Save for riding her horse, Imo stubbornly stayed in her bedroom and smoked cigarettes; Noah continued his work, tight-lipped; Honora acted as though Imogen's presence at home was perfectly normal; Cook rolled her eyes but still prepared Imo's favourite titbits of food for her. As for me, I went to the library to carry out some research, kept a careful eye on Imo and bided my time until she was ready to spit it all out.

–

Imo's explosion finally came one evening in May.

'This is worse than a bloody police cell!' she shouted when I popped my head around her door to bid her goodnight.

Noah had imparted a few pieces of information to me about Imo's arrest, but it was very much the bare bones: she had stolen a credit card and was apprehended when she forged a signature and tried to use it.

Looking at her pointedly, I perched on her bed. 'You've chosen to hide in here, Imogen. You've turned down the opportunity to attend a college in Doncaster and make some new friends.'

She pushed a pile of textbooks away. 'I already know the whole syllabus backwards. Why would I want to hang out with some spotty teenagers who are so stupid they have to re-sit their exams?'

I paused for a while. 'Seems to me there's only one stupid person around here.'

'Only being caught and that wasn't my fault.' She glared. 'You and Mummy had no idea what I was doing, so I'd say that's pretty smart.'

She was right; we'd trusted her. We'd been hood-winked and blind, but she had *no idea* how much Noah had told me either. 'So why did you do it?' I bluffed.

'I'm sick of being poor, for starters. I have to practically beg Mummy for money, which is totally humiliating.' She shrugged. 'So, I like being taken places and bought stuff. It's nice to feel special too.'

Despite the fizz of alarm in my chest, I kept my expression blank and waited for more.

'And anyway, I enjoy it.'

My worst fears were being realised. 'Enjoy what?'

'Well, you wouldn't know, would you, *Mrs* Shaw. Still a bloody virgin at forty-three.' She gave a sneery laugh. 'Though I don't suppose you'd give a *penis* the time of day even if it was offered.'

I didn't reply; she was being cruel and crass when there was no need, and she knew it.

She hung her head and picked at a scab on her knee. 'I was always thinking about it, needing to… you know, going to the toilets at school at break, waiting for the next lesson so I could have another… fix, I suppose.'

Masturbating, I assumed. Remembering the headmistress's complaint about Imo's sexualised talk and behaviour at primary school, I inwardly nodded. Was her precociousness from listening at windows and doors? Reading inappropriate books in the library? Or was it simply inherited from the dark side of the Percy line?

'Then I went on holiday with Camilla for real and met…' She gave me a sidelong glance. 'My friend. He liked me very much and wanted to be my…'

Her sugar daddy, her abuser at only fourteen.

As though reading my thoughts, she sighed. 'It's fine, Milly. He's… gone.' She covered her face. 'It was horrible. He was grunting, and I thought he was enjoying himself, then he suddenly… collapsed, I suppose. I was scared I'd be in trouble, so I quickly packed my case to get out of there, but then I realised I—'

'Had no money.'

The anger returns to her eyes. 'Exactly. No. Bloody. Money. Have you any idea how mortifying it was at Ivor's to never have any? To be constantly making excuses for not joining in, well, pretty much everything? So yes, I took the bit of cash he had and his credit card. It worked a couple of times, then it didn't and the police came.'

'What happened to your...' I gritted my teeth. 'Your friend?'

'Died, I suppose.'

'And then?'

Though she nonchalantly lifted her shoulders, her cheeks burned. 'My flight was only a couple of hours away, and I was worried about missing it, so I... Well, I offered the *poliziotto* a trade to let me go.'

'You propositioned a police officer?'

'I know; that *was* stupid. Look, you won't tell Mummy, will you?' With a peculiar look, she grasped my hand. 'Mummy doesn't understand me like you do. She's not as—'

'As what, Imogen?'

We both spun around to the doorway. I don't know how long Vivienne had been listening, but her face was bone white. 'As strong? You lied, you cheated, you prostituted yourself, you stole. But do you know what is even worse than all that? You didn't call for help. A man was dying and you ran away. A *strong* person would have done the decent, Christian thing by staying and accepting the consequences. I'm ashamed of you, Imogen, deeply ashamed.'

Vivienne's angry speech and her feelings of shame got through to Imogen in a way I would never have imagined. I understood Imo's behaviour and actions were much more than selfishness and greed, but that's how Viv saw them. Even though a man in his fifties had groomed and abused her daughter, she couldn't get over the fact that Imo had bolted and left him to die alone. Was he already dead, or could he have survived if help had been called? It was a question she asked me each night before sleep.

Many a time, I wanted to share my deep fears about historic sexual deviancies with Vivienne and whether they could be passed down the Percy line, but as things turned out, Imogen became a changed person. After another week of disappearing or hiding away, she came to her mummy's sitting room, knelt by her sofa and begged for a second chance: she was deeply unhappy; she had what she called 'obsessive thoughts' constantly circling in her head; she was prepared and indeed wanted to see a therapist or a psychiatrist who might help her overcome or at least handle them. She was desperate to be rid of them as much as anyone.

Like a weight lifted off her, Vivienne embraced the poor girl and readily agreed it would be a fresh start. I made a few discreet enquiries, found a private mental health clinic in Doncaster, and Viv drove her there twice a week.

After a few hourly sessions with Imo alone, her doctor asked Vivienne to join them.

'Imogen and I have talked this through, and we think we've found a way forward,' she said.

'Oh yes?'

'Imogen considers herself a "freak". She most certainly isn't, but she needs to discover that for herself, so I feel a residential addiction rehab centre would be greatly beneficial to her. I'd suggest a month's stay to begin with. That'll give her time to settle in and meet like-minded people. She'd be rubbing shoulders, learning, growing and getting better with other sufferers who have a range of addictions from alcohol to prescription drugs, from gambling to shopping.' She smiled at Imogen. 'I guarantee you'll soon discover you aren't a freak, nor are you alone.'

Vivienne returned from the consultation and filled me in. 'Imogen's all for it, which is wonderful, but the cost is extortionate.'

The next words on her lips were the usual, 'Oh, Milly, how on earth will we pay?' But this time I had an answer. My research at the library had come good; quality and scarcity of the vintage were the key, and the contents of the Rutherford cellar ticked both boxes. I'd already contacted several investors who were interested in buying, but on balance, I thought we'd profit more at auction.

'Oh Milly, you are so clever!' Vivienne declared.

I felt somewhat pleased myself: we were sitting on a treasure trove of fine wine.

Chapter 55

1988

Duncan

Although Duncan has been staring at Jana's postcards for a good half hour, he's still reeling from bewilderment when the desk phone shrills. He's tempted not to answer. Suppose Imogen is calling? What will he say? Because despite Vivienne's prattle about confused postmen, he's certain something else is going on here. Jana has clearly addressed each one to him at the Ridings with no mention of Rutherford; the earlier ones arrived safely, so why not these? And if they were piling up on the ornate side table in her hallway, why didn't Vivienne bring them earlier? Why did she bring them at all?

The caller doesn't give up, so he steels himself and picks up the receiver.

'Hello?'

'It's Mum. What took you so long?'

'Sorry, I was having a beer outside.'

'Dad wants a word.'

He tries to cover his general agitation with a quip. 'His PA now, are you, Mum? He'll be having you type letters for him next. Put him on.'

'He wants to talk to you in person. That's why I'm calling. You can fetch us cod and chips on your way in.'

'Right.' His neck feels hot and itchy. 'Did Dad say why?'

'Why what?'

'Why he needs to talk to me in person?'

'Business, I expect. Her ladyship turned up in her car. Even though she didn't have an appointment, she wafted me off with a "Thank you, Connie, you are kind letting me borrow Noah for a couple of minutes". Then she had the gall to close me out with my own bedroom door.'

'Her ladyship?'

'Vivienne, of course. Who else.'

Sweat trickles down Duncan's spine. A personal visit to both son and father cannot be a coincidence. He just can't quite get a handle on why.

'OK. What time shall I come?'

'I'm peckish now, so the sooner the better. Plenty of salt and vinegar on those chips.'

—

'Let's get it while it's hot,' his dad says when he takes through his dinner on a tray. 'We can talk later.'

Duncan wasn't hungry when he bought himself the portion of fish, but as he glances at his dad's grim expression, he feels positively sick.

'OK. I'll eat in the kitchen with Mum and see you in a bit.'

He tries to swallow down the meal. 'Fancy helping me out?' he asks, gesturing to his food.

'What's going on with you two?' Connie asks. 'You've both got faces like a wet Monday.' She scrapes the cod onto her plate. 'Glad I'm working tonight. Leave you flaming miseries to each other.'

When she leaves the house with a slam and hairspray in her wake, Duncan takes a big breath and goes through to his dad. 'You wanted a word.'

'Aye. Take a seat,' he replies, but falls silent for some time. He finally seems to come to a decision. 'Word has it you've been... been seeing Imogen Percy.'

Feeling deeply ashamed, Duncan looks at his hands. He knows without a doubt he and Imo have been spotted having sex.

'Your love life should be none of my beeswax, but in this case it is.' His eyes burning, Noah glares. 'What the hell are you playing at, son? You have a lovely girl both your mother and I like.' He shakes his head. 'In life it never does to mix business and pleasure anyway, but in this instance, it's more than that. Mum talks a lot of rubbish about the Percys, but she's right about keeping them at arm's length. Take my word for it; they are a complicated lot.'

His dad is generally reticent, so it's a fairly long speech, yet Duncan senses a lot has been omitted. He doesn't know what to say but finds his immediate thoughts popping out. 'Several of my postcards from Jana ended up at Rutherford so I didn't see them until just now. Do you know anything about that?'

'No, I don't.' His dad looks at him fixedly. 'But I can guess.' He clears his throat. 'Apparently, the girl is going on holiday for a while. When she comes back, you just leave it. Civil but distant, professional. However charming the lass might seem, you leave it be. It's all been contained; it's now in the past.'

'How long for? Her holiday?'

'I don't know for sure, but a month was mentioned.' He peers at Duncan intently. 'It's in the past. It was a mistake you'll put behind you. Yes?'

'Yes.'

'Trust me, lad, you're much better off without her.'

It's a heavy weight off Duncan's shoulders, and his father's clear disapproval will help his resolve. Yet he can't help but wonder what Imo did to cause it.

Chapter 56

Present Day

Christie

With no idea what to do with myself, I stumble down the Riding's staircase and breathlessly tell Lillian I have to attend a work emergency, that I'm so sorry but I will be in touch. Then I climb into my VW and blindly drive until I'm out of sight.

I yank the car into the first lay-by I find and rest my head on the steering wheel. In that iota of time in Duncan's bedroom, did I really think the photograph was evidence that my mum was alive? Yes, no. I don't bloody know. Yet the hope was certainly there.

Hot tears squeeze from my eyes. How desperate am I, how fucking needy? I was staring at a photograph of a young woman in her early twenties, one who had Whitney curls and big shoulder pads. A snap taken three years before I was even born.

A sob bubbles up. How damaged is my psyche that for a moment I thought I'd actually found her?

The steady April drizzle blurs the windscreen. What does it all mean? Jana and Duncan were clearly boyfriend and girlfriend at university. Why else would she visit the Ridings? But those images were from the 1980s. She went missing in 1999. Is there a connection? Any sane person would say no, but her scarf was at the bothy, *the* scarf she was wearing that June day.

Yet I know that isn't foolproof. There's no evidence it's hers or that she left it there in 1999; she might have had a penchant for leopard print back in the Eighties.

Something nags in a far recess of my mind, another link I can't quite grasp through my agitation. Needing to calm my frenetic thoughts, I turn on the wipers and watch their regular, steady movement until my heartbeat slows.

What does everything mean? Duncan Watkins, a missing girlfriend, a dead wife. No, not a dead wife but a murdered one; even his beloved daughter thinks so. And what did Lillian once say about Duncan killing her long-dead uncle?

I summon up the inscription on Freddie's grave, but my eyes slip to Imogen's dedication. Oh God, that's it. She died in 1999, the same year I last saw my mum.

–

Trying to handle the panic, I stay immobile in the driver's seat for some time.

My rational self knows I'm not dying, but it's hard to rise above the sharp pains in my chest. I've never had a heart attack, but I'm certain this is how it must feel. I focus on breathing in and out, in and out, as slowly as I'm able, but when a vehicle pulls up and an elderly man asks if I've broken down, I know I have to get a grip and do something.

I turn on the ignition and propel the car forward with shaky arms and legs. What now? I ask myself. What now? My dad is the obvious answer, but I need to think about that too. Mum always said they met and dated at university. Did she have a fling with Duncan Watkins behind his back? And is my imagination simply in free-fall anyway? If I shared my theories with him, would I cause him unnecessary hurt?

At the road sign for Sprotbrough, I take a huge breath. OJ will calm me; he'll listen and be rational and give me a gentle but objective talking-to like he did on Monday. Relief already kicking in, I park in Village Vet's car park, pull out my mobile and send a text:

> Hi, I've been at the Ridings to see Lillian today, so I'm here. Do you have time for a drink before I drive back?

There's no reply for a few minutes, but my phone eventually pings.

> I have a couple more appointments, then a break. Come in and Amy will make you a coffee.

Then:

> PS What a lovely surprise xx

Hoping I don't look as deranged as I feel, I hop up the steps, walk through the handsome building's glassy porch and into a busy reception area.

'Is it Christie?' a young girl asks from the counter. She's Amy, presumably. 'Take a seat. Mr Cullen won't be long. Tea or coffee?'

'Tea please,' I manage through a new surge of anxiety. But as I look around the room, my pulse slows. There are four dogs, three cats and a rabbit with their owners, all of whom look as tense as me. It'll be fine. OJ is used to highly strung and stressed animals; I'm just a different species of such. My eyes sweep the eclectic mix of equine paintings hung on the walls, finally resting on the silver plaque by the desk.

Belinda P Cullen MRCVS

Peter M Cullen MRCVS

Oliver-J Cullen MRCVS

Veterinary Surgeons

Despite my agitation, I smile. Not wanting to be just another 'date', I never did ask OJ for his actual names. So, the 'O' stands for Oliver. J for James, maybe? I read further down and note the practice was established in 1988, the year before OJ was born, which means he was probably brought up in this very house and attended the village primary school.

Oliver. Ollie. Why does the name ring a bell? I squeeze my memory and eventually recall trickles back. The boy Lillian loved who was mad about horses. What did she say? *Something horrible had happened and he wanted to talk about it. But I didn't.*

Yet OJ all but denied knowing her.

Chapter 57

1988

Duncan

Duncan spends Saturday slumped in an armchair. He can't get a real grip on his emotions. He feels raw and scared and sad and exhausted. He feels angry, ashamed and disgusted with himself. But he also feels overwhelming relief. His dad could have wiped the floor with him, but he didn't; his mum clearly doesn't know what's been going on; Imo has gone away and their relationship has been 'contained', whatever that means; best of all, Jana has been in touch; she still loves him.

He has read the postcards again and again, but each time he's skipped over the news from Phnom Penh or Kampot or Siem Reap and gone to her parting words:

Love you and miss you so much!

As for the one from Phuket, it makes his blood boil. But he can only blame himself; he was weak, he was foolish; he let his dick rule his head.

He looks at Jana's tiny scrawl again:

Where are you on Sundays? I've tried calling three times! Hope everything is OK. I love you xx

–

Remembering Thailand is six hours ahead of the United Kingdom, Duncan gets up at six on Sunday morning, sits at the study desk and stares at the telephone. He knows Jana is thoughtful and wouldn't wake him so early, but there is no way on God's earth he'll miss today's call. If she calls. If she hasn't already taken his absence as a sign that he's gone off her. Or a bloody huge clue that he's been shagging a woman behind her back. The remorse, the self-disgust, makes him feel physically sick, and yet like Pavlov's dogs, he finds his body stirring in every bloody room in the house because it's a reminder; he and Imo had sex there – on the lounge sofa, the kitchen table, the dining room rug; on the grimy scullery room floor; against the study door and of course in the bed, the bath and the shower.

He pictures his father's grim expression, that steady gaze loaded with all the things he didn't say, and he steels himself with resolve. Duncan Watkins has been given a second chance; between Noah and Vivienne, the last crazy few weeks have somehow been buried. How lucky is that? And though he was flattered and intrigued, infatuated and obsessed with Imogen, he's sure of one thing: he never truly loved her. And solid, real attachment is what endures. Jana is the person he loves, the one he always will. He's certain of that.

As he spreads out the photographs of Jana he dug out last night, a thought occurs. Today is the first of September, a new month. And it's pouring with rain outside. The heat, the must, the humidity and madness of August has passed. Today will be a brand-new start.

The telephone finally peals at noon, and though he's been waiting and longing for it, Duncan has to take a moment to steady his racing heart before answering.

'Hello?'

'Duncan! You're there. I left it until now in case you were having a lie-in.'

It's Jana, her warm tones clear as though she were in the next room.

He finds his own utterance cracking. 'I'm so sorry—'

'What for?'

'For missing your calls. I didn't know you'd tried.' Endeavouring to contain his anger, he takes a gulp of air. 'The post went haywire. Your end or mine, I don't know, but a whole bunch of your postcards landed on the mat at once.'

He feels guilt blend with the rage. He's already lying to Jana because of her. Because of himself too. 'So, I've been here by the phone all morning. God, it's so nice to hear from you. I'd almost forgotten—'

'Me? I hope not.'

'God, not you, not at all. Just your beautiful voice.' It's all he can do to hold back the tears. 'I've missed you so much. When will you be home?'

'That's why I'm calling. I have a job interview I don't want to miss, so I'm coming back two weeks earlier than planned. Marsha is staying for the full whack, so I wondered if you fancy meeting me at the airport? You know, a grand romantic reunion at the gate?'

'Try to stop me. So…'

'Manchester on the 14th. I'm due in around two in the afternoon. I might not look my best but hey ho.'

'As long as you bring your smile, I'm sorted.'

'That's perfect then. When I see you, I'll definitely have that.'

Chapter 58

Present Day

Christie

All I know is that I have to get out of Village Vet's waiting room as gracefully as I'm able. My chair loudly scrapes the tiled floor as I stand, and all eyes turn to me. Then Amy appears from a door and beckons me over. 'I've put your coffee in the sitting room. Mr Cullen says he'll meet you...'

But I turn away, walk to the exit and scuttle back to my car. Perhaps it's paranoia brought on by anxiety, but something doesn't add up here. If I discovered the whole village practised witchcraft, right this minute I wouldn't be surprised. Everything feels too, too connected, incestuous almost. The Cullens clearly know the Percys; the Percys and the Watkins united by marriage, so of course Belinda Cullen will have known Duncan and Imogen; of course *Ollie* knows Lillian. What did he say when I asked the direct question? '*No, not at all, I barely know her.*' Yet he turned up at the Ridings that first visit, and when Lillian saw him, she hid.

Then there's my mum in the mix. Maybe it was years before she went missing, but she was outside the Ridings in that snapshot. What the hell does it mean?

Back in the safety of my home, I lock the front door, make my way upstairs on jelly legs, kneel at the bedding box and open it. Tears blinding my eyes, I carefully remove what's left of my mother: clothes, ornaments, trinkets, a camera, notebooks, jewellery, shoes, boots and hats. Her books are still on the shelves in the lounge, and if she kept a diary, it isn't here. But there are several photograph albums, and a picture tells a story, so they say.

Though I know there'll be a million images of me as a baby, a toddler, an infant, a girl, I pick out the one marked 'university' and the last two years of her life, then climb beneath my duvet. Registering my own description of 1998 and 1999 as the last years of 'her life', the tears flow again. I've been convinced my mum is *somewhere* for the previous twenty-three years; do I really believe she is dead? Pushing that thought away, I decide not to bother with the Nineties as the police went through them. Instead, I take a breath and try to glean something of my mother from a decade before.

–

I wake to the sound of the doorbell. Expecting it to be the dead of night, I glance at my phone. It's actually seven-thirty in the evening. From a combination of trauma and crying, I clearly fell asleep.

Ignoring my caller, I fall back against the pillow and recount the story I learned from the photographs. With her big hair and big smile, Jana Fox went to Newcastle University, dated Alistair Morfett for a year and Duncan Watkins for two. She went travelling to South East Asia with Auntie Marsha, then returned to Alistair. It's not an unusual tale, but why did Duncan go from the university student with an adoring gaze to the dead-eyed man in Lillian's photos? And as she had put it, how did her parents go from young love to Imogen's grave?

The ding of a text brings me back from my reverie.

> Please open up. I don't know what I did to upset you, but I won't leave until you tell me.

My nose burns with emotion again. For once in my life, I let my heart rule my head; I wholly, completely trusted OJ, but I no longer know what to think.

> Come on, Christie. If you're dumping me, please give me the courtesy of an explanation.

Then:

> Simple honesty isn't much to ask, is it?

I find myself bashing the keys:

> How very poetic.

> What does that mean?

You asking for simple honesty when you can't manage it yourself.

I've been completely straight with you about everything, Christie. Right from the start I knew something good was going on and I had no intention of ballsing it up.

I roughly wipe the tears from my cheeks. I so want that to be true. Perhaps it's an occupational hazard, but I know when someone is lying. I should have known it from his evasive behaviour during our FaceTime call last week, but I guess I just didn't want to see it.

Just tell me. Please.

You lied about knowing Lillian Watkins.

I don't know her. I'd say hello if I saw her, but not as a friend.

You went to school with her.

Yes, twenty plus years ago.

When I don't respond to that, he texts again:

> I don't understand, Christie. What's
> bothering you so much?

Quickly inhaling, I take a wild guess:

> What happenod to you and Lillian at the
> bothy when you were ten?

There's a pause for many seconds, but a reply eventually comes:

> In all honesty I'm not sure. It was a long,
> long time ago.

Chapter 59

Duncan

Finding a new energy, Duncan passes the next ten days toiling long hours on the land. He makes himself a healthy dinner, then spends an evening in each room dusting and sprucing. Expunging the memory of Imogen? Perhaps, but he wants the house to look its best for when Jana moves in, which surely she will once she's spent some time with her folks in Leeds, said hi to her friends and family. They virtually lived together in Newcastle, so it feels like the natural progression of their relationship. Her job interview is at the university in Sheffield and that's only twenty miles away, a commutable drive until his mum and dad return to the Ridings. Then they can find a place of their own.

He now walks along the pedestrian high street and smiles. Life is finally coming together. He told his mum that Jana was due back on the fourteenth, and she was clearly delighted.

'I do love that girl. She's so sunny and easy-going.' She nudged Duncan with her elbow. 'And a good conversationalist and listener, which makes a change around these parts with you and your dad and whatever you might be thinking tightly clamped in your heads.'

Duncan laughed inwardly at that. Thank Christ his mum hadn't known what was constantly whipping in his skull like a spinning wheel during August. But maybe that's why he now feels so light, why he has this burst of vitality, and in all honesty it's wonderful not to have Imogen constantly there like an earworm, tempting, coaxing, both sweet and demanding. His chest still burns with anger when he thinks about the missing postcards, though. And did Imo deliberately keep him away from the Ridings on a Sunday because she'd read them? Yet he can't blame her completely. He was an adult; he was obsessed with having her, invading her. He could have simply resisted her advances. Couldn't he?

Yet that's precisely what he worries about. He's almost stopped squinting against the sunshine and scanning the land for a glimpse of red hair, but what if there is a next time? Could he say no? Could he fight Imogen's will? He absolutely wants to, but what if his body rebelled? Would his resolve and his deep, deep remorse hold up?

He nods and peers into the jeweller's shop window. That's why he's here, why he's spending every last penny of his savings on a ring. It's why he'll go on bended knee at the airport on Saturday and ask Jana Fox to marry him.

–

Friday drags unbearably. His dad is able to sit up long enough to do the more complex accounts, thank God, but there's still paperwork to do, invoices to clear, temporary workmen to pay. And the damned ledgers, of course. He's now taken to completing them after dinner each day, but in August he was distracted and fell behind. He shudders to think what he was doing between toiling, inspecting and mending – and who witnessed it – but he pictures the solitaire diamond sparkling on its velvet pillow and repeats his dad's words like a mantra: *It's all been contained; it's now in the past.*

He looks again at the plethora of documents spread across the desk. The excitement at seeing Jana tomorrow is so strong that it's a struggle to concentrate, but he's nearly finished. Then he'll go for a long run, meet up with Andy and a few others from the footie team for a beer or two, come home and have an early night.

–

Though the temperature has substantially dropped since the summer months, Duncan is sweating profusely on the last leg to the Ridings. As the house comes into view, he pulls himself up short. Bloody hell, Vivienne's Citroën is in the driveway. What does she want? There has been no mention of meetings or tours of the estate since she turned up with the envelope, but maybe it's that; perhaps more postcards have found their way to the big house.

He cautiously approaches the car. When he looks through the window, it isn't Vivienne's blonde hair but Imogen's red.

She opens the door and steps out. 'May I come in?' she asks politely. 'It'll only take five minutes.'

He wants to scream 'No!' but he has to be sensible. She is his employer's daughter; in all likelihood she'll be his patron one day. What did his dad say? Civil but distant, professional. He puffs out his agitation. It's fine; she's wearing jodhpurs, boots and her smart riding jacket. And her tresses are in a neat bun. She doesn't look as though she's here for—

As ever, she seems to read his mind. 'It's nothing like that. I need to have a word about something.'

Civil. Distant. Professional. 'Of course. Come in.' In the hallway, he gestures to the study. 'Take a seat.'

She does as she's told, and when he sits opposite, there's a sense of huge relief. She's just the slightly strange-looking posh girl he used to occasionally see on horseback or at the stables. He doesn't fancy her at all. It's as though the blip of August never happened. He almost wants to thank her for removing the image of the voracious temptress from his psyche.

He keeps his eyes averted from the jeweller's gift bag on the bookcase. 'So, what did you want to talk about?'

Her hands are folded in her lap. She addresses them. 'I need your help in making a decision.'

'Oh yes?'

'I'm pregnant.'

As though she's slapped him, he jerks back. 'What?'

'I missed two periods, so I did a test. It was positive, so I guess I must be...' She glances up before looking away again. 'Seven or so weeks pregnant.'

It feels as though his heart has simply stopped beating. 'What are you going to do?' he eventually squeezes from his throat.

Her gaze huge and vulnerable, she finally looks at him. 'I guess that's up to you.'

Chapter 60

Present Day

Christie

> In all honesty I'm not sure. It was a long, long time ago.

I stare at OJ's text for several beats, then I tumble down the stairs, scrabble with my keys and fling open the door. He's already belting up in his Land Rover.

'You said you wanted to be completely straight with me,' I shout into his passenger window.

He winds it down and spreads his hands. 'I am trying to be.'

His expression seems so sombre I'm afraid of what he'll say. Did he do something inappropriate to Lillian at the bothy? Is that why she didn't want to talk about it? Why she was so uncomfortable about scattering Duncan's ashes there? Yet I don't want OJ to leave. Something tells me that if he goes now, he might never come back.

'And your name,' I splutter through my tears. 'Why didn't you just tell me you were called Oliver? Did you think I might make the connection?'

Clearly trying to add up my erratic assault, he frowns. 'Everyone calls me OJ.'

'And why were you so evasive about your mum knowing Duncan and Imogen? She's the family vet; she must have.'

He sighs and steps out of the car. 'Same answer to both as it happens.' He wraps me in his arms and holds me tightly for several seconds. 'Come on. Let's go in, grab a beer and talk.'

–

OJ sits on the sofa, so I take the chair. I desperately want him to cuddle me, to make everything better, but I need some answers to help me out of this spiral of panic and doubt, and this man is the start.

'So, what do you want to know?' he asks.

I don't feel brave enough to deal with the bothy part yet. 'What you said about your name and your mum.'

'OK.' He takes a swig of his lager. 'It's foolish, I guess, but it's all based on fear.'

It's my turn to frown. 'Fear of what?'

'Fear of becoming him.'

Though I'm not sure where he's going with this, I wait for him to explain.

'When I was at primary school, I had a pretty bad temper. When you're this size, it's dangerous. I'm not saying the other end of my fist didn't deserve it, but I broke a nose or two and got a reputation as trouble. The headteacher had no time for it – understandably I suppose – and instead of looking further than the superficial angry boy, he demonised me. When that happens, you give up and become the person everyone thinks you are.' He smiles thinly and taps his temple. 'You're the expert; I'm sure you know all this.'

I bite my lip at that comment; all my university education and training doesn't help me to help myself.

'Anyway, this story has a happy ending. There's always someone good who offers a nugget of hope. In my case it was an elderly teacher who'd come back to cover a maternity leave. She took me to one side and said something to the effect of "You are you; you aren't him; you're going into high school, so it's time for a clean sheet; there's a kind, sensitive boy in that body; you can do this; I have faith in you."' He smiles. 'She's as old as the hills, but I still pop in for a cuppa when I'm out her way.'

'So "him" is your dad?' I ask.

OJ nods. 'I'm Oliver-John, same as him. He's generally known as Jonny, but a new name felt right for a new start, so OJ was born. Simples.'

The hurt passing through his gaze tells me it was far from that, but he steps over and takes both my hands. 'Enough about me. What happened today? What's thrown you?'

Though I wish I could stop them, the tears start up again. He fetches a wad of tissues and perches on the pouffe. 'So, you went to see Lillian at the Ridings…'

'Yes.' I blow my nose and take a breath to steady myself, but the words come out in a tumble, nonetheless. 'My mum and my dad went to Newcastle Uni, but she dated them both. There's a whole photo album of them upstairs, but there were two photographs in *his* wardrobe, Duncan's wardrobe. It could be a whole crazy twist of fate, but she was there at the Ridings, standing right in front of the house and looking so…' My voice cracks. 'So happy. Add that to the scarf I found, and it has to be more than just a coincidence, right?'

OJ rubs his head. 'Wow. So you're saying your mum went out with Duncan Watkins?'

'Yes, for two years. She went travelling, then got back with my dad.'

Pausing, I picture my parents sitting companionably side by side on the sofa, Dad listening to music and Mum with yet another tome on psychology. Every now and then, he'd put his headphones to her ear and she'd listen, smile and give him the thumbs up.

'They never married, but they had me, lived here and were happy.'

OJ peers at me. 'But?'

'God, I don't know; I was only eight, and I never breathed a word to anybody, but when I looked back on the day Mum went missing... She was, well, giddy, I suppose, and wearing silky underwear.'

'You think she was going to meet a lover?'

'Yes.'

'When was this?'

'Well, that's another thing...' Imogen's memorial flashes in, especially the creepy steps down to the tomb. 'Imogen died, and my mum went missing the same year.'

'And this was?'

'Nineteen ninety-nine.'

'Nineteen ninety-nine.' OJ repeats slowly. His forehead creased in thought, he falls silent for some time. Then he takes a breath and his gaze focuses again. 'It's still foggy, but I'll tell you what I remember.'

'About...?'

'About that day I was with Lillian at the bothy.'

Chapter 61

1988

Duncan

The engagement ring box pulsates in Duncan's pocket as he drives along the Woodhead Pass towards Manchester. He still hasn't decided whether to tell Jana the truth. His mind thrashing with possible outcomes, he barely slept a wink last night, and this morning it still feels as though he's stuck in mud, unable to come to any conclusion. Except it's no longer mud, is it? It's quicksand, and he's running out of time.

'What do you mean it's up to me?' he asked Imogen yesterday, still reeling from shock.

She dropped her head again, but not before he saw the hurt in her eyes, the onset of tears. Christ, she wasn't expecting him to declare his love, suggest the two of them give it a go, live together or even get hitched, was she? They barely knew each other; the relationship was simply a summer holiday type of fling. Of course, he knew it took two to make a baby, but his mind was all over the place; it was difficult to function, so he had to leave the room, pace the hallway for a few minutes and breathe.

'Seriously, Imo,' he said when he returned. He could see she'd been crying and he didn't want to be unkind, but he intended to marry someone else. Jana was coming home, and he'd bought her a ring, for God's sake! 'Why would it be up to me?'

When she didn't reply, he had to swallow back the words *I don't love you!* and try another tack. 'I mean, you don't want to be stuck with a plodding idiot like me. Or a screaming kid. You're so young and incredibly clever; you should be going to university and changing the world.' He cleared his throat. 'Look, I'd find the money to pay and go with you to the doctor or a clinic or whatever is needed...'

She looked truly appalled, scared and alarmed. 'You want me to have an abortion? Have them do whatever invasive thing they do to get rid of it?'

Christ, he felt rotten. 'It isn't up to me; it's your body, so your decision, but...' He crouched down by her side. 'Look, I'm as naive about these things as you are, and I'd be frightened of the unknown too, yet it's what people agree to do in these types of situations. I understand it's scary, but I know girls from uni who've been through the same, and they say it wasn't that bad, that in all honesty it was more a relief than—'

'Than what?'

Tears were now streaming down Imo's pale cheeks, but he had to be honest and get the words out.

'Than bringing an unwanted or unloved baby into the world.' He paused, then took a breath. 'You wouldn't want that either, would you?'

As though a spasm of pain was passing through her body, Imo shuddered. 'You're right. I wouldn't.' Her chin wobbled but she lifted it and nodded. 'OK, understood. I have no idea where to start – my GP, I suppose, but I'll do whatever I need to do.'

Duncan now parks the car in the arrivals terminal, looks at his watch and hurries out. He was stuck behind a line of lorries, so the journey over the hills took longer than he'd thought, but at least he's made up his mind. Before leaving the Ridings, Imogen gave a brave smile, then tiptoed up to kiss him on his cheek. 'Don't worry, I won't tell anyone,' she said. 'Have a happy life.'

He's been given another reprieve, another blessing. Only a fool wouldn't take it.

–

Her tender kiss still burning his lips, Duncan listens to Jana's happy prattle and drives towards Leeds. It didn't feel appropriate to make an idiot of himself by declaring his love at the busy airport gate, so he simply held her tightly instead.

She handed over her backpack. 'Please take this and throw it in the first bin you spot. I don't want to see it or the contents ever again.' She laughed. 'Though maybe hang fire until I've doled out my pressies. I bought you something I think you'll really like. I can't wait for you to see it...'

So the jewellery box is still there in his pocket, beating with a heart of its own. When should he make his proposal? Maybe pull up at a service station? Or wait until they're at her mum's house? Hand it over before they get out of the car, or maybe find a time when they're inside?

'I bought you a pressie too,' he could say, then wait until she looks at the tiny inscription inside the gold band: *I love you, Jana. I always will*, before asking her to marry him. And he does love her, he really, really does. He's sure of that more than ever.

He finally pulls up outside her mum's semi. 'Home sweet home,' he says. 'I bet your mum's so excited to see you.'

But instead of climbing out, Jana turns with a frown. 'What is it, Duncan?' she asks. 'Something's wrong, I can tell.'

It's the perfect time to grin and brandish the ring like a magician, but he can't. Instead, he opens his mouth, and his whole world falls out in five rushed sentences.

'I had a relationship in your absence. With Imogen Percy. It ended, but yesterday I discovered she's pregnant. I love you more than you'll ever know, but I have to do the honourable thing.'

Tears shoot to his eyes. He knew he'd do this, didn't he? In the early hours he'd known it. He couldn't put Imo through the trauma of an abortion. Terminating a life just isn't him; he couldn't live with the guilt. And any child of his would never really be unwanted or unloved.

He takes a huge, shuddery breath. 'So, if she'll have me, I'll marry her.'

Chapter 62

1986

Milly

We had a lovely few days before driving Imo to the Manor Clinic. We laughed as we leafed through its glossy brochure.

'It looks like from home to home,' I said, raising my eyebrows at the Rutherford-type building. 'Except there'll be a houseful there, not just Mummy, Granny and me rattling around these old walls.'

'Let's hope *their* walls don't have the yellow damp patches or peeling away wallpaper one longs to tug at,' Imo replied. She laughed. 'Or perhaps one *has* tugged at and made a bit of a mess!'

'I wouldn't have them any other way,' Viv replied. Then, 'Well, that isn't strictly true. A lick of paint everywhere would be wonderful, wouldn't it? Maybe modernise the kitchen. Buy a new sofa suite. Only my sitting room has kept up with the times.'

'What planet are you on, Mummy? No one has orange couches or swivel chairs these days. That furniture must be over twenty years old.'

'Which is extremely modern for the Percy family...'

'True. I suspect they'll have something a bit more *wipe-able* at the Manor. After all, it's a glorified loony bin.'

'Imogen!'

'It's fine, Mummy. I'm cool with it. I have an addiction and I want to overcome it.'

We were all about being open, truthful and honest these days. It was part of Imo's therapy: as painful or as embarrassing as it was at times, we were to acknowledge what had happened in the past so we could start a clean sheet and build trust going forward. Secrecy was bad for us all, but for Imo in particular. Secrecy and its veil of silence had allowed her addictions to grow, thrive and eventually dominate. Frankness with Viv and me was an integral part of tackling this, so we were to listen when Imo wanted to share, even if it was uncomfortable. Secrecy was a thing of the past.

Of course, in practice, it wasn't. One couldn't expect total honesty if one didn't give it, and in reality, Viv 'listened' but didn't really hear. And sometimes the truth took time to dribble out, like poor old Honora and the harrowing domestic abuse she'd suffered throughout her marriage. Not just forced intercourse whenever the fancy took Henry, but other depraved sexual acts by him, which only dementia had allowed her to voice via her 'stories'.

–

It was nice for each of us to spend a few hours with our girl alone.

Imo accompanied Honora on her walks with the dog, and Vivienne took over her packing. Though Imogen never bothered to look at them, let alone wear them, she confessed to a stash of expensive gifts in the drawer at the bottom of her wardrobe. Viv studiously averted her eyes, raked through the hangers and discovered – much to her delight – that none of her daughter's clothes fitted any more. Imo would never be as tall as her, but she'd definitely had a growth spurt, and she'd spent the last few years mostly in school uniform. It was the perfect excuse to drive into town in the old Citroën, have lunch and squander a few pounds from my wine sales on new outfits.

My one-to-one time was more lying on Imo's bed before sleep and having cosy chats like we used to. It was amazing how much one could learn over a mug of hot cocoa. Imo didn't disclose the identity of the man in Venice, but I discovered he wasn't the only 'sugar daddy' who'd contributed to her treasure trove in return for favours.

It was important not to show my shock, especially when I discovered he was a respectable and married local bigwig I had actually heard of, but the thought of those disgusting individuals made me shudder.

'You are not the freak or the loony, not by a long shot, Imo. Those men are. At fourteen you were just a baby. You might not realise it, but even at sixteen, you're still one now.'

She rolled her eyes at that. 'Yeah, ironic.'

'What does that mean?' I asked. But she wasn't for divulging that little secret yet. It turned out she had good reason not to.

Chapter 63

Present Day

Christie

Terrified of what OJ's about to impart regarding the bothy, I delay the moment by nipping to the toilet and washing my face. When I look up at my reflection, Jana stares back: same hair, same lips, same age. Only my eyes tell me and my departed mother apart.

'What happened to you, Mum?' I ask. For I'm now sure OJ's disclosure won't be about him and Lillian or any childhood misunderstanding or jinks, but about her.

When I return to the lounge, OJ is back on the sofa. He pats the cushion, so I sit beside him and allow his strong arms to warm my whole shivering being for a few minutes.

I eventually pull away. 'Tell me,' I say.

'OK, so... When I was nine or so, Mum got me a weekend job at Rutherford's livery stables. Mucking out, feeding, grooming, riding. The new horse barn was amazing, and being paid for something I loved was great. The downside was having to put up with a girl from my class, but it turned out she was a good kid who loved animals too, so when I finished my chores, we hung out, chatted, ate sandwiches, climbed trees, told each other spooky stories. And if it was raining, we'd trek over to the bothy for shelter. I think she was unhappy and I felt sorry for her.'

He glances at me. 'Sorry, I'm digressing.'

'It's fine. I want to hear it all. Why was Lillian unhappy?'

'A lonely only child and…' He grimaces. 'That was tactless. Sorry.'

'It's OK. That's why I want three.'

He kisses my nose. 'Three kids, eh?'

Despite the sheer anxiety, I find myself smiling. 'Yes, but maybe one at a time.'

'Order duly noted.' He goes back to his story. 'Yeah, so Lillian. She didn't have many friends and her mum was flighty, to say the least. Yet I think she preferred her absence.'

'Her parents rowed?'

'Yes.'

'Were they violent at all?'

'She never said it in terms, but I think so.' He clears his throat. 'Anyway, this particular Sunday, Lillian must have been at her granny's because she brought the dog. The weather turned, so we made for the bothy, chucking a ball through the woods for the collie to chase. When we got to the garden, the dog didn't appear, so we went back to investigate. He was in a hollow, scratching at the loose earth.'

I swallow. 'What had he found?'

OJ sighs. 'This is where my memory gets fuzzy, but at the time I thought it was a soil-covered hand. Me and Lillian both stared for a second, then I grabbed the collie and we belted out of there. We were both so freaked out, we didn't know what to think. I know it sounds crazy, but we just went home and didn't say anything to our parents. I pretty much had nightmares for a week, but I had to do my weekend stint at the stables, so I steeled myself to look again the following Saturday. All I found near the surface were leaves and tree roots. Some looked like fingers, so I convinced myself that's what we'd seen, and maybe we had, but then rumour had it that—'

'That Imogen Watkins had gone missing?'

'Yes. And that the police were questioning Duncan. When I tried to broach what we'd seen with Lillian, she clammed up and didn't want to talk about it. She pretty much blanked me after that.'

'God, poor girl; poor woman.'

I picture Lillian's troubled face at the Devonshire. No wonder she was so defensive and scared; she loved her dad dearly but was certain he'd killed her mother, and she'd keep that secret deeply hidden for over twenty years until confessing it to me that day. No wonder she had mental health problems and self-harmed in the past. No wonder she was so confused by Duncan's wishes for the scattering of his ashes…

But today she was in a much better place with her positivity and baking. I realise that I really do care for her welfare. And yes, not just as a nurse, but as a close friend.

So exhausted from emotion, I settle against OJ's shoulder and almost fall asleep, but eventually my torpid mind cranks up again.

'But Imogen Percy was later found,' I say. 'She had died in a driving accident. The police dropped their investigation, so it must have been kosher.'

I sit back and stare at OJ. 'So, if you did see a hand in that hollow, who did it belong to?' Nausea hitting, I lower my head. 'My mum. It was hers, wasn't it? For whatever reason, she came to see Duncan at the bothy that day and left her scarf. Maybe to rekindle their university relationship? But something went wrong. They rowed, or perhaps she found out he'd done something to get rid of Imogen. I don't know – tampering with her brakes, paying someone to drive her off the road.'

I try to focus. Can it really be true? Could my mother be buried in the woods? 'The hand,' I say to OJ. 'Was there a ring or anything else to identify it? Painted nails or the like?'

'I honestly don't know, Christie. I'm so sorry I can't be more definitive about what I saw either that Sunday or when I went back the following week. Life moved on. I glimpsed Lillian at Imogen's funeral, then she went off to boarding school. She might remember more than me, but I doubt she'd want to talk about it. Still, I suppose you could ask.'

'No,' I reply slowly. 'No. She's no longer my patient as such, but I still owe her a duty of care to look after her wellbeing and…'

A strange certainty hits me. Duncan's ashes request was remorse, wasn't it? Perhaps the first page of the 'wishes' letter explained more – that it was an accident of some sort, a lover's tiff – but at the end of the day, he killed my mum and made me motherless.

I look at OJ and nod. 'I'd be accusing her father of yet another death.'

Chapter 64

1986

Milly

I never told Vivienne about Imogen's situation; despite all the promises of candour going forward, it would have simply been too painful for her to learn.

In truth I should have known, as all the signs were there in the weeks before Imo was admitted to the Manor. Though still a petite girl, I'd noticed she was a touch chubbier, her breasts a little larger, and occasionally she pushed her favourite food away on the grounds she'd 'gone off it'.

Now chairlady of the church committee, Vivienne was at a fundraising event when the call came through. It was from the director of the Manor Clinic himself.

'Is that Mrs Percy, Imogen's mother?' he asked.

Something about his brisk tone made me pause before answering. 'Yes, it is,' I replied.

'We have a problem with Imogen, I'm afraid.' Unlike Mrs Fleming and her dithering, he came straight to the point. 'She has confessed to being two to three months pregnant and she's insisting on keeping it. That's as far as the conversation has gone.' He cleared his throat. 'Our hands are tied, Mrs Percy. Imogen doesn't have a mental health condition which would warrant a section or any "enforced action", if you like, so in the absence of her consent, nature will take its course. The question is where we go from here. She has made excellent progress with us, and I'm happy to extend her stay in the short term if your finances allow it, but after that... Well, let's put it this way, we're not a maternity unit, and we don't have facilities for a baby.'

My head spun, but I used my confident voice. 'Let me have a word with Imogen and I'll get back to you.'

—

I considered calling Imo straight back and challenging her, but I decided to see her in person. Vivienne was mildly surprised I was ringing the changes by visiting my old gran during the week, but I made my way to the village, took a bus into Doncaster, a train out to Chester, followed by another bus and a very long walk. My feet ached, and I was exhausted by the time I reached the Manor, yet Imogen wasn't for talking at first, let alone relenting.

'I don't know what you're doing here. I've decided,' she eventually said.

'Decided what, exactly?'

'To continue with the pregnancy.'

'And what then?' I asked. She seemed thrown by such a simple question. 'Will you keep the baby or have it adopted? Surely you should already have the answer to that.'

'How will I know until I've seen it?'

It was the sort of comment I expected but not the one I wanted to hear. The patter of little feet around Rutherford again would make my heart soar, but Imogen wasn't mother material. Maggie had been far from loving with me, but these days I had a better understanding of that. I took a breath to say something, but Imo spoke again.

'I'm not having another abortion.'

Another abortion. I tried not to let my shock show. 'Oh yes?'

'Sinclair arranged for some woman to do it at her house and it was horrible. I'm not going through the blood and the agony ever again, so that's that.'

–

Imogen remained resolute for some time. But when the foetus began to move, she turned on a sixpence, said she'd made a mistake and wanted a termination. It was quietly put into effect by the staff at the Manor, and by then her two-month stay was up. The team leader advised Viv that Imogen was 'ready to face the world, socialise and put all her learning, therapy and ways of handling her addictions into practice'.

'It will be so wonderful to have Imo home,' Vivienne said when she put down the phone. 'But the *world* and *socialising*… Well, she's hardly going to get that here, is she?'

I had already formed a potential plan in the event of Imogen's continued pregnancy. Vivienne's brother and his French Canadian wife had been enchanted by her when they'd visited last summer. 'What about a trip to see Maxwell and Gabrielle?' I suggested. 'They've offered to have her to stay several times.'

'Quebec? That's many hours away even by aeroplane, Milly. Longer than that damned train to Bournemouth.'

'True, but with a different language and way of life, it will be an education of sorts.'

The doubt fell away from Viv's face. 'Oh, Milly, you're wonderful; what would I do without you? Yes, finishing school! That's what we'll say if anyone asks.'

Chapter 65

Present Day

Christie

I'm still in bed at noon on Saturday and staring at the ceiling. The day, the house and the world feel still and surreal, but that's not surprising because I'm frozen too. I know it's trauma and shock, but in a way I'm making the most of it because I know the pain will come. I know I won't be able to stand by without finding out the truth, even if I have to walk all the way to Rutherford and scratch up the soil with my bare hands.

It's OJ's turn to work at the surgery this weekend, so he had to leave me first thing this morning. 'I love you, and you'll never get rid of me. You know that, don't you?' he said at the door.

'Get rid of you? Hmm, in your case, I might need the assistance of a crane,' I replied.

'I think you mean a stork. The two birds aren't one and the same as people think. Cranes are in the family Gruidae while storks are in Ciconiidae...'

'Fascinating. I'm not sure a stork will help with the lifting or digging, though.'

He grinned. 'True, but it will bring all those babies.'

Maybe our humour is a little dark, but it got me through last night. A little tender lovemaking too. But now I'm on my own, I've reverted to thoughts of OJ's shocking discovery at the bothy.

'You know I'll need to find out whether you saw my mum's hand that day,' I said to him in the early hours.

'I do, but think it through first. It's Percy land, so you can't do anything without permission; otherwise, it's trespass. What about involving the same police who investigated her disappearance? That might be the best move, but I imagine they'd contact your dad. Then there's Lillian and how the whole thing might impact her mental health and your friendship.' He grimaced. 'It's a dreadful metaphor to use in the circumstances, but you might be opening a can of worms. And suppose I was wrong? Suppose it was the furtive imagination of a ten-year-old boy after exchanging spooky tales? What if I simply saw tree roots?'

I now rock my sweaty head on the pillow. God, what should I do? I close my eyes, and the image of my beautiful mother pops up, the woman I used to see in bus stop queues or in the dentist's waiting room or in a busy wine bar. But if we dig and find her, she'll simply be bones. Is that a good thing or a bad thing? I just can't decide.

–

By two o'clock I'm up, showered, dressed and in the car. Not only have I fully thawed, I've made a decision.

It feels strange to bypass the entrance to the Ridings and motor through the main gates towards Rutherford House. I look from left to right as I pass through the budding parklands, but surely I won't be spotted. Lillian hasn't yet visited the main house, and when I called her for a chat before leaving Sheffield and idly enquired, she said she had no intention of doing so.

'Funny you should ask. Milly says Granny wants to see me now I'm back. Well, if she's so keen, she can make the effort and drive over.'

'Maybe she's been ill or struggles with her mobility.'

'Nope. She's being stubborn. Dad's not here any more, but she clearly considers the Ridings tainted.'

'Didn't she get on with him?'

'Maybe once, but…'

Though Lillian deftly changed the subject, it was the information I required: after Imogen's death, there was clearly no love lost between Vivienne Percy and Duncan Watkins.

Coming back to the present, I gaze at the huge dwelling ahead. It's as magnificent as it was in the photographs, but in person there's a definite sense of decay. If I wasn't so nervous, I'm sure I would take in each detail of its sheer yet jaded splendour, the white elevations now turned a shade of grey, the handsome windows in the two wings unnaturally dark. Its corroding, Gothic grandeur sends a shiver down my spine, but I try to block out Lillian's stories about hauntings and curses and stay focused on the reason I'm here. I duly take a deep breath of resolve, drive past overgrown lawns towards the double staircase, park up and climb out. The rain cooling my hot cheeks, I hurry up the steps to the imposing front entrance and search for a bell. After a minute of hopping from foot to foot, I try again with the knocker.

The door finally opens and Mrs Shaw appears. She looks at me curiously, then the penny drops at the same time as her face. 'You're from the Devonshire. Is it Lillian?'

'Sorry, no, nothing like that. I'm not here as a nurse. It's about something personal, in fact.' The woman squints at me suspiciously and inches the door to, so I quickly speak again. 'Please could I have a word with Mrs Percy? I promise I'm not a salesperson or a from a religious cult. I'd like to ask her permission for something...'

My fake smile and friendly manner are clearly not working, so I inhale to change tack, but an eloquent enunciation filters through.

'Who is it, Milly?'

'Please may I have a word, Mrs Percy?' I say over the small woman's head. I find my voice cracking. 'It's very important to me.'

Five minutes later I'm ensconced on a worn velvet couch in a shabby parlour at the front of the house.

The lady who graciously introduced herself as Vivienne Percy now addresses me. Though she must be well into her seventies, she's still blonde, stylish and attractive. 'How may I help you?' she asks.

I look at the china cup in my hand. On the way I'd contemplated some cock and bull story about being an amateur archaeologist or wildlife biologist needing soil samples, but now I'm here, the simple truth feels right, and besides, I've already shed a couple of traitorous tears.

'It's a very long story, but I'd like permission to dig up a small area of your land.'

It's freezing in the lofty room, but neither woman seems to notice. Instead, they both sit straight-backed and study me politely. 'Oh yes?'

'The thing is, I wouldn't want Lillian to know.'

They glance at each other then. 'Why on earth not?'

The tears shoot out again. 'Because my mother went missing over twenty years ago. She once dated Lillian's father. I know I'm grasping at straws, but I need answers about what became of her.' I pull out a tissue. 'But I don't want to upset Lillian as her nurse or her friend. Not unless I have to.'

Vivienne dips her head. 'And where would you want to dig? I'm afraid the Ridings doesn't belong to us.'

The door bangs on its jamb and a flurry of cold air breezes through the room; if I believed in spirits, I'd say one was walking right past me.

I rub the chill from my arms. 'The bothy garden. Well, near there, in the woods.'

Two sets of eyes stare as though I've lost the plot. Perhaps I have. I sense their civil patience is wearing thin, so I grasp at *something* to show I'm not as deranged as I must appear. 'My boyfriend will help me excavate and make good. We won't touch the grass, and you won't know we've been.'

Vivienne stands and gestures me out of the room. 'Well, let me think about it.'

I step into the hallway. 'My boyfriend, he's...' Wondering where they keep their dog, I glance around the vast, shadowy area and look up to the almost black tiers above. Ghosts or not, I don't blame Lillian for not wanting to live here. 'He's your vet. Or at least your vet's son.'

Although I feel bad for mentioning it without OJ's permission, a smile breaks Vivienne's stately expression. 'Oliver-John? How lovely! We've known him since he was knee high. He's such a delight.' She pats my shoulder. 'Don't worry, we won't say anything to Lillian. We'll have a little think, and now I know who to call.'

Chapter 66

Milly

When Imo turned eighteen in May, she decided to fly back from Quebec and apply for university in this country. What with her lack of O and A levels, it turned out to be more tricky than she'd imagined, but she lifted her chin and said she'd take the necessary exams at a college in Doncaster and apply again next year. I was very pleased about that. I liked her pluckiness and tenacity, her willingness to look at the long term rather than her needs in the moment. That was the young woman I wanted her to be.

As May and June passed it was wonderful to have her home, even if she and Viv did chatter away in French at times. Imo had always been a chameleon, so it was no surprise to see she'd changed again after her stint in Canada. Much to Vivienne's delight, she presented as the charming daughter freshly back from finishing school, and she graciously accompanied her mother to church fetes and charity events in the village, even volunteering to help cover the reception desk at the local probation service.

However, by mid-July, Imogen became distant and secretive again, ditching her mother and the voluntary work and disappearing for hours. Even our regular bedtime natters seemed a thing of the past, and I worried she was no longer being open with me, even partly.

'It is disappointing,' Vivienne said, 'but hardly surprising. Imo's young and beautiful and wants to have fun. I'm sure I wouldn't have hung around with middle-aged ladies discussing jam, or indeed with petty criminals, when I was that age. It was Christian of her to do it while it lasted. What she really needs are some friends. Even better, to meet a nice young fellow and fall in love.'

From Imogen's bright eyes and her furtive behaviour as sweltering August passed, I guessed she already had, and when Honora reported seeing 'coupling in the grounds of Rutherford' with an aghast expression, I knew it wasn't the ramblings of a confused old lady with dementia, but Imo and a boy. Not just a boy, but the Watkins lad. Why I hadn't gleaned that earlier, I had no idea. After Noah's roof accident, young Duncan had been standing in for him at the Ridings, and from the way Imo had gawped at him over the years, I knew she'd had a crush on him from being very small.

I certainly didn't condone outdoor intimacy, and I wouldn't have dreamed of mentioning that aspect to Viv, yet otherwise I didn't disapprove. When Imo was still confiding in me, she'd said that total abstinence from sex with herself or others had helped her obsessive thoughts during her time at the Manor – and presumably in Canada – but if the subject of her affections was around the same age, surely that was a sign the therapy had worked, and she was now as 'normal' as she could ever be. I had no time for that airhead Connie Watkins, but Noah was a good man, and what was the harm in a little romance for our Imo?

After mulling for a while, I decided to broach it with Vivienne. Instead of the indulgence I'd expected, her response was terse. 'The Watkins boy? Are you certain they're an item?' she asked, tight-cheeked. 'And how long have you known?'

When I prevaricated on both points, she marched up to Imo's bedroom and returned with a bundle of postcards. 'Hidden,' she said. 'Hidden beneath Imo's mattress. You are clearly correct about your suspicions, Milly, but look at this. The young man already has a girlfriend.'

Same as I had after the Venice incident, I wondered whose side Vivienne was on, yet before I could take a breath, she was scooping up her handbag and striding to her car.

'Where are you going?' I shouted after her.

'To speak to Noah; see what he makes of it and, if necessary, put this right,' she answered over her shoulder.

Once she had gone, I sighed at my feelings of redundancy. Speaking to Noah Watkins and putting things right used to be my department. However, when Vivienne returned from the village an hour later, I couldn't help but smile a secret smile at her opening words.

'I'm shocked to the core, Milly.'

'Why? What did Noah *make of it*?'

Viv recounted Noah's reaction and my smugness soon vanished: Duncan had made a foolish mistake by getting involved with Imogen, but she was a deeply troubled young lady; he would not under any circumstances encourage or condone a relationship between his son and her. Duncan already had a beautiful lass he intended to marry one day; Imogen had clearly seduced his boy, and wherever she'd been sent to for treatment the last time, she needed to go back there.

Somewhat offended, Vivienne had apparently challenged him. 'How can you possibly know who seduced who?'

'I have a bloody good idea.' Noah clearly struggled with saying it but must have felt that he had to. 'On the way back from Venice,' he muttered. 'Aye, she even tried it on with me.'

That did it for Vivienne, of course. If there was one thing she couldn't stand, it was what others might think, so she told Noah that Imo would go on a month's 'holiday' and it wouldn't be spoken of again.

Poor old Imo. In truth, I thought it was a little unfair, but no one saw fit to consult me.

—

I'd always loved listening to the distant chime of church bells on the Sabbath, yet I desultorily tromped the fields with the new puppy that mid-September Sunday. I'd felt unsettled for the past few weeks and today was no exception. Imo had been dispatched to the Manor for over fourteen days now, and she hadn't been in touch with me. I hated feeling out of the loop, and Viv had faithfully promised that I wasn't, but I sensed my firm hold on events and my general influence at Rutherford was weakening.

Wondering how Imo was coping, I ambled back towards the house, but as I turned for the path to the rear, I glimpsed a tall figure loping up the perron to Rutherford's entrance.

I quickly scurried towards him. 'Hello?' I called. 'Can I help you?'

'Oh, hi.' He retraced his steps and towered over me with a nervous smile. 'Hello, Mrs Shaw.' He held out his hand. 'I'm sure you don't remember me, but I'm Duncan Watkins. I'm here to see Imogen. Is she in?'

'No, I'm sorry...' I began, somewhat confounded by his shocking presence and his assumption she would be. Thinking how to put it, I stalled. 'Mrs Percy is at St Mary's, but if it's a matter of business, you could—'

But to my astonishment, the front door fired open and Imogen ran out, her clothes somewhat crushed as though she'd only just woken up.

'Sorry, Milly, I came back late last night and didn't want to wake you and Mummy.' Then to Duncan, 'Hello you. You came.' A huge beam on her face, she reached out a hand and tugged him to the veranda. 'Come on in and let me show you around my house.'

Chapter 67

Present Day

Christie

I decided not to tell OJ about my visit to Rutherford until I saw him in person the following week. I'm getting to know him pretty well, but I have no idea how he'll react to me mentioning our connection to Vivienne and frankly using it to get my own ends.

He's due any minute, so I pace my small lounge and mentally prepare my speech. The doorbell pings so I hurry to open it, peck his lips and say, 'I have something I need to tell you.'

'I know,' he says, stepping in.

'Oh God. Really?'

'Yup. Mum received a call from Vivienne this afternoon, as it happens.'

I cringe. 'She called your mother?'

'She did.' He lifts a paper take-out bag. 'Malabar matthi for two. One rice, two naan breads and ten popadoms.'

I laugh nervously. I'm struggling to gauge his mood. 'Are you sure ten is enough?'

'Put it this way; I'm starving.' He pulls out a chair and sits at the set table.

I'm really not hungry, but I spoon food into my bowl and give him a chance to eat. 'I'm sorry,' I say eventually. 'I should have asked you first, but it was on the spur of the moment. God, I can't believe she called your mum. I feel really bad.'

'So you should. Bit of a shock for my old mum to discover she isn't my whole world.'

'What did Vivienne say?'

'Nothing specific, thank God. Something along the lines of "Tell Oliver-John we're fine with his lovely girl-friend's request". "Girlfriend?" Mum replied...'

'So you haven't told her about—'

'Nope.'

'Really?' I usually know when he's teasing, but in all truth, I feel winded and fragile, my judgement unreliable right now.

He puts down his cutlery and gathers me in his arms. 'Of course I've told Mum about my stunning new woman. Both she and Pete are gagging to meet you, but I didn't want to push you into the lion's den too soon.' He sighs. 'And I know I'm being overly jokey, but in all honesty, this whole thing about your mum is so huge, I don't know how to handle it. Not for me but for you. I know you need answers, but I worry about you constantly. Should I have told you when my memory is so sketchy? Have I done more harm than good? Because if your mum is buried at the bothy, there's no turning back for you, for your dad or Lillian.'

My stomach churns with anxiety, but I force a smile. 'Don't fret on my account. I'm stronger than I look.'

–

What with my shifts and OJ's and the rainy weather, we struggle to find a day to visit what I inwardly call my mum's grave. By the time we meet in the pub car park at seven o'clock on a Wednesday morning, ten days have passed, and I'm almost faint with anxiety, loss of appetite and sleep.

When I slip into the front seat of OJ's Land Rover, he puts a hand to my cheek. 'You're wasting away. Are you still sure about this?'

'Yes. I've come this far; I can't stop now.'

'OK. If we find anything at all, we put our tools down and report it to the police. Yes?'

It's what we've already agreed, so I nod.

From Lillian's stay at the Devonshire, I know she usually struggles to wake as her medication makes her groggy. Yet still I'm fretful when we arrive at the bothy. Suppose she's stopped taking it? Suppose she decides to walk here? The scattering of Duncan's ashes hasn't been mentioned since the day I bolted away from the Ridings. Suppose she decides to do it by herself? If anyone else happened upon OJ's car parked outside the barn or busying himself around here, it wouldn't seem odd, but Lillian would instantly know why he was in that particular spot and digging. And though I'm still desperate for answers, I feel awful for betraying my friend. Because I'm certain we'll find something. No, not *something* but bones in the remnants of the clothes I last saw Jana in; the fully formed skeleton I've been dreaming about every night, but with her beautiful teeth and hair.

OJ doesn't ask me if I'm sure again. Instead, he hops over the square of grass to the woods beyond and moves around the nearby hollow for a while. He eventually pats the trunk of the huge beech tree looming above, presses his shovel a few inches into the ground and carefully slices the mossy top away. Then he kneels down, examines and shakes each clod until the softer, looser soil is exposed. I dumbly watch. I have a spade too, but my limbs feel so weak, I'd be of no use.

He continues his gentle excavation like an archaeologist searching for treasure. 'I'd suggest you stay in the car or the bothy, but I know you won't,' he says over his shoulder after a while. He strips off his jacket and hands it to me. 'Sit on this.'

I perch on a grassy mound and continue to observe him gingerly dig, spread and examine each layer of earth. The care and tenderness he's giving to his mission bring tears to my eyes, yet still I will him to hurry, to find my waiting mum.

I have no idea how much time passes, but OJ's T-shirt becomes so wet with sweat, it sticks to his torso, and his face muddies from his wiping the perspiration away from his eyes. After a chilly start, the dappled sun creeps through the trees. I know it's a balmy late April day, but the warmth doesn't register. My own bones feel like ice, yet none of my mother's appear.

After quarrying a good foot in depth, OJ stands and stretches and steps to me. 'Nothing, Christie. I honestly think I'd have found something by now.' He drops his head. 'I'm so very sorry; this is definitely the place, but I was mistaken. Whatever I saw was…' He gestures over to the exposed rhizomes. 'Roots.'

I know he's suffering too, that he found himself between a rock and a hard place, but I can't give him the love and redemption he clearly needs just now. I'm stunned, I'm hollow, I'm barely functioning.

'Look, I'll gladly carry on digging, but…'

'It's fine,' I mutter. 'You're right; she's not there.' I manage to force myself upright and gesture to the bothy. 'I just need to...'

'OK. I'll be... fixing things here. I'll come in and get washed in a bit, then we should get a bite to eat.'

I stumble across the grass. 'I really am so sorry, Christie,' I hear OJ say on the breeze, but I don't turn or acknowledge it. Instead, I make my way to the only piece of my mum I'll find today, maybe ever. I carefully unearth the scarf from beneath the garments on the coat stand and put it to my face. Then I leave the old building and head along the tree-lined track to the pub car park, hoping that somehow I'll find my way.

Chapter 68

1988

Duncan

'Hello, you. You came,' Imo says. She grasps Duncan's hand and tugs him towards the veranda. 'Come on in, and let me show you around my house.'

He follows her into the domed hallway and immediately feels the old shiver. He hasn't been in here since Freddie's funeral twelve years ago. Was Imo milling with the mourners that day? He doesn't know. All he can remember is terror, a certainty that someone or something non-human knew what he'd done and would punish him if he didn't get out of there.

'Duncan!'

He reverts to his intended. Pretty, trim and smiling, and her hair tousled as though she's only just up, she reaches up on tiptoes to his lips. Aware of Mrs Shaw's gaze burning his back, he responds with a chaste kiss. Christ, he's confused already. Imo is showing no surprise that he's here, and yet the housekeeper was clearly gobsmacked to see him, and especially her. She mustn't know that Imo came back early from her holiday or the reason for it. Oh God. Is Imogen really pregnant? Yes, yes, she is. He saw the fear, the hurt, the innocence in her eyes only two days ago. She couldn't possibly have had an abortion between then and now, could she?

'Come on, handsome,' she's now saying, pulling him through one of the two archways. 'Let me give you a tour.'

He doesn't feel remotely handsome, attractive, good or nice. He feels like a complete and utter shit. Jana didn't shout or accuse or make a scene in the car yesterday. She simply cried. She let him take her into his arms, and she sobbed against his chest until his shirt was soaked. Then she climbed out, removed her rucksack from the boot and walked to her mum's front door without looking back. All he was left with were her tears, and by the time he was back at the Ridings, they had dried and disappeared as effectively as she had.

Dragging himself back to today, he lets Imo lead him in and out of lofty rooms, which were once clearly opulent but now are jaded and worn. With a huge effort, he tunes into what she is saying.

'The house is Palladian, which means the design was copied from the Venetian architect Andrea Palladio.' She gestures around a vast, dank-smelling chamber. 'This is the second drawing room. We never come in here, but as you can see the wallpaper is made of velvet.'

'God, yes,' he says, automatically touching it. It's a far cry from how his mother redecorated the Ridings when she lived there. She maintained the flavour of an old property, but everything was clean and simple and wholly preferable to this overindulgence.

Imo slips her slim arms around his neck. 'Isn't it all wonderful? Or at least could be if it was tarted up. Just think, this will be ours one day!'

He was never one for literature or poetry, but he clearly remembers *The Rime of the Ancient Mariner* and that albatross: this mansion, Imogen Percy… And the child?

Anxiety rising, he gently touches her belly. 'Is everything…'

'Of course it is. I knew you'd change your mind.' She softly kisses him. 'You don't know how glad I am you did, how happy I am that you're here.'

How the hell did she know when he didn't know himself? But his fickle body responds to her sweetness, her innocence, the baby, his baby growing inside her.

'Let's go upstairs,' she says.

He follows her up the grand staircase to the first landing and looks down to the marbled floor below. This is exactly where he saw movement, a glint in the shadows that day.

Imo's voice flutters in with his shudder. 'This one was Freddie's bedroom.'

'Oh right.' He doesn't want to even peep in, so he gestures to a large door at the end of the corridor. 'Where does that lead to?'

'The east wing. It's boarded up,' she says dismissively. She catches his arm. 'And this is mine.'

Stepping over the threshold, he glances around the large space. He knows the Percys have struggled financially, but there's everything here one would expect of a spoilt child, from an elaborate doll's house to a handsome rocking horse and everything in between.

Imo lies on the neatly made bed and pulls up her top to expose her stomach. 'Come and give our peanut a kiss.'

'A peanut?' he says, emotion gripping his windpipe.

'Or a baked bean, but I think peanut sounds nicer, don't you?'

'Yes,' he croaks. He can do this; he really can.

He kneels down and plants his lips on her soft, pale skin, but a flash of the other Imogen hits the back of his eyes. The pill-popping one who disappears somewhere else; the laughing temptress who can down a row of shots in a minute, then challenge him to do the same.

Sitting back, he clears his throat. He has to start as he means to go on. 'A clean page, Imo. It isn't just the two of us having fun any more. We have a baby on the way, so no drugs, smoking or heavy boozing, no riding without a hat. A healthy lifestyle and good food. Yes?'

'Of course.'

'I mean it, Imogen.'

'Yes, Duncan. Whatever you say, I'll do it.' Her gaze is so shiny, her smile so sweet. 'I promise, my darling, absolutely.'

Chapter 69

Christie

My breath shallow, I drive straight from the pub car park to home. All I know is that I need my dad and my dog. That's as far as my thoughts will go. So, I grab my overnight bag and shove in the few things my torpid mind can process – purse, toothbrush, pyjamas, leggings, T-shirt, jumper. And yes, clean underwear.

The Uber soon arrives, but when I open the door to leave, I realise I'm still shivering from the cold, so I swap my jacket for a winter-weight one and dash into the taxi. It isn't until I'm on the train to Aberdeen and settling in for the long journey that I realise my mobile is still in the pocket of my other coat.

I shrug at the loss of my lifeline to work, to the world, to everyone and everything. It's hardly important in the scheme of things. I had planned to text my dad and warn him I was coming, but other than that, it's a good thing, even serendipity. I need to escape, to free my mind from my mum, Duncan Watkins, Rutherford House and the Ridings. I need to close my eyes and just sleep.

After six hours of blindly staring at the passing countryside on my journey, I'm exhausted when I reach my dad's mid-row villa in Cove Bay. With its grey veneer, it isn't the prettiest of houses; he didn't have masses of money to spare, certainly not after transferring our Sheffield home into my name. And it isn't all bad; on Coast Road you can hear and smell the sea.

As ever it's raining, so I press the bell and huddle beneath the door roof as I wait. The windows are in darkness, so it isn't a surprise when there's no answer. Finally kicking myself for forgetting my mobile, I look at my watch, but I soon calm down. It's six o'clock; my man-of-habit father is sure to appear soon to give himself time to prepare his dinner and have it on the table by seven.

I consider moving out of sight to the rear of the terrace. However, I know from my last visit that a high fence surrounds Dad's postage-stamp garden and that he keeps the gate locked, so I have no option but to hunker down and loiter in his doorway. As the dusk becomes darker, I feel my eyelids droop, and despite the damp and the low temperature freezing my bones, the mercy of sleep pulls me in.

—

I wake to concerned eyes and the mild aroma of baking.

'Christie, love, it's Ruthie. Ally's neighbour called me.' She hitches me up to my feet. 'He's away until Friday evening, love.'

I thought I was no longer capable of tears, but they flow as if I've turned on a tap. 'Oh God. I needed to see him. And Sammy.'

'Well, that works out perfectly.' Her expression both sad and compassionate, she takes my elbow with one hand, my bag in the other. 'Sammy's staying with me, and so must you. Come on, it isn't far. Looks like you need feeding up.'

Though I struggle to wake, let alone walk, she guides me to a homely looking dormer bungalow. When she opens the front door, my mutt sleepily stands from his basket and stretches, then does another take when he realises who his visitor is.

'Oh bless.' Ruthie chuckles. 'When he's had his fill, go on through and make yourself at home.'

It takes a while to settle Sammy's clear delight, but once we're in the sitting room, Ruthie appears again, strips my outer garments and pulls a thick jumper over my shoulders with a tut.

'You're freezing. You'll catch your death. Right, I'll put on the fire and get you some broth. Will leek and potato do you?'

'Yes. Thank you.'

The 'fire' is a three-bar electric heater, and chewing the hunk of bread my host offers is a struggle, but I manage to down the soup under her and Sammy's inspection.

Though she doesn't ask what's going on, Ruthie's pale gaze seems to. And it's kind, understanding.

'I thought I'd found Mum,' I say. 'I thought I'd finally found her and could, you know...'

She folds me in her arms and rocks me until the fresh round of tears pass. Her warm embrace is the closest thing

I've had to a mother's for twenty-three years. 'Move on?' she asks when she pulls away.

I nod. 'But I can't. I still feel totally lost. Maybe if I'd had a brother or a sister to share the load…' Embarrassed by my self-pity, I glance at a photograph of Ruthie surrounded by smiling kids on the sideboard. 'It looks like you have a massive brood of children.'

She looks too. 'Children but not children. Foster kids.'

'Ah, how lovely.'

'We tried, but it didn't happen.'

She clocks me peering at one of her and Dad. 'Ally's at some recording studios in New York this week,' she says. 'Seems he hasn't quite retired yet. And why would he with talent like that? Rubbing shoulders with the up-and-coming pop stars. A George Martin of our time.'

'That's true.' Her evident pride in my dad's achievements is touching, but I frown as I take in more images of him and Ruthie as much younger people with a backdrop of various cities.

Scratching Sammy's chest, she addresses him. 'I turned down the Big Apple for you, didn't I?' She comes back to me. 'We could have used kennels, but he's still settling in. Maybe next time, eh?'

I swallow and gesture to the framed images. 'So you and Dad…' Ruthie must have accompanied him on his job trips for years. Why didn't I know that? 'How long is it now? You know, the two of you?' I manage.

'Oh, let me think… it must be getting on for twenty—' She slaps a plump hand to her mouth. 'You didn't know?'

There's no point pretending. 'No. No, I didn't.'

'Oh, love, I'm sorry. He always said he would when the time was right, and I just assumed…'

Winded by the revelation, I pause to work it out. 'So you and Dad have had a… a what? A long-distance relationship for years?'

'More a holiday romance, I suppose. All the fun bits. Which is why I insisted he buy his own place up here. See how we cope seeing each other every week.' She raises her eyebrows. 'Not that he's ever over there for more than two minutes.'

'But you mentioned children…'

'Aye, they never came.'

'So, if it was that serious, why didn't you buy a place together a long time ago?'

'You, love, of course, his special girl. It was your happiness and stability that really counted.' Her smile is thin but not mean-spirited. 'And as it happened, you were indeed special.'

'Why?'

'Well, after the tests, it turned out he'd… he'd *made* you very much against the odds.'

Chapter 70

1988

Milly

The news that Imogen would be having a child in March took a great deal of adjusting for everyone concerned. I was frankly miffed that she hadn't confided in me about the romance in the first place, let alone the pregnancy. Fortunately, I had gleaned that something more than just dating was going on between her and Duncan when he unexpectedly appeared on Rutherford's steps, so I wasn't totally surprised when Imo dashed down the staircase the moment Vivienne arrived home from church.

'I know,' she said, wafting away her mother's surprise at her presence. 'I discharged myself early, which at eighteen I'm fully entitled to do. Anyway, I'll explain when you've taken off your coat, powdered your lovely nose and gone to fetch Granny.' She gestured to the front sitting room. 'Family meeting in there in fifteen minutes.' She looked at me pointedly. 'No whispering to Mummy before then.'

Vivienne eyed me questioningly, but I decided not to get involved. She hadn't taken the news about Imo and Duncan well the last time, and I felt she'd held back a little from me ever since. 'You get Honora and I'll see to refreshments,' I said instead, quickly departing for the kitchen.

Honora and Viv were settled in the wingbacks when I returned with a tea tray. 'What on earth is going on, Milly? Why isn't she…' Viv started, but the door opened behind me, and Imogen floated in holding her lover's hand.

I had no idea what might be going through poor Honora's mind, and I couldn't bring myself to look at Viv, so I poured the hot drinks, sat in an armchair and waited for Imo to speak from the sofa.

'Two things,' she eventually said. 'Firstly, Duncan will be joining us for lunch today, if that's all right with Cook.'

I rather think she enjoyed Vivienne's slapped expression; after all, it had been she who'd firmly taken the lead on the pair's parting and Imo's return to the Manor.

Imo delicately sipped from her teacup. 'Secondly, we're delighted to announce our engagement.'

Vivienne gasped with shock, but more was on the tip of Imo's tongue. 'Oh yes, and a third thing. A new little Watkins is on its way.'

From her bemused expression, Viv was clearly struggling to keep up, but Imogen smiled her sweetest smile and said, 'Which will make you a grandma, Mummy. And…' She laughed. 'And, Granny, you'll have the esteemed title of great-grandmother!'

I watched the different emotions pass through my mistress's eyes. They weren't married! What would people think? The vicar, his wife and the members of the Lady's Guild? But the baby card triumphed as I knew it would.

'Goodness,' she said, putting a hand to her chest. 'Goodness, what a surprise, but congratulations are clearly in order.' She leaned forward to her mother-in-law and spoke loudly as usual, even though the poor woman had perfect hearing. 'It's lovely news, isn't it, Honora? Imogen and Duncan are going to be parents in…' She looked at the happy couple.

'We think March,' Duncan said, finally speaking.

'March, Honora. The onset of spring.'

Honora imperiously turned to Duncan. 'And where will you live, young man?'

His cheeks coloured. 'The Ridings for now, then we'll see.'

'And do I have your guarantee you'll keep your…' She gave a little cough. 'I believe the young people call it shagging these days.' Viv spluttered but Honora continued doggedly. 'Do I have your assurance you'll keep your open-air rutting to your own land?'

–

'Oh Lord, how on earth is Noah going to take it?' Vivienne said repeatedly that night.

We weren't privy to the conversation, so we could only imagine what passed between Duncan and his parents, but I suspect Connie's initial horror was superseded by the prospect of a newborn and all the joy that went with it. Noah remained housebound, so neither me nor Vivienne saw him, but by Christmas he was tentatively on his feet, and he joined the 'family' meal at the Ridings. He was undoubtedly grave and tight-lipped, but he'd always been reticent, so anyone looking in wouldn't have known what a viper's nest of secrets there were within those four walls. Connie, with all her puerile prattle, was the most oblivious, but Duncan wasn't far behind. Neither of them knew about Imo's 'sugar daddy' exploits nor the severity and the treatment of her addictions, and of course, no one except me was aware of the two previous pregnancies.

All in all, I was the curator of Imo's dark side and much more. But that was absolutely fine. Like my mother before me, I was the housekeeper who saw, sensed and heard everything but kept my own counsel. More than anything, I wanted our girl to be happy, and I prayed to God each night that she'd have an easy birth and a perfect, healthy baby.

Chapter 71

Present Day

Christie

Ruthie is truly lovely, yet it's a relief to discover I'll have the bungalow to myself during daytime hours until my dad comes back from his work jaunt. It turns out that she has her own business, a craft-cum-wool shop in the village. Though she usually takes Sammy for company, she leaves him with me, so I spend Thursday and Friday either sleeping with him at my feet or walking him along the shingle beach until we're both windswept and salted out.

Thank goodness my thoughts are shallow. If I dwell for too long, I'll feel a shedload of guilt: guilt for being the needy daughter who held Dad back from having a regular relationship for the past twenty years; guilt for putting a load on OJ's shoulders and secretly blaming him for the empty grave; guilt for phoning in sick at work when they're already short-staffed; guilt for neglecting Lillian. In fairness, I did try to find a number for the Ridings so I could explain about my missing mobile, but nothing was listed. As for OJ, I'm perfectly aware I could contact him at his surgery, but I'm not ready to speak to him yet.

Then, if I'm honest, there's the slight needle about Ruthie. She is hard to dislike, but I can't help feeling piqued that she's stolen both my dad and my dog. I have to remind myself I'm a thirty-one-year-old adult and that *Ally* can do what he likes, but he clearly started the relationship when I was – what? – around twelve or thirteen, *and* he astonishingly tried for more kids. Suppose conception had worked? Would he have deigned to mention it to me then?

And suppose Mum had come back? I have to breathe through that particular thought. She didn't come back; she won't come back; my mother is dead; I just haven't found her yet.

–

His face taut with worry, Dad arrives at the bungalow on Friday evening.

'Christie, thank goodness,' he says the moment he sees me.

He's clearly heard the story of his girlfriend scraping me from the wet ground via his nosey neighbour. Still, without that SOS and Ruthie's care and sustenance, I'd probably still be on his doorstep, a fact I have to remind myself of when she drags Dad into the kitchen. To warn or reprimand him about his failure to be honest, in all likelihood. I'd have bashed out my anger and dismay by text rather than waiting to do it in person, so her restraint is admirable; after all, he has let us *both* down.

With a hangdog expression, he returns to the lounge and sits in the armchair.

'I'm sorry, love,' he says. He glances at the line of photographs. 'It's always the same with these things. You fully intend to say something at the right moment, but when is that? You only realise when it has passed, so then you wait for the next time, and suddenly your daughter has gone from girl to adult to young professional, and just saying it becomes so huge you can't get the words out.' He sighs. 'And I knew you'd see it as a betrayal of Mum, that you'd tell Auntie Marsha, that she'd inform the Fox clan... It was cowardly, of course, but I wasn't ready for the grief.'

He's right; there would have been 'grief'. Marsha and that side of the family are loud and opinionated, but they're forgiving too. He should have told me and them. He should have done it for poor Ruthie too.

'I know I wasn't truthful but...' He pats his chest. 'Some things get lodged in here, and it's easier not to examine them closely. It's too painful when you do.'

God, no one knows that better than me. 'Exactly.' I try for a wry smile. 'Now I know who to blame for that aspect of my personality.'

He doesn't reply but looks at his hands. 'Hurtful too,' he says eventually. 'Deep, astonishing hurt even now when I think about it.'

With a jolt, I twig he isn't referring to Mum's disappearance but something else, *someone* else. I decide to just ask. 'Did Mum have an affair?'

'Yes.'

'When she went missing?'

'I don't know. Possibly then.'

Alarm bells clanging, I sit up straight. 'Then why didn't you tell the police? It would have been a major line of enquiry.'

'I didn't know then. I was completely oblivious. A bloody ignorant fool, in fact.'

Sweat dances on my spine; I already know the answer, don't I? But it's floating, just out of my reach. 'I don't understand what you're saying.'

He takes a deep breath. 'Ruthie wanted a child. She was giving up so much else, I couldn't deny her that. We tried for a couple of years, and when nothing happened, we went for fertility tests.' He clears his throat. 'I have a very low sperm count, Christie. Conceiving a baby isn't impossible, but it's highly—'

'But you had me,' I find myself shouting. 'Your special girl!'

'Maybe, but…' He gently takes me by the hand and leads me to the mirror above the hearth. 'Not a lot of blue-eyed daughters outgrow their brown-eyed dads. Besides… and it doesn't make me love you an iota less than I always have… you look like him.'

'Who?'

He moves to a drawer and pulls something out. 'The son of the man who sent this.'

Wholly confused, I take the envelope. It's addressed to 'Jana Fox'.

'I don't understand.' I peer at last year's postmark. 'Why would someone be writing to Mum?'

'It eventually found its way to me. Read it.'

I sit at the card table and slip out a letter headed with an address in Alicante. 'It's from Noah,' I whisper. 'Gramps.'

'You know him?'

'No. He's my friend's…' I snap around to Alistair. 'Who do I look like?' I demand.

'A man she dated at university called Duncan Watkins.' He pats my shoulder. 'I'm afraid he's—'

'Dead. I know.'

'So… Did you meet him?'

'No. He was my...' My patient, my friend, my *sister's* father.

My heart thumping, I revert to Noah's missive and read it.

> *Dear Jana,*
>
> *I don't know if you remember us, but Connie and me remember you, and we both think of you with great fondness.*
>
> *I'm sorry to inform you that our beloved Duncan died unexpectedly a few months ago. Along with his will, he left a letter of wishes dated only this year, so you must have been very much in his thoughts. He asked that the enclosed be passed onto you with his deepest love and his everlasting regret that he never gave it to you in person.*
>
> *I hope you are having a joyous, full life.*
> *Best wishes,*
> *Noah Watkins*

Alistair hands me a black velvet box. 'This came with it.'

'Have you looked in it?' I ask.

He shakes his head. 'Too distressing. Duncan broke her heart. I thought I'd helped her to pick up the pieces and be happy again, but at some point she must have got back with him.'

Too overwhelmed to focus on any one of the emotions fighting for dominance, I inhale deeply, then cautiously open the lid. It's clearly an engagement ring, its small but brilliant diamond bursting with love.

Alistair peers at the treasure too. 'I asked her to marry me more than once. She sweetly turned me down.' He dabs his eyes. 'It looks as though there's an engraving on the inside.'

I carefully pluck it from its cushion, lift it to the light and nod in acknowledgement.

'*I love you, Jana,*' it says. '*I always will.*'

Chapter 72

1989

Duncan

Though months have now passed, thoughts of Jana still wheedle in when Duncan's alone at work. He looks to the sky and firmly pushes them away with his mantra: he's made a decision – and a vow – to love and protect Imo, and especially their baby, so that's that. Yet it doesn't stop the sadness that overwhelms him in the dead of night when the noises of the woods filter through. He flips his head to Imo, takes in the glint and silky spread of her hair and the outline of her ever-growing belly, and tries to get a handle on his self-pity.

He and Imo waited until Noah was fit enough to travel, and though Vivienne would have preferred the local church, they had a simple wedding service at the registry office in Doncaster, followed by a meal where everyone was as polite and civilised to each other as they had been at the Christmas get-together. Without the parental acquiescence on both sides, it could have been a disaster, but so far his life with Imo has been fine. She's reined in her excesses and eats properly for two; she attends all her antenatal appointments and classes, walks daily to the village to pick up provisions, has sedate horse rides wearing her hat, and seems genuinely happy with her lot.

Yet there's a disconnect he can't quite put his finger on. He knows Imo loves him very much in her own way, indeed he catches her looking at him with an intensity of emotion that almost scares him, but he doesn't *feel* it. They still have sex, and for the build-up and peak the old passion is there, but there's a strange hollow afterwards – no pillow talk, no exchange of funny stories or feelings or worries. No intimacy, somehow. Imo immediately falls asleep, and he's left with the shell of a person he doesn't know at all.

–

Duncan removes his boots at the scullery door, then he stretches his aching back and limbs before going in. He's still toiling the estate grounds from dawn to dusk, or so it feels. It's now March, and though Noah is able to stand and walk for a short while, his rehabilitation is slow.

'I'm sorry, son,' he says to Duncan repeatedly. 'I was as fit as a fiddle, so I suppose I thought I could recover faster than the docs and physiotherapist advised, but—'

'But it turns out he's not Superman after all, that he's just human like the rest of us,' Connie replies with her duck face.

So all in all, work is as full-on as ever. Duncan made time for Imo's antenatal appointments at first, and he was there for her devastatingly wonderful first scan, but Vivienne and Mrs Shaw are a constant presence, so it's easier for him to back off and listen to the reports when Imo gets back. Yet he's still somewhat shocked when he flops down at the kitchen table and Imo says:

'I've decided on a home birth.'

'What? That's in two weeks.'

'Exactly, so the baby could come at any time now.'

'OK…' Anxiety hitting, he takes a deep breath. 'It's obviously your choice, but isn't it safer to go into hospital? Suppose there are complications?'

'There won't be.' Imo gives one of her winning smiles. 'Please, Duncan, don't make a fuss. It's what I want.' She gives him a peculiar look. 'And I have been a really good girl, haven't I? I've done everything you asked for…' She rubs her belly. 'For Peanut.'

It's more a flaming Space Hopper these days. God knows how she'll get it out of her petite frame. In all honesty, the thought terrifies him.

'Right.' He tries to adjust his frazzled mind. 'We'll have to buy the… the equipment in. I don't know, special towels, antiseptic and plastic sheets? And what about pain relief? Yes, we'll need everything sorted, the midwife on call at the drop of a hat…'

'Don't worry, it's already in hand. Mummy and Milly…'

With a sinking heart, he knows what she'll say next.

'Mummy and Milly have prepared my old bedroom.' She squeezes his hand. 'You don't mind, do you? It's a family tradition. I was born at Rutherford, so it's only right and proper that the new little Percy is too.'

–

Imo goes into labour on the following Monday afternoon. Praying Imo won't call the new baby 'a little Percy' in front of his mum, Duncan takes a huge breath and telephones her. He has already told her it'll be a home birth but was too cowardly to mention it would be in the big house.

'Mum, it's happening. Imogen has regular contractions. She's…' He steels himself for the onslaught. 'We're at Rutherford. I'll call you again as soon as the baby arrives…'

'Oh my God!' Connie replies. 'It's the fourteenth. When did she start? First babies take their time. You took…' He hears her muttering to herself. 'Eighteen hours, which means tomorrow.'

Completely thrown by her reaction, he takes another breath. 'Well, tomorrow is OK, isn't it?'

'No, it's the fifteenth. Put Millicent Shaw on the phone.'

–

With Duncan banned to the parlour until near the very end, the newborn is wrapped in a clean sheet and placed in his arms by the midwife, Milly Shaw. He has no idea what was said between his mother and her, but when he peers at his daughter's tiny features, the hall clock strikes midnight.

'A beautiful girl,' he says, his voice cracked with emotion. 'We have a gorgeous daughter, Imo.' He kisses her forehead. 'Well done, Imo. She's just perfect, isn't she?'

Clearly groggy, Imo hitches herself up. 'She? Not Freddie?'

A shiver passes through him. They'd discussed names for both sexes, but 'Freddie' had never come up. 'No, she's a little girl, so if you still like the name Lillian…'

Tears seep from Imogen's eyes. 'It's Freddie's birthday. I thought…'

Smiling sadly, Vivienne looks at her watch. 'It is now, Imo. But little Lillian was born yesterday, which is just lovely. What do they say about Monday's child? Fair of face.'

Knowing he'll devote his life to this helpless little being, Duncan smiles at the housekeeper. 'Thank you so much for stepping in. I'm already loath to let her go.' He stands and addresses his new baby. 'Hey, little stunner, do you want to say hello to Mummy? Maybe have a small feed?'

But Imogen slithers back down the bed. 'I'm tired.' She rocks her head to Duncan. 'Seeing as you're so keen, you can feed her yourself.'

Chapter 73

Christie

I catch an early train back to Sheffield on Sunday, but my thrashing mind helps the long journey to pass. There's so much to take in: Alistair Morfett began another relationship three years after my mum went missing. He isn't my biological dad. He discovered that a decade ago when he had fertility tests but loved me just the same. I have an older half-sibling. My former patient Lillian Watkins is my sister, for goodness' sake!

But it's thoughts of Duncan Watkins which grip me the most. He is my real father, and I've maligned him, misjudged him, misunderstood him. He had nothing to do with the disappearance of my mum. He clearly loved her deeply; he wrote a letter of wishes only last year, believing she was still alive.

Tears prick my eyes. Me, Dad and the Fox family had so many unanswered questions after Mum's disappearance, but if she did still meet up with her lover – which I'm convinced she did – we weren't alone. Duncan's 'dead-eyed' look in the photographs isn't guilt; it's devastation, unhappiness, heartache. Jana left him out of the blue without an explanation. How must that have felt when he couldn't share it with a soul?

Heat hits my cheeks. It isn't on the same scale by any means, but I've done the same to OJ, haven't I? Though conflicted, he went out of his way to help me search for Mum; he was clearly weighed down with the responsibility of his memory playing tricks, but instead of thanking him and comforting him, I ran off. And he won't know I haven't had my mobile for the past four days. He'll have sent texts of concern, which have gone unanswered. Bloody hell; what will he think of me?

I picture the look of love which shines from his eyes. It'll be fine; he'll understand once I've explained everything. And despite only knowing him for a short time, I love him too, I really do. Perhaps it's not exactly *closure*, but something has shifted inside me. Instead of raking up or dwelling on the past, I want to move forward and build our future together.

–

As soon as I'm home, I grab my discarded jacket and fumble in the pocket for my phone.

Taking a big breath, I sit on my bottom stair and look at the messages through squinted eyes. Oh God, there are several from OJ ranging from:

> Hey are you OK?

to

> Please call me I'm worried

to

> You're not being fair, Christie. What on earth am I supposed to think? You're not at home; you're not at work; where are you?

Then finally:

> Seriously, Christie. This is doing my head in. Please get in touch.

I quickly compose a text:

> I'm home. I've been at my dad's and accidentally left my mobile here. So sorry for not replying before now. Are you free to talk?

Breath stuck in my chest, I grip the phone, willing a reply to appear. I don't have to wait long.

> No thanks, Christie. I'm pleased to hear you are alive and not injured or in hospital or dead, but we've been here before, so that's it for me.

Dumbfounded, I stare at the screen. He can't be serious, surely?

> What do you mean by that's it?

> I think we're best going our own ways.

> You're dumping me?

> No. Parting as friends. I wish you all the luck in the world.

I scrabble to call him and listen to the ringtone but he doesn't answer, so I bash the keys with my thumbs.

> You said you loved me!

He doesn't reply for a while. Then after a good five minutes:

> Sorry, Christie. I know you're having a really tough time, but I need constancy and communication. Being in an uncertain relationship isn't good for me. My shortcomings, not yours, but I have to be honest with myself this time round. Sorry.

Winded with astonishment and dismay, I bend double. What the hell have I done? And he's right, isn't he? I've run off twice without telling him why. I didn't get in touch with him for four days even though I knew he'd be worried. And yes, if the boot was on the other foot, I'd be livid; I wouldn't be jilting him so nicely; he'd be getting it with both barrels.

Tears slither down my cheeks. I haven't been rational over the last couple of weeks; my behaviour on Wednesday was possibly psychosis; a break from reality brought on by trauma. But he doesn't know that. All he knows from my own admission is that I have a tendency to finish relationships on a knee-jerk basis. And I'm aware he's insecure; he recently went through a horrible break-up, mostly based on a lack of talking things through, for goodness' sake. I need to make it up to him; I must make it right. But how?

Like serendipity, my mobile rings in my hand. I quickly glance at the name, but the caller is Lillian.

'Finally! I've been worried.'

'Sorry, I've been in Aberdeen visiting my dad, and I accidentally left my mobile here. I've only just got in, actually, so I haven't had chance to read your messages. I hope it wasn't anything urgent.'

'Not urgent, no, but a bit odd.'

I shake myself back from my distress about OJ. *Odd.* Surely not so odd as what I'll impart to her about our blood ties. *If* I tell her. I need to think about that.

'Oh right. What's odd?' I ask.

'Are you free this afternoon? If you come over, I can show you.'

Chapter 74

1989

Duncan

The first few weeks of little Lillian's life seem to whizz by. In truth, Duncan can't get enough of her. So excited to get back and take over parental duties, he gets up even earlier, works like a maniac and arrives home at lunchtime.

Exhausted after the birth, Imo pretty much stays in bed all morning, but that's fine, too, as Vivienne and Milly arrive early, feed the baby and take her to visit Honora or go for long walks around the grounds with the pram.

Worried that Connie might feel pushed out, he visits the bungalow with Lillian for a cup of tea most days around four. 'Where's Imogen?' his mum asks today. 'She is welcome, Duncan.'

'She's still a little stunned and needs to rest.'

'Has the health visitor been to check up on everything?'

He knows what she's thinking; six weeks have now passed; he's really worried about postnatal depression himself. 'Yes. She has one-to-one chats with Imo and says everything is fine.'

'Hmm. Shouldn't a new mum be bonding with the baby instead of farming her out every morning to Vivienne and the witch?' Connie pulls her duck face. 'Yes, they go into the village for a coffee and show Lillian off to all and sundry, so I've heard.'

That concerned Duncan too, yet when he privately raised it with the health visitor, she said that maternal bonding takes more time with some mothers than others and that forcing the issue won't help. But how much flaming time does she mean? He thinks about getting the anxiety off his chest, but it feels disloyal to poor Imo, who had to give birth, after all.

'She feeds Lillian and plays with her in the evenings. Anyhow, I thought you and the *witch* were best pals these days,' he says instead.

His mum folds her arms. 'You know my thoughts about that old house. Better safe than sorry is what I say.' Then her face softens. 'How are *you* coping, love? You do look tired.'

–

Unsure how much longer he can manage the half days and keep his head above water, Duncan arrives home on Friday at lunchtime as usual. To his surprise, Vivienne's old Citroën isn't parked on the drive.

He makes his way around the back to the scullery, but when he bobs his head in the kitchen, Imogen is at the table eating toast with Lillian in her bouncy chair at her side.

Tears of relief shoot to his eyes, but he covers the emotion with a smile. 'Hey, you pretty ladies,' he says. He pours from the teapot and sits opposite with his mug. 'So what have you two been up to? No Granny and Milly today?'

Imo snorts. 'I thought it was time. Much as I love them, they can get a bit much, especially together. Divide and rule is the thing with that pair.'

He doesn't really know what she means, but he's delighted to see his wife and child hanging out as a team. It's also nice to have his house back, just for their family unit. He gestures to the window. 'It's a beautiful May day. How about the three of us go out for lunch? We can drive somewhere or walk into the village.'

Imo claps the crumbs from her palms. 'Thanks, but I've eaten.'

'OK. I can grab some food here, then we can make the most of the sunshine.'

'Sweet, but I've had her all morning.' She stands and kisses his cheek. 'Now you're here, I'm off for a canter.'

–

Imo's horse riding or 'nipping out' in Duncan's old car becomes a daily and weekend event. He understands having a baby is full-on and that Imo is trying her best to be a good mum during her stints every morning. He completely gets she needs exercise and time to herself, but he does Lillian's night feeds on top of everything else, and he's got to the point where he's so exhausted he feels like a shit employee and an even worse dad.

Of all people, it's his mum who takes him in hand. 'You're not coping, are you, love?' she says on one of his visits.

Unable to reply, he busies himself with Lillian's car seat. But Connie persists. 'Dad told me not to interfere, but look at you. You're a wreck. Where's madam gone now?'

In all honesty, he doesn't know where Imo is. He still catches her looking at him with a sort of desperation in her eyes, and they'll watch some inane television together before bed, but otherwise they barely speak. The moment his head hits the pillow, he's out like a light until Lillian's hungry cries wake him. Then, when he sets out for the fields at six in the morning, he leaves them both sleeping.

He takes a shuddery breath to defend his absent wife, but Connie reaches her arms around his chest. 'Oh, love, I'm here.' She holds him for some time before pulling away. 'Right, that's it,' she says. 'I'm handing in my notice at the Wheatsheaf.'

He wipes away his traitor's tears. 'Why would you do that? You love working there.'

'Because you're my son and I love you more.' She puts a hand on her chubby hip. 'So, from Monday week, I'll be coming over to look after you and our Lilly.'

Chapter 75

Present Day

Christie

Before leaving the house, I send OJ a photograph of the letter Noah Watkins sent to Jana with a message saying:

> My dad gave me this on Friday along with a diamond ring. I was so wrong about Duncan Watkins; he clearly thought my mum was alive a year or so ago. I discovered other mind-blowing stuff I'd love to share! I was also wholly wrong to treat you so badly. I'm so sorry. Please let me explain.

I follow it up with:

> I love you and like you and fancy you and need you very much. Please don't desert me.

I figure that even if the latter plea doesn't work, intrigue might bring OJ round. It doesn't; my mobile stays stubbornly silent, and the closer I get to Doncaster, the more my heart slumps. I don't quite know why, but I'm in a much better mental place than I was this time last week. Although I have shockingly discovered my dad isn't my biological father, I'm OK with it so far, and there has been that sea change about Mum, which makes me much calmer: I haven't found her yet, but I'm certain she's dead, so maybe acceptance is finally settling in. All good news, surely? But tears prick my eyes as I drive. What's the point of any of it if I don't have OJ by my side?

When I finally reach the Sprotbrough junction, I don't head towards the Ridings but drive the other way and pull into Village Vet's car park. Amy, the receptionist, will undoubtedly think it's the deranged woman making a resurgence, but I have to do something to win OJ back. Before I can change my mind, I quickly hop up the steps, stride through the porch and turn the entrance handle. It's locked, so I peer through the glass. Save for a woman at the reception desk, the waiting room is empty. She glances up, and I instantly know from her looks that it's the head of the practice, Belinda Cullen.

Already cringing with embarrassment, I watch her approach and unlock the door.

'We're closed for today, I'm afraid,' she says crisply.

Though I'd like to bolt yet again, I steel myself. 'I'm actually here to see OJ if he's in.'

She eyes me curiously. 'He isn't. And you are…?'

'A friend of his. I was just passing so…' I step back. 'No worries. Sorry to bother you. Another time.'

'Are you Christie?' She seems to sense my dismay as her demeanour softens. 'He and Pete were called out to an emergency at a farm in the back of beyond.' She gestures me in. 'I was just about to pour a coffee.'

'Only if it's—'

'It is. Come on through.'

I dumbly follow her to a kitchen overlooking a huge garden where Casper is catching a few rays of early May sunshine. Without asking if I want one, she fills two cups from a carafe and sits at the table, so I do the same. 'Thank you.'

'Not at all. Milk?' She dips her head to peer at me as she pours. 'Is there anything I can help with in OJ's absence?'

Though I do my utmost to stop it, a tear trickles down my nose. Quickly wiping it away, I grope for humour. 'I don't think grovelling is something I can do via his mum.' She looks at me questioningly. 'I went off to Aberdeen to see my father, who turned out not to be my real father at all, which I certainly wasn't expecting, and he's had a relationship with a woman I didn't know about for the past twenty years…'

Bloody hell, what's wrong with me, splurging like this? Maybe I'm not chilled about things after all.

I laugh a fake laugh. 'But at least my dog was pleased to see me.'

'Goodness, poor you. Have you ever met your biological father?'

'No, he died a year ago, so…' I take a deep, steadying breath. 'But the point is that I let OJ down by not telling him my plans, mostly because I didn't know them myself.' I genuinely chuckle this time. 'I'm honestly not usually this… this manic or flighty. In fact, I'm usually described by my patients as measured and calm…' The words reminding me of my Lillian mission, I look at my watch. 'Actually, being measured and calm is supposed to be the reason I'm here. Sorry about the coffee, but I'd better get off. I said I'd be there by four.'

The front door is ajar at the Ridings, but my concern is soon assuaged by the aroma of baking.

'I'm in here,' Lillian calls from the kitchen.

When I join her, she glances over her shoulder. 'Are you OK?'

'Sure,' I say with forced brightness. 'Anything I can do to help?'

She nods to a bag of rubbish. 'Maybe put that in the outside bin?'

'Sure.'

As I return, I almost collide with Lillian kicking away a small pile of cigarette butts. Her expression is peculiar when she catches my eye. Maybe she's embarrassed about not quitting smoking after all, or perhaps it's me. Is it obvious I've been crying?

'I'll just nip to the loo,' I mutter.

'Go straight through after and make yourself comfortable. I'll just pour water in the teapot.'

I feel much better after washing my face, so I amble to the dining room, pull out a beautifully crafted chair and take in the spread of sandwiches, scones and mini buns. 'Wow, thank you!' I say as Lillian enters the room.

'A pleasure, but no running off from me today, otherwise I'll get very fat.' She laughs. 'I hate waste. Come on. Help yourself to tea and tuck in.'

I study my sister-friend as I eat. She has put on some weight and she looks very well. My eyes slip to a framed portrait of her and Duncan on the wall. God, that's my father. And yes, my eyes and my nose are most definitely his. But how will Lillian take it? Her dad was unfaithful to her mum after only a year or so of having her.

She interrupts my mulling. 'Seems I'm not the only one either.'

'You've lost me.'

'Not the only one you ran away from. I had a visit from Ollie.'

Just when I thought today couldn't get worse. 'Oh right,' I reply. 'What did he say?'

'Not a lot. He wondered if I'd happened to see or hear from you.'

My cheeks burn. 'Sorry. I guess I should have mentioned we were—'

'It's fine, Christie.' She reaches for my hand. 'I don't think girl code counts that far back. Less hair, but he's still cute, though.'

A jolt of sadness hits that I've let him slip through my fingers, yet it's wonderful to witness Lillian's transformation into this relaxed, smiley person. 'So, are you in the market for a guy?' I ask.

She glances at the portrait of her dad. 'Maybe I'll get there one day.'

I take a breath to come clean about the bothy excavation, to say something about the vivid imagination of children; bloody hell, the vivid imagination of me as an adult too, but Lillian stands and fetches her mobile from the sideboard. 'So,' she says, 'the thing that's odd. I decided to be brave and go through Dad's photographs.'

I'd forgotten her phone used to be Duncan's. 'Wow, good on you.'

She pulls her chair next to mine. 'They got on pretty well before, but after Mum died, Granny broke off any contact with Dad. She didn't visit here and hasn't since I came home, which, as you know, I'm pretty hacked off about.' She swipes through several images of the main house. 'But Dad never went there either, so why was he interested in taking so many photos of Rutherford?'

Chapter 76

Milly

Though Imogen continued to turn up at Rutherford and dump little Lillian on us whenever it suited her, me and Viv mainly watched Duncan's life crumble from the sidelines.

The poor lad worked hard, so he didn't know that pretty much from giving birth, Imo was up and about every morning the moment his back was turned. In fairness, I think she still loved him very much, but as I feared, she just wasn't mother material, and it really troubled her to see him so doting on the baby. Instead of recognising it as the fatherly love she'd never had – or maybe because of it – she saw it as a rejection of her. Then there'd been those seven long months of pretending to be someone she wasn't during her pregnancy; I suspected it felt like a kettle constantly bubbling behind the sweet smile. Both the kettle and the baby had finally popped, and she needed to let the steam out.

Between us, me and Viv spied the evidence for ourselves. I found the remains of white powder and empty spirit bottles in her Rutherford bedroom, and Viv saw her openly cavorting with Jonny Cullen in the village park with her very own eyes.

'I know she took pity on him when she worked at the probation office, but he's a married man who's just had his second child. Lord knows what they're doing hanging around those disgusting old toilets. Smoking like school children, do you think, Milly?'

They might have been sharing a cigarette, but I feared they were *sharing* more than just that.

As ever, Viv was appalled at the prospect of having the family's dirty laundry washed in public. 'What on earth should we do, Milly?' she asked.

'We'll have to take her to task,' I replied.

—

As evidenced by our expulsion from the Ridings, Imogen didn't take our 'shocking interference' well. Indeed, she was so angry when we challenged her that she saw fit to see us out with the decorative poker from the hearth. Still, I couldn't help but smirk when the cavalry arrived. A silly airhead and a gossip Connie Watkins might have been, but she wasn't one for backing down, and there was no doubt she loved her son and her grandchild.

Chapter 77

1990

Duncan

Having his mum over to help every afternoon is quite simply a lifesaver. It allows Duncan to work, but it isn't just that. She feeds and changes and plays with Lillian, then when she naps, she tidies and cleans the house, changes bedding and programmes the washing machine, and if she has time, she prepares a casserole or a salad for tea.

Then there's Connie's love. When he arrives back to relieve her at four-thirty, she sits him down at the table and says: 'I've bought you these new biscuits to try. You always did like caramel. Tell me about your day, love. Has the carpenter finished those flaming livery stables yet?' Or 'How many fences has it been this week, then?' And 'What's happening tomorrow? Don't forget what I said about "All work and no play". You're allowed a holiday. That's what farmhands or subcontractors are for.' Or 'How's that friend of yours Stiggy? Now he always made me laugh. It'd do you good to give him a call, even have him to stay for a weekend. And what about Andy Maher? He's a good lad too, and he's only down the road. I'll gladly babysit.' And always, 'I know a new baby is tough, love, but she's a blessing, and it will get easier, I promise.'

Imo hasn't yet said much about his mum's visits, but Duncan knows she doesn't approve from her comments. 'Goodness, we'll have poor Lillibud sounding right Yorkshire if we're not very careful.' 'Let's hope she isn't being fed a diet of cake. It's all Connie can do to fit through the door these days.' 'Good job Lillibud only likes picture books at this stage. Let's face it, Connie isn't the brightest button in the box.'

Though unnecessary and hurtful, Duncan tries to ignore the swipes and let them pass, but halfway through his and Connie's teatime chat on Friday, Imo swans in.

God knows what's rattled her cage, but she pulls out a chair and looks at Connie down her nose. 'You know you bore him senseless with your blathering, don't you? We're very grateful for your services, but you finished fifteen minutes ago, so why don't you just hop it rather than hanging around where you're not wanted?'

Both shocked and appalled, Duncan gapes for a beat. Then he rallies. 'She doesn't bore me, and she's very much wanted, Imogen. I like our chats; look forward to them, in fact.'

Imo guffaws. 'Oh right.' She puts a theatrical palm to her mouth. 'Not what he says behind your back.'

The penny drops that this is exactly what she meant by 'rule and divide'.

'My time with Mum isn't a joke or something for you to sneer at, Imogen. She listens; we communicate. That's what people do when they love someone.'

'*Love someone?*' She sits back, clearly stung. 'You think I don't love you?'

'I have no idea. We barely speak. Do you? Do you love Lillian?'

'No, Duncan.' Her eyes burning, Imo glares. 'That isn't the crux, is it? The real question is, do you love me? Have you ever?'

Beneath the table, Connie squeezes his hand, and somehow he knows that despite everything, she's willing him to say yes. But seconds pass, and he just can't get that single word out of his mouth.

Imogen juts up her chin. 'There we have it,' she says in a clipped tone. 'I'm going out. Don't wait up.'

When the door clicks to, Duncan buries his head in his arms. His mum finally speaks. 'I'm so very sorry to add to your troubles, love, but there was something else I wanted to say.'

She waits until she has eye contact. 'Your dad – well, he's the last person to make a fuss, but he's still in a lot of pain, so we've decided on that move to the Costa Blanca, and we're off for a recce if his back is up to the flight. I know it's well before any of us expected, and we're going to take it in stages, but the warmer weather is just what he needs...'

'Dad's retiring? He won't be moving back in here?'

'This house will be yours, and he'll do it all legally, but... Sorry, love. No, he won't.'

–

Not caring where Imo is and quite frankly glad of the freedom without her, Duncan listens to the hooting owls and rutting deer at midnight. Yet instead of feeling soulful, his chest is full of fire, partly from three large brandies but mostly from resolve. Through his own bloody fault, he's been in the tailspin of Imogen for over a year now. The chaos is still there and always will be with a child to consider and care for, but he's only twenty-two, and he has to find a way to live a life alongside it.

He opens the side drawer and pulls out his old diary. His mum is right; he can invite Stiggy over to stay, but a pub date with Andy can be arranged right now; it's Friday, and he'll be rolling back home after five pints and a kebab. He flips open the index to search out his number but finds himself staring at the name 'Jana Fox' instead. She was and still is the love of his life. How did he get everything so horribly wrong? On impulse, he scoops up the handset, punches in her number and listens to the ringtone. But he immediately reprimands himself for his weakness. Connie would be furious at an incoming call at this late hour, and Jana will hardly still live with her mum. And yet, by some miracle, she answers.

'Hello?'

'Jana! It's Duncan.'

'What the fuck, Duncan? It's Marsha. Why are you calling? Are you pissed?'

God, yes, he is. Drunk and deluded. 'God, I'm sorry, Marsha. I have no idea what I thought I was doing. I'll let you—'

'Hey, not so fast. I've wanted to give you a mouthful for a bloody year. What the fuck, Duncan? You broke her heart. You were supposed to love her.'

'I did. I do.'

'So you let your prick rule your head? Well, more fool you. Do you know what most people do? They just say N-O. Simple. And if they're spineless and do it anyway, they use a bloody condom, they don't get a girl they hardly know pregnant.'

'I know. She's beautiful, though. My baby that is. Lillian.' Then, 'How's Jana? I think about her every day.'

'Well, you have no fucking right to.' She seems to relent. 'She got the job at the uni in Sheffield and…' He waits for her to say it and she does. 'She got back with Alistair, and they bought a place together.' After a moment, she sniggers. 'Or should I call him Sheena?'

'You remember that?'

'Course I do. I really liked you, Duncan; we all did. I thought you'd be my brother-in-law one day.'

Christ, he wants to cry. To sob his bloody heart out. 'And is she happy? Jana?'

'Yeah, yeah, she is.'

Chapter 78

Present Day

Christie

When we've finished our high tea, we sit on the sofa and closely study the images on Duncan's phone.

'They're all taken at night,' I say.

'Yes. And nearly all identical.'

'Nearly? They all seem the same to me.'

'Agreed, but look. It's dim, but it's there in a few of them.' She taps at a window on the screen. 'There's a light peeping through the shutters.'

'OK…' I say slowly. 'But why is that odd? Your granny and Milly live there.'

'That's the east wing, Christie. It was boarded up years before I was even born.'

'Maybe they've moved into that side.'

'No, Granny loves her retro rooms.'

'Perhaps Mrs Shaw then?'

'She shares with Granny.'

I raise my eyebrows, but Lillian shrugs. 'Maybe they are that way inclined. Or maybe Milly's just a dog who sleeps at her mistress's feet.'

As ever, I'm curious. 'Where do the real dogs sleep?'

'The last one died years ago. How did you know about them?'

'You must have said something. Or I just made an assumption. Horses and hounds and all that.'

Oh God, these days I'm getting into a tangle about who told me what, and I still need to decide if and when to tell Lillian about the first page of Duncan's 'letter of wishes'. And the flaming rest. But the dog point disturbs me. OJ said his mother went there to treat them, didn't he? Why would he say that if they didn't exist?

Goosebumps prickling my skin, I quickly change the subject. 'So what are you thinking about the glow through the casement?'

'Why was Dad so interested in it?' She lifts her eyebrows. 'When she didn't think I was listening, my grandma in Spain used to say Milly was a witch.'

I have to remind myself that Connie Watkins is shockingly my grandma too. But the time to say something isn't now.

I laugh a little nervously. 'So, there's a cauldron and pointy hat behind that window?'

'Well, you never know. Fascinating, though, don't you think? I'd love to find out what's been stashed in there.'

I carefully study her. This is the woman who was terrified of her old bedroom, and yet there's no apparent fear today. Is she mentally well? She does seem a bit high, but she's never been diagnosed with attention deficit hyperactivity or bipolar disorder. In all honesty, I think she's just enjoying the mystery, which is a huge improvement on her thinking her dad is a murderer.

'I guess so. How do you plan to find out?'

'By taking a look, of course.' She smiles. 'I have keys, so it's just a question of sneaking in.'

'You vowed you'd never step inside there again!'

'That was living or sleeping. A little visit is another thing. And besides, there are a few bits and bobs I want to collect from my bedroom without Granny knowing I've been there.'

'So this is just a ruse to get your stuff without losing face?'

'Well, I suppose there is that. Which is why I'd have to go when they're asleep.'

Certain of what will come next, I quickly look for excuses. 'But it's supposed to be haunted, isn't it?'

She looks at me pointedly. 'Granted, you never said so, but you thought they were dreams or hallucinations. Who knows, maybe they were. Anyway, I'll be fine if you're...' She grasps my hand. 'Come with me. Please, Christie? If nothing else, it'll be a laugh.'

Chapter 79

1990

Duncan

Imogen stays away from the Ridings on both Friday and Saturday night. Part of Duncan wishes she'd just go forever, but there's Lillian to think of. She's only six months old, a really good little girl who's blonde and smiley and can now sit up with help. Her cuteness makes everyone else go weak at the knees; he's at a loss why it has no impact on Imo, why she'd just disappear for forty-eight hours without saying something to someone.

Suspecting she might simply be at the big house, he swallows his pride and phones Vivienne on Sunday morning. 'I don't suppose Imogen is with you? It's my fault, I guess, but she left after an argument on Friday teatime and hasn't come back since.'

'Oh, Duncan, I'm so sorry, but no. She can be a bit hot-headed at times. Did she take the car?'

'No, it's still in the driveway.'

'Goodness. Well, I guess she can't be far. I'll have a word with Milly, and if we have any ideas, we'll call you back.'

They don't call him back, but an hour or so later, he hears the crunch of her approach from the open kitchen window. Grappling with the urge to shout, he scoops up Lillian from her play mat and inhales the soapy scent of her hair.

'Where have you been, Imogen?' he asks when she saunters in.

'What does it matter to you?'

'It matters because we both care about you.'

'You *cared* for Freddie, and look what happened to him.'

'What the...' He should know by now to expect the unexpected from Imogen, but her comment still winds him. 'Freddie died a long time ago.'

Taking Lillian from him, she kisses her nose. '*We*,' she says to her. 'What does Daddy know about what you think, hey? People should never make assumptions about what's going on in someone else's head.' She pulls a sad face. 'Daddy loves you, but he doesn't love me.'

'Enough, Imogen.' He won't be blackmailed by her absence or manipulated into making false declarations. 'It isn't acceptable to run off without telling me where you are going or when you'll be back. I've been worried about you.'

She shrugs and passes the baby back. 'I've been at Rutherford, OK? Just needed a bit of time out.' She raises her eyebrows. 'If you don't believe me, ask Milly.'

–

Imo is all sweetness and light on Monday and Tuesday. She says there's no need for Connie to come over as she'll be at home all day. She's true to her word, reading books with Lillian, tidying up after herself and preparing French onion soup for dinner one day and bœuf à la Bourguignonne the next.

'Remember the last time I made you this?' she asks as they eat.

On some level, he knows that she's playing with his head, but he so wants a normal life, he goes with it.

'It was delicious then, and it's delicious today. Thank you for making the effort.'

'Did you love me then?'

'Imo…'

'Because that's the night we made Lillian. And you love her, so…'

'Then yes.'

'And what about now?'

Right now, I want to sleep, to escape, to wind back the fucking clock and live another life; right now, I'm swinging between hatred and fear; right now, I'd like to put my hands around your throat and squeeze the very life out of you, he wants to scream.

But she's worn him down, and he's desperately aware she always will.

'Yes, I love you, Imogen,' he says. 'I loved you then and I do now.'

Chapter 80

Present Day

Christie

Lillian assures me her granny and Milly are creatures of habit, that the front door will be locked and bolted by nine-thirty and the bedroom lights extinguished by ten.

I can't help but feel I'm being led into trouble, but Lillian is so very charming; the pull is irresistible. I'm due at work tomorrow at noon, so I shouldn't really be holding her hand and giggling with both hilarity and fear like a kid at Halloween as we make our way through another dark tree-lined shortcut, this time to the rear of Rutherford House. But it's a welcome break from the other thoughts churning my mind – Dad and Ruthie, Mum and Duncan, the complete fool I made of myself beneath Belinda Cullen's shrewd gaze – and especially the fact OJ still hasn't replied. My phone is now on silent for this furtive mission, and not listening out for a notification is frankly a relief.

Although Lillian has a torch, every hoot, sigh and rustle seems inordinately loud, and when I spot a pair of glowing eyes, I nearly pee myself. With her deer-like stride, Lillian is gracefully nimble, whereas I stumble repeatedly.

'If I fall and break my neck, you know it'll be all your fault,' I eventually hiss.

'Shh,' she replies. 'We're here.' She peers around a privet hedge. 'We're heading for that door to the scullery. Wait here until I unlock it. Keep on the grass; the shale is noisy.'

'OK,' I squeeze out through my ridiculous terror.

When she's opened up, I follow her torchlight through a vintage kitchen, then along a panelled corridor, and though I creep, I'm certain the simple rustle of my jacket will wake the eerie, silent world inside this old building. Expecting her to find a rear set of stairs which lead to her bedroom, I continue to tiptoe after her, but when we emerge from the darkness, we're in the domed hallway. It's as breezy, dank, and as bloody central as it was on my visit. I want to demand why on earth we've come somewhere so open and echoey where we're bound to be caught, but Lillian darts across the marble floor and scoops a hoop of keys from a side table.

'Left there in case of fire. Apart from everything else, Milly is very practical,' she whispers when she comes back. She gestures to the floor above. 'Up we go...'

I can't believe she's taking the sweeping main staircase, but I do as I'm told, scuttling behind her to the top, then around the first landing until we reach a huge door.

'Is this the way to your room?' I hiss, but Lillian is peering at each label on the huge bunch of keys. She eventually selects one, puts a finger to her lips and inserts it into the old keyhole.

As the lock loudly scrapes, I deduce this must be the east wing entrance. Bloody hell, it feels far more like trespass than a visit to Lillian's private space. What the heck am I doing? I'm barely breathing and my heart is madly thrashing, and yet my instinct to get the hell out is superseded by nosiness. Pushing away thoughts of curses, witchcraft and spells, I focus on the likelihood of freezing, lofty rooms cluttered with antique cupboards and tables, statues and paintings covered with dust sheets.

I'm wrong on all counts. From what I can gather from Lillian's dull beam, it's a suite of empty spaces divided by walls. And though the windows are boarded up, surprising heat pumps through the old, panelled radiators. When we finally reach a closed door, Lillian looks over her shoulder, then turns the white porcelain knob. I'm frankly terrified about what we'll find inside, but I reason the furniture and period pieces will simply be stashed in there, which is why it's so warm.

I step over the threshold and bingo, I'm right. My shoulders slump with relief, but Lillian snaps on the central chandelier.

'What on earth are you doing?' I ask, spinning around.

But Lillian isn't standing beside the light switch; it's… it's the housekeeper, Mrs Shaw.

Chapter 81

1990

Duncan

Connie telephones the Ridings first thing on Saturday morning.

'Hello, love.'

'Hi Mum. Are you and Dad all packed for your trip?'

In truth, Duncan feels so despondent and low, it's all he can do to stop himself begging her to take him with them to Spain.

'That's why I'm calling. I know it's short notice, but could you drive us to the airport this afternoon? We planned to take a taxi, but on second thoughts, they might not be amenable to several stops to allow Dad to stretch his back.'

'I didn't realise it was that bad, Mum. Will he be OK on a two-and-a-half-hour flight?'

'Once we're in the air, he can walk up and down the aisle. Shall we say here at four? Vivienne's happy to have Lilly if Imogen… if she has other plans.'

He glances at Imo. She always busies herself leafing through a book or magazine when he's on the telephone, but he senses she listens. For what, he doesn't know. He hasn't got an existence beyond these four walls. Except the meadows, the gardens and outbuildings that comprise the estate, he supposes, and thank Christ for that.

'Mum's asking if—'

She wafts a hand. 'It's fine. Whatever Connie wants, Connie—'

'Thanks,' he quickly interrupts, then goes back to the call. 'Imo is around this afternoon, so no need for... I'll see you later.'

-

Pulling up on the bungalow drive, Duncan takes a moment to compose a smile before climbing out. But the front door immediately opens and his mum appears, dragging a suitcase behind her.

He hurries to help. 'Here, let me take that.'

'Thanks, love, but seeing as I'll be the mule for the foreseeable, I'm best getting used to it. The sooner we find somewhere permanent in the sunshine the better.' She kisses Duncan on the cheek and chuckles. 'Then I'm going to sit on my arse, drink sangria and catch the rays.' She calls over to his dad. 'Aren't I, Noah?'

'You are.'

'Think you'll manage a bit of waitering for your beloved? You know, to the bar and back?'

'Aye, I'll work on it.'

Duncan fixes that smile. 'And a few San Miguels for you, Dad? Sounds perfect.'

Two weeks' holiday is one thing, but he really, really doesn't want his parents to leave here forever. He knows it's childish to feel so needy, but he'll have no one to turn to. He's already flailing, and soon he'll be lost.

As though reading his thoughts, Connie smooths his hair. 'Don't forget we'll expect lots of visits from you and

Lilly when we live there full time. She'll love the sand and sea, and it'll give you an excuse to get away from the Ridings. In the meantime…' She presses some keys into his palm. 'A spare for when you need a breather. Just until we sell it, mind.'

He already has his old set from when he lived here, but he doesn't like to belittle her thoughtfulness. And maybe it would be good to lie on his old bed and just cry. 'Thanks, Mum.'

'Her idea, not mine.' His dad pats his back. 'But on balance, I think she's right.' He abruptly pulls him into his arms. 'I love you, son. I know I'm not much of an orator, but I do, very much. You stood up and did the right thing, not once but twice, even though neither was what you wanted. I'm proud of you, lad.'

Duncan takes a deep breath, but his tears seep out. Connie takes over the hug. 'Come here, you daft thing.' She pecks his forehead. 'We'll see you in two weeks with a pair of maracas and a dolly wearing a Flamenco dress for Lillian. Then you'll wish we stayed.' She looks over his shoulder. 'Right, the cab is here.'

Completely thrown, he watches the taxi driver hop out and heft the suitcase into his boot. 'I thought I was driving you…'

'Change of plan.' Connie nods to the open front door. 'Lock up will you, love? Wouldn't do to be burgled. Oh, and make sure Dad has turned off the hob.'

Once the cab has disappeared, he trudges inside. Everyone surrounding him seems to have lost the plot, but maybe it's him. Christ, wouldn't it be something if the last eighteen months were simply a horrible dream. He could wake up and do everything differently.

At the entrance to the kitchen, he stops in his tracks. What the…?

Jana Fox is sitting at his mum's Formica table.

–

'You spoke to Marsha,' Jana says when he's finally finished fumbling with the kettle, the coffee jar and cups.

'Yes, sorry about that. Calling the house was out of order, and at that time especially. My mum would have gone ballistic.' His lips twitch. Despite not knowing why on earth Jana is here, it's so lovely to see her. 'But Marsha didn't let me go until she'd given me a mouthful, as she put it.'

'Good for her.'

'Yeah.' He catches the gold band on his finger. The wedding handcuffs, the ones he locked himself. Jana isn't wearing one. 'Far less than I deserved.'

'She said you had a baby girl.'

He nods. The ring is the manacle, not her, not Lillian. 'She's incredible; I'm totally smitten.'

'And Imogen?'

He doesn't want to talk about her; he doesn't want her to infect the few minutes he has with this woman he still dearly loves. 'Why are you here?' he asks instead.

It's Jana's turn to look away. 'Marsha said you sounded unhappy, so I called your mum to have our usual chat and—'

'You kept in touch with her?'

'Yes, from time to time. You know, for a general catch up rather than talk about…' She smiles thinly. 'Anyway, she was out, so I spoke to your dad. He… well, he apologised, I guess. He said he'd been wrong to dump the Rutherford job and all the responsibility on your shoulders. He'd got used to the loneliness so hadn't registered how much it would impact you, and of course he was a grown man, not a…'

Lowering his head to hide the tears, Duncan nods. A boy. Because that's what he is. A needy only child who desperately wants someone to look after him. He has tried to man up and miserably failed. The only light is Lillian, and even that has started to dim.

Jana clears her throat. 'And he said Imogen was guileful…'

'Guileful?'

'Yes. That you'd been a bloody fool and done the unforgivable, but that…'

'But what?'

'That you'd probably fallen into a trap.'

Duncan breathes deeply. Duped, ensnared, manipulated, played. On some level, he knows that, but it's too traumatic to go there. He can't turn back the clock and undo the damage. And he wouldn't want a life without Lillian.

'Betraying you was reprehensible,' he finally mutters.

'It was, Duncan. You broke my heart, but…' She gazes with glistening eyes. 'It never stopped me missing you, thinking about you, loving you.'

As she pulls back her chair, he inwardly nods. She's leaving; she's punished him in the worst possible way by declaring her love. But she holds out her hand. 'I guess we don't have that much time,' she says. 'Let's make the most of it.'

Chapter 82

Present Day

Christie

Stuck for words, I gape at the petite woman in the doorway. Her grey hair is cropped short in an elfin-style cut, and without her black wig, she looks younger somehow.

'So it *was* you,' I hear Lillian croak behind me.

Surprised by her tone, I turn and take in my friend's cheeks, blanched almost white with... Shock? Or is it anger? Wondering what the hell is going on, I glance around the old-fashioned yet cosy room. It has a sofa, matching cushions and velvet drapes, an elegant sideboard, a walnut table with high-backed, handsome chairs. And beyond it, a four-poster bed. Oh God, how embarrassing; we've clearly invaded Mrs Shaw's personal living space. Maybe she and Vivienne were romantically an item and they've split up. Or perhaps she comes in here to smoke, as there's the stench of stale cigarettes in the air.

I return to the housekeeper and take a breath to apologise or say something to break the tense silence, but her cold stare stops me short.

She addresses Lillian. 'So this is *her*.'

'Who? What do you mean?'

'My husband's bastard, that's who.'

Comprehension slowly creeping, I take in the woman's opaque gaze. I was wrong; it isn't Mrs Shaw, is it? She has a similar build and green eyes, but... *My husband's bastard*... Oh my God, it can't be, can it? The *wasp* is supposed to be long dead.

'Daddy's bastard?' Lillian's sharp intonation makes me jump from my skin. 'What's that supposed to mean?'

'He was rutting behind my back.' Imogen tilts her head. 'Oh, poor Lillibud. Didn't your new bestie tell you?'

'Tell me what?' She snaps around to me. 'What haven't you told me, Christie?'

'I'm so sorry, Lillian.' I lift my hands. 'I should have said something earlier, but I have literally only just found out.'

'Found out what?'

'That Alistair – my dad – isn't my biological father. That your dad – Duncan – is,' I say weakly.

I'm trying to process the bombshell of Imogen Watkins being alive, but the clear hurt is etched on Lillian's face. 'So, I wasn't Daddy's—'

'Beloved golden girl, no,' her mother says, interrupting. 'At least not his only one.'

'We were friends,' Lillian says to me. 'I told you everything...'

I scrabble to make sense of this surreal, surreal moment. 'Yes, friends. And now we're sisters, too. An amazing thing, surely?'

Yet I understand her feelings of betrayal. Even though Alistair and Ruthie didn't manage to conceive, their intention to do so had felt like a stab through my heart when it finally sunk in.

'He didn't know about me, Lillian,' I breathlessly continue. 'Your dad had no idea that my mum had disappeared, let alone that I was his, so…'

My mum, my *still* missing mother… I inhale deeply from my diaphragm. Alarm bells are clattering and clanging in my head, but I simply can't go there right now. The best I can do is to deal with one problem at a time.

I hold out an arm of earnest entreaty. 'So you *were* his only, much-loved child, Lillian,' I add.

'Only because I saw to that.' Imogen's sneery rasp breaks the intense moment.

'Saw to what?' I ask, spinning back to the woman.

'Him never knowing.' A triumphant glint sparkles in her eyes. 'The stupid bitch wrote him a letter. God knows why; they shagged often enough; she could have told him in person. "*Darling Duncan, until now I never knew for sure, so I didn't say anything, but little Christie is yours.*" I suppose she thought I was away, that I wouldn't be around to intercept a handwritten fucking envelope to my husband.' She theatrically gestures around the four walls. 'More fool her. I always was good at hiding.'

Like a wasp you can't bat away, and yet you can't quite work out where it is either, I remember. Despite the cold, cold dread that bolts through my very being, I'm calm and analytical. 'This letter,' I ask Imogen. 'What did you do with it?'

She frowns as though thrown, then shrugs. 'Dealt with it before it could reach his baby blues.'

'Why did you care if you already knew Duncan was seeing my mum?'

'I had no intention of letting him leave me.' She stares without blinking. 'Ever.'

The deepest of pain grips my chest. I'm finally certain of the truth, the devastating truth. 'Is that why you killed Jana? They met in the bothy, didn't they? But you turned up instead, murdered her and buried her in the hollow.'

I glance at Lillian's stunned features. 'The hand you and Ollie saw in the woods?' I say. 'The reason you thought your dad had killed her? That was my mother, Jana Fox. Neither you nor he were imagining it or crazy.'

I go back to the evil, evil woman. 'Then you moved her, didn't you? Where did you put her?' I demand. Yet I already know the answer to that. I've pictured those steps down to the Percy family vault often enough in my dreams. 'She was my beautiful, kind and loving mother,' I yell, looming over her. 'She was the love of Duncan's life. You killed her and took her from us both. You interred her with fucking strangers.'

Imogen's stance remains fiery and defiant. 'No. *You* killed her. If you hadn't been born, they'd both still be alive and shagging every few months. Have you any idea how much that *killed* me? But I lived with it because he came back to my bed every night; he stayed; he still loved me. Then you got poorly and had a blood test or some other such excuse to tempt him away from me. *You* ruined my life; you made me do it; you took me away from my husband; you made me a prisoner.'

Her jaw set, Lillian finally speaks. 'An inmate who escaped. One who came into my bedroom and *haunted* me when I was only ten. Have *you* any idea how terrified I was? A ghost I could sense and see, hear and smell. Did you even consider how that would affect me throughout my life? Thinking I'm odd and weird and fucking, fucking crazy?'

Imogen puts a hand to her heart. 'I missed you; I wanted to see you.'

'You had no right to see me! I thought Daddy had murdered you; the police thought he had murdered you. It tore me apart.'

'Well, that was put right after a little while, wasn't it, darling? And I didn't know about what you'd spotted at the bothy. So it really wasn't Mummy's fault.' Replacing her contrite expression with a smirk, she reverts to me. 'So, *little Christie*. I was coming to find you, but you've appeared like magic.'

'It wasn't exactly divine, was it, though?' Lillian says. 'You tricked me here.'

'Oh, Lillibud, you always were so easy to... shall we say misdirect? A light in a window. A few cigarette stubs at the back door. Photographs on Daddy's old phone. A subliminal sighting of me.' She gives me a withering look. 'You too. A strategically placed photograph and the scarf. I knew then you were the bastard, but I had to be sure. Then you saved me the bother of another expedition behind Mummy's back by turning up at the front door of all things.' She mimics me. '"*My boyfriend will help me excavate and make good. We won't touch the grass, and you won't know we've been.*" And now you're here in the dead of night, just as I hoped.'

Lillian moves in front of me. 'What for? What do you want with Christie?'

'Did you know she dug her own grave? That was rather poetic.'

'Leave her alone.'

'Just listen, Lillibud. This is the girl who ruined my life, our lives, darling. It's all her fault, *all* her fault, and she has to be punished.' Arms open, she steps towards her.

340

'We're blood, you and I, so I know you understand, that you won't—'

'You're insane.' Lillian shoves her away. 'We're leaving.'

Though Imogen stumbles, she lithely moves to the hearth, scoops up the poker and wields it. 'No, you're not.'

'Try and stop us. I'm not scared of—' Lillian begins, but a split second later, she's dropped to the ground.

Open-mouthed, I gape at this deranged woman. Her daughter is out cold and bleeding from her head, yet her expression is jubilant. 'See, I'm stronger than I look.' She brings her weapon to my throat. 'You've plagued me for twenty-three years. Now it's your turn to suffer.'

Chapter 83

1990s

Duncan

Only meeting Jana from time to time isn't perfect, but she breathes life into Duncan. Knowing he'll see her when he can is enough for him to cope, to work hard and look after Lillian, to deal with Imogen's increasingly erratic behaviour, her disappearances, her mood swings, her violence. She has taken to throwing cups and pots and vases and plates at the walls, and he knows it's only a matter of time before she hurls them at him.

On some level he knows she's frustrated, that she needs a reaction from him rather than his passive response to her tantrums. But what can he do? Pin her against the wall by her throat and yell? Tell her to clear up the broken china herself? Tell her to fuck off and leave him and Lillian alone? Kill her, so he knows she really has gone forever? But he has a child to think of. He sees little Lillian flinch when Imo is on a rant. He knows her huge eyes are questioning and scared. And when she starts to talk, her early words are: 'Where Momma?'

Focusing on Jana and her love is the invisible elastic band he snaps when he thinks he can't take a moment more of Imogen's bile, when she blows smoke in his face and says:

'*You killed Freddie. I was there, watching. You were a snivelling little coward who did nothing. Don't bother to deny it. Who do you think went into the bothy afterwards and tidied up your mess? You as good as pushed him off that bannister.*' Snap.

'*How do you know Lillibud is yours? You thought I was an innocent virgin, didn't you? What a simpleton you were and still are!*' Snap.

'*Two abortions before Lillibud. Perhaps I should have had a third.*' Snap.

'*Remember your drink being spiked? Guess who that was? Yes, Jonny Cullen, but he did it for me! He might be the biggest dumbass in the village, but boy can he fuck.*' Snap.

—

Jana and Duncan's trysts are relatively easy at first. Under the guise of seeing a supplier or checking up on the bungalow, they meet and make love in his old bedroom. Though their time together is disappointingly short, at least the property recession works in their favour, and it feels like a miracle until Jana turns up and announces she's pregnant with Alistair's child, and that in all fairness to him and the growing baby, they should have a break. But in truth, they can't. So they continue their romance both before and after Christie is born.

His mum and dad's house finally sells. 'Where now?' Jana asks.

'We'll work out something. We have to.'

As the months pass, they meet for a few hours in a hotel room between Sheffield and Doncaster, but it's so bloody frustrating when they both fall asleep or want to stay chatting and cuddling until morning. Jana suggests an overnight stay when Alistair's working away, but Duncan

can't take that risk. He knows Imo is watching him. And though she regularly disappears on a 'road trip' for an indefinite time in her mother's old car, his babysitters are Vivienne and Milly, her allies and possibly her spies.

He manages a couple of fleeting afternoon visits to Jana's cottage in Sheffield and says hi to her stunning blue-eyed baby girl, but the travelling simply lessens their time together. Though he feels bad that she has to come to him, he eventually says, 'The new livery barn is up and running, so no one goes to the old stables any more. I know it's not ideal, and you deserve so much better, but there is running water, a kettle and a comfortable bed...' He gives a crooked smile. 'How about meeting at the bothy?'

Chapter 84

Present Day

Christie

The poker still against my throat, Imogen speaks. 'Sit. There are things I need to say to you.'

I flick my eyes to Lillian's prone figure. I have no idea if she's breathing, but blood is trickling from the gash above her temple.

'I will listen, I promise,' I say in a calm tone. 'But your daughter has a head injury and needs urgent assistance.'

'It's wrought iron and French,' Imogen says conversationally, as though I haven't spoken. 'Eighteenth century, Louis XV, so a valuable antique.'

'Lillian is bleeding, Imogen. Please, an ambulance first, then we can—'

She presses her *antique* into the hollow of my neck. 'Like a knife through butter if you say another word.'

Though I have to cough several times when she releases the pressure, I try to stay unruffled. She hasn't killed me yet. Whatever she wants to say is more important to her right now. And I have to keep her talking until I can somehow disarm her and holler for help.

'Is that how you killed my mum?' I ask.

She bears down again for a second or two. 'I told you to shut up.'

'Come on, you want to show off, don't you?' I manage to splutter. 'Tell me how clever – and strong – you've been. Let me guess. You waited in the shadows of the woods until Jana appeared, then you crept into the bothy and…' Anger fizzles through me as I recover my breath. 'Did you strangle her with the scarf? Because blood would have got everywhere, including on yourself. And what better way to hide her body than in your own coffin.' Despite renewed pressure on my windpipe, I clap. 'What a masterful plan. Did you snoop around on the day of your funeral too? Was it fun to witness your own brilliance, or was it a tad disappointing because Duncan didn't shed a tear?' The notion of that dark and hostile Percy vault fuels my rage. 'He was glad you were gone, wasn't he? The only mourning he did was for Jana.'

'Shut up!' she yells. Though her spittle flies, her fury distracts her from the mission in hand. 'You have no idea what it's like to be me.' She smacks her forehead. 'To constantly live with the claustrophobia of my own psyche; to have obsessive, unwanted and intrusive thoughts and images and anxiety and disgust. To loathe myself deeply, yet revere myself too. But despite all that, Duncan – my Duncan – he—'

'Loved you? Are you sure about that? Because I've looked at his photographs and seen no happiness there.' I understand this woman has a severe psychiatric disorder and that I'm being cruel, but I have to attend to my sister. 'Let's count the months between your marriage and Lillian's birth. Strikes me the poor man was trapped rather than remotely in love. Did he even like you?'

'He loved me because he told me.'

346

'Did you know he bought Jana a ring?'

'That's a lie.'

'A beautiful sparkling solitaire engraved with words of sheer adoration. It's mine now, so I have it at home. Guess what it says?'

She hesitates for a beat, so I quickly reach for the metal rod. But Imogen is too fast. 'You're lying!' she screams, lifting her weapon.

Knowing I've pushed her to the limit, I scrunch my eyelids and prepare myself for the sickening blow, but the thud of terror in my ears is heightened by loud clattering and movement, then finally, words: 'Don't move a bloody inch.'

Praying there has been some kind of Lazarus moment, I snap around to Lillian, but she's still on the floor, unconscious or dead. Reality filters through as I ease out my trapped breath. The voice belongs to OJ, and when I turn back, he's holding the poker in one hand and his mobile in the other.

'Ambulance urgently needed,' he says. 'Straight away.'

–

The hysterical words, *'Tell me what it said! Fucking tell me what the inscription said!'* still ringing in my ears and a blanket around my shoulders, I dumbly watch the police activity around me. Imogen has been taken away, but Vivienne Percy and Mrs Shaw have stayed in a huddle, anxiously watching the paramedics tend to Lillian, roll her onto a stretcher and carry her out. My knight in shining armour holds my hand and remains by my side until a suited officer introduces himself.

'I know you've been through a traumatic experience, Ms Morfett...'

'Christie is fine.'

'Thank you, Christie. I understand you're a nurse, so you'll appreciate the importance of getting a preliminary statement from you as soon as possible.' He pulls a wry face. 'Which means now, I'm afraid, while everything is fresh.'

I take a breath to agree, but OJ speaks first. 'It's past one o'clock. She's had a dreadful shock and needs to be checked by the medics. I think it can wait until tomorrow.'

The officer points a pen at his chest. 'And you are?'

'Oliver-John Cullen, Christie's boyfriend,' he says.

Chapter 85

1999

Milly

It was a shame to watch Imo's relationship with Duncan go from bad to worse. The lad tried hard to make the marriage work, but it was as if the scales were suddenly lifted from his eyes, enabling him to finally see the manipulative, scheming, demanding version of his wife. And she was all those things, I couldn't deny it. Yet it wasn't all her fault; she was ruled by her genes, her upbringing and her demons. I truly believed she tried to overcome her obsessions, but when one of them was Duncan himself... Well, it wasn't pretty to see her jealous of her own child.

During Lillian's early life, I developed a grudging respect for Connie Watkins. She still looked at me as though I was the devil incarnate, but she was there with hands-on help after Imo had summarily dismissed me and Viv from the house.

She called me before moving to Alicante full time. 'My lad needs help. That baby will suffer if you don't step up and do something about it.'

We did 'step up', as she put it, going daily to the Ridings in the face of Imo's obvious disapproval, and discreetly doing chores as well as childcare. On the one hand, the tension seemed to ease from Duncan's shoulders, but on the other, Imo became even more flighty, indulging her daughter one week, then disappearing the next. As Lillian got older, she spent more anchored time with us at Rutherford, but I could tell from the little lass's timidity that the damage was already done.

–

Imogen had told me and Viv she'd be away for a week, so it was a surprise to hear the scrape of her keys in the scullery lock in mid-June. Why she pretended to us she was with her 'finishing school' pals, we didn't know. We were, after all, the ones who knew her the best and still loved her very much, warts and all. Perhaps these friends were people she'd met in Canada, but I suspected they were the 'like-minded' folk she'd rubbed shoulders with at the Manor, the same ones she got her supply of pills and powder from.

I was spooning batter into cupcakes for Lillian to decorate in the morning, so I looked up expectantly. 'Hello?' I called. 'Is that you, Imo?'

When she didn't reply, I shook off a shiver and looked out at the early evening outside. 'Imogen? Where are you?'

'Here.' Her pupils were dilated, so I immediately knew she'd taken something, but as she moved further into the light, I saw that her face, her hands and her white frock were smeary with dirt.

'What on earth…?' I began.

'Digging. It isn't as easy as it looks.' She peered at her fingernails. 'They'll take some scrubbing. Thank God I found a trowel.'

Though I prayed she'd developed an interest in horticulture, I already knew from her sidelong glance that she'd done something wicked. As though surprised it was there, she unravelled a leopard print scarf from around her neck and fingered it for a moment or two. Barely respiring, I waited for her devastating confession, whatever it might be today.

'She had it coming, Milly.'

'Who did?'

'Darling Jana.' She leaned towards me and theatrically whispered. 'The baby is next.'

My heart was already in spasm, but those words were bone chilling. The priority was not to let her escape, so I led her to the table and sat her down, then casually locked the door and rang the old bell to alert Vivienne.

'Let's start at the beginning, shall we?' I said, delving deep to present the reliable, practical housekeeper. 'Who is Jana? Someone you know?'

'They shagged at the bothy. I mean, that's pretty insulting, on Percy soil.' She looked at her grimy palms. 'Which is where she is now.'

'What do you mean, Imogen?'

'In her grave.'

'Is she dead?'

She snorted derisively. 'One doesn't generally inter people who are breathing.'

'Are you sure?'

'Oh yes.'

I took a deep, steadying breath. 'And who is the baby?'

'Duncan's bastard. *Little Christie*, she's called.' She scraped back her chair. 'That's right, I need to find her, so I can—'

'Sit down, Imogen!'

Vivienne had appeared from upstairs. Her face taut with fury, she strode towards her daughter. Quite honestly, I thought she intended to hit her. 'What exactly have you done this time?'

Clearly alarmed at her mother's anger, Imogen shrank away and swallowed. 'This.' She slid a folded piece of paper across the table. 'So I'm not to blame. She is, and she had to be... punished.'

'You are always to blame, Imogen. You always have been.' Viv scooped up the letter and read it, visibly shuddered, then passed it to me. 'What now?' she asked when I'd perused it.

'The police,' I replied quietly, slipping the note in my pocket. 'Imogen is ill; she's a danger and has to be detained.' I rubbed Vivienne's arm. 'It won't be prison, I'm sure, with her medical history. I'm afraid there's no other way.'

'There has to be.' Viv snapped away from my touch. 'I've had a bellyful of sympathy or staring for the past thirty years. Theo and doctors, Freddie's death and...' She pointed a trembling finger at her daughter. 'Her. From Noah to headmistresses and medics and parents – her again and again.' She straightened herself regally and slowly inhaled. 'I'm respected and have a nice life in this village. This time I'm not prepared to be humiliated or pitied or laughed at. I'd rather visit her dead in a grave than alive in a prison cell. Do you hear me? This is your fault, Milly. It's down to you to find a solution.'

–

'Oh dear,' Imo said once Vivienne had left. 'Mummy's very cross, and you're not allowed to dob me in.'

As only Imo could, she'd already recovered from her mother's lambast. I sat down opposite her. 'You need psychiatric help, Imogen. The proper medicines to make you better. If you had anything about you, you'd hand yourself in.'

'And you'd still be in trouble with Mummy. How you'd hate that.'

'Shh. I'm thinking.' *Dead in a grave…* As dreadful as the situation was, a vague idea was already slotting into place. 'And don't look so smug. Your walkabouts will be a thing of the past for starters.'

She shrugged. 'Only some of it was walking…'

'And what is that supposed to mean?'

'My little nest in the east wing. With my stash of goodies, I've stayed there for days.' She sniggered. 'Don't tell me I managed to get one over on you, Millicent Shaw? You must be losing your touch.'

I stared at her smug expression for a while. She had hoodwinked me, but it made sense of her magically appearing from nowhere, not just recently, but for many years. 'Well, at least that solves one problem. We won't have to pay for a forged passport to get you to flaming Canada or the like.'

She guffawed again. 'I very much doubt Gabrielle would want me darkening her door again.'

'This isn't a joke, Imogen.' I glared. 'You have taken a young woman's life and deprived a child of her mother. You'll wipe that smile from your face and do as you're told. Right…' I reverted to logistics. 'We'll need to move the body and hide it as soon as we can. The cellar will do for now, but neither of us are strong enough to carry a dead weight.'

Imo stood. 'Leave that one with me.' Clearly pleased with herself, she looked down at her dress. 'I'd better have a shower and change into something nice. I need to get down to the pub.'

Chapter 86

Present Day

Christie

Snug against my boyfriend's shoulder, I lie in my bed and speak intermittently. For ease and speed after we left Rutherford, I thought he might invite me to stay at his family house. He seemed to consider it as we approached the surgery, then he said, 'There's no traffic at this time. I'll have you home in twenty minutes.'

I peer up at his troubled face. He's treating me as if I'm fragile and might easily break, yet he seems distant too.

'Thank God,' he says again. 'Thank God I got there the moment I did.' He kisses my forehead. 'Losing you doesn't bear thinking about.'

'Do you think Lillian will be OK?' I ask.

He checked her vital signs and put her in the recovery position before the paramedics arrived but hasn't said much since. 'With a penetrating head injury, a bleed on the brain is possible, but she's in the right place,' he replies, then falls silent again.

Though I don't think I can cope with more trauma right now, I take a quick breath. 'OJ?'

'Yup?'

'Something's wrong. Is it Lillian? Do you think she won't make it?'

'No, it's not...' He pauses as though shifting his thoughts. 'These things are unpredictable, as you know, but she recovered consciousness, so I'd say that's hopeful.'

'Then what is it? What aren't you telling me?'

'Nothing. You've had a dreadful shock. Why don't you try and get some sleep now.'

I pull away and look at him intently. 'You're not going to dump me twice in one day, are you?'

He smiles faintly. 'It's Monday now, so...'

'Just tell me. Whatever it is, just say it.'

His brow furrows. 'You've been through a lot. I don't want to add to the load.'

Tears prick the back of my eyes. 'Now you're freaking me out. Seriously, you're not going to leave me, are you? I'm really sorry for bolting; I should have explained what was going on in my head, and I promise I will if it ever happens again. I won't shut you out.'

He rakes a strand of my hair behind an ear. 'I'm sorry too. It took the birth of twin bull calves and a lecture from Pete to realise I did the same to you but by text. I shut you down and didn't explain.'

'I like the sound of Pete.'

'Yeah, he's great.'

'So, what do you need to tell me?'

He sighs. 'I'm guessing you think I turned up at Rutherford in the nick of time because Vivienne heard a commotion and called me?'

I'm thrown by his question. 'Goodness, I don't know; I haven't thought much of it through yet.' I steel myself for something I won't want to hear. 'I take it that isn't what happened?'

'Do you remember asking me why I was so evasive about my mum knowing Imogen? I think our conversation moved on at the time, but the answer is that I was non-committal because that's how my mum has always been about her, both when I was a kid and later if her name came up in conversation. I had no idea why, but I suspected her reticence was something to do with my dad. It wasn't unheard of for him to make a play for a woman. Anyhow, when I arrived back home from Brook Farm last night, Mum told me you'd visited...'

I have no idea where this story is going, but I cringe. 'God, sorry about that, well, outburst. She must think I'm crackers.'

He gives me a strange look. 'Thank God you did, Christie. So, Mum told me what you'd said about discovering your dad wasn't your biological father. I added that info to the letter Noah had sent to your mum, and it was obvious that Duncan was the guy in question. But Mum was already beside herself with agitation. She surmised from your comment when you left that you'd gone to the Ridings; she insisted I immediately go there and check you were OK. So I did. Your car was there, but you weren't, so I belted to the main house and saw the light on in the east wing. The rest you know.'

'Right, I see. But...' My torpid mind struggles to catch up. 'Why wouldn't I be *OK* at the Ridings?'

He takes a shuddery breath. 'She knew about Imogen.'

'What?' The wasp; she knew about the wasp? I find myself inching away. 'What do you mean?'

'I'm so sorry, Christie, I don't have the full story yet, but she hurriedly told me that Imogen was alive and living in the east wing. I'm still taking it in myself, and I know it's dreadful, simply horrendous. That's why I didn't want to burden you with it yet. But...' He rubs his cropped hair. 'But we have to be truthful with each other, yes?'

I dumbly nod.

'OK...' He swallows. 'Mum said she didn't know for several years, so she had no part in your mum's death or the cover-up, but at some point she spotted Imogen in the shadows at the big house. She struggled to believe her own eyes and left, but she couldn't let it go, so she decided to broach it with Vivienne. Long story short, she was confronted by Imogen herself. I guess there must have been some dialogue about who'd actually been buried in the family vault.' He grimaces. 'The conversation ended with Imogen making it clear that if she was going down, she'd take my father with her.'

Trying to process what he's saying, I cover my face. 'So... so your dad was involved in my mum's murder?' I ask eventually.

'Mum says she never asked him. She knew Imogen had him wrapped around her little finger, but she doubted he'd do anything so extreme. He was a petty thief, a bully and a cheat, not a murderer. But she was still besotted with Dad and couldn't take that risk, so she agreed to remain silent.' His expression bleak, OJ spreads his hands. 'I obliterated that man from my thoughts years ago, but I'm appalled with her, and I completely understand if being with me will be a constant reminder of your loss and your unanswered questions for so many years.'

'Why are you telling me this?'

'Honesty is everything, Christie.'

Yet he stopped me from speaking to the detective. 'But you want me to lie for her?'

358

'No, not at all. She has to take the consequences for the choices she made. She knows that, and she'll confess to the police.'

I flop back against the mattress. 'She covered up a crime. She was...' I grope for the expression. 'An accessory after the fact.'

'I know.'

My mind is gluey with shock, but I try to process the facts. This is the man I love. I don't want to lose him. Yet his mother... Christ, it's bloody unbelievable. 'She definitely knew nothing at the time?'

'No, she didn't.'

'And had no part in my mum's death?'

'None at all.'

'Why is honesty everything?'

'Because I love you, I want to marry you, set up a home and have kids with you, Christie. There's no other way.'

It's what I want too. What I need to guide me through all *this*. To recover my mum's body, finally say goodbye and give her a proper resting place. To be strong for my sister and help her through her injuries and trauma. 'What if I was fine with Belinda continuing to stay silent?'

OJ takes my hand. 'It would be incredibly forgiving and generous of you, but Imogen will be questioned at length by the police. Who knows what she'll say.'

Though the wasp's furious expression flashes in, I'm suddenly exhausted, sleep pulling me down. 'Don't go anywhere, will you?' I mutter.

'I won't.' He kisses my forehead. 'That's the one thing you don't need to worry about.'

Chapter 87

Present Day

Milly

As is my wont every night, I double-lock the great door, look up to the shadowy first tier above me, then down to the hard marble below. Perhaps it's only me who can see it, but the pale pink blood stain is still there, like Freddie himself.

I wearily climb the staircase, pad to the east wing door and turn the key out of habit. Imogen was strictly forbidden by Vivienne to leave the house itself, but we only locked Imo in her quarters if she was having a manic episode or if we knew visitors were due. Many a time we had a close escape when someone called unexpectedly, and it was unfortunate that Belinda Cullen came on spec to check on our little dog during his last days. Imogen's demand to have a private audience with the veterinary – followed by her blackmail – was both alarming and embarrassing, especially for Viv, but it was fortuitous too. We were able to offload the ordeal we experienced during Imo's dark days when she declared she was off to hunt that poor baby down, when she'd scratch, kick and bite as we struggled to restrain her. Thank goodness Belinda was able to help by 'prescribing' her with much needed sedatives.

Breathing deeply, I inhale the aroma of Rutherford House. How funny that I vowed never to go into service like my mother, yet this has been my home since I was sixteen. During those sixty-three years I've done unpalatable things, and some shame me more than others, but they've all been in the name of love.

Of course, I didn't kill Jana, and I was presented with a fait accompli that evening by Imogen, but I did feel ashamed for covering up the truth about her death. The woman had a partner and a child, and though I didn't witness their grief, their anguish and frustration at their lack of simply knowing what had happened to their loved one, I could see their devastation through Duncan's hollow eyes. He existed and smiled and went through the motions for Lillian, yet he stooped and decayed a little more as each year passed. My heart went out to him, but Imo was my priority, and she had to come first. I'd already 'stepped up' at the Ridings when Connie and Noah went off to Spain, so I continued to keep an eye on the lad, taking him a casserole or a pie every week, even though he was a fully grown man in his thirties and forties. When he reached fifty, he seemed to slump even more, and when I popped in to see him one evening with an offering, he was cutting up a pile of photographs. Knowing they were of his love, I decided then he should see her missive, so I hurried back to Rutherford to unearth it, stole in again and left it by his bedside. When I returned in the morning to collect my oven dish, he wasn't in the kitchen or already out and about on the land but cold in his bed.

Did I do right or wrong? I have no idea, but when I gently tugged Jana's letter from his hand, I like to think it was the former, as he looked relaxed, peaceful, and the most contented I'd seen him for over two decades. He'd died in his sleep knowing Jana loved him and that little Christie was his.

My meeting with Sinclair Stephens, Member of Parliament, was another kettle of fish. I had no hesitation in reminding him of the 'back street' abortion he'd arranged for Imo at the age of fourteen and the evidence of their association she'd been smart enough to retain.

'Arranging for a car to career off the road into a lake, then misidentifying the body and the cause of death isn't something I can arrange with the click of my fingers,' he spluttered.

Yet, somehow, he did once ten days had passed. Viv was sad to lose her old Citroën, but the police duly contacted Duncan to advise him of his wife's tragic death. 'Swerving to avoid an oncoming vehicle', the RTA report concluded. She was identified by her dental records, and due to the bloating by water, a viewing of her corpse wasn't recommended. We had a lovely funeral, and everyone mourned, including that oaf Jonny Cullen, who'd carried poor Jana's dead body for half a mile under one arm just because Imo told him to.

I'll never understand why an intelligent woman like Belinda got involved with a scoundrel like him, but I suppose one doesn't always choose who one loves or know what lengths one will go to for that person. What became of him, I don't know, but bad pennies usually turn up and so far he hasn't.

I was dreadfully sorry for Lillian's 'loss' of her mother, but Duncan, Viv and me were there for the little lass, and in truth she was far better off without her. We didn't realise that Imo was 'haunting' the poor child until the damage was done, so we decided it was best to send Lillian to a nice boarding school with the money Honora had left in her will. Duncan didn't want her to go, but we put forward a good case: we were getting doddery, Noah and Connie were in Spain, he had to work, and Lillian needed more than just Oliver-John as a friend. In short, it was what was best for *her*, so he reluctantly agreed.

I sigh at the thought of our beautiful Lillian. After hearing the commotion and scurrying to Imo's nest on Sunday night, it was such a frightful shock to see her immobile body by the hearth. So very similar to how I found Freddie, I felt the life drain from me, but Oliver-John was astonishingly there and tending to her. He looked up and blew out a long puff of relief. 'Thank God, she's breathing,' he said.

This afternoon I visited the hospital and watched her from the shadows. I know she won't want to see me and Viv yet, but she will one day, I'm sure. She's Imo's daughter, after all, and there's something about blood, isn't there? Despite everything, it is thicker, murkier, more sticky than water. And occasionally I see Imo in her face, a glint of her wilfulness and sometimes that loss of focus as though she's gone somewhere else.

Today she was in the arms of the Watkins family – Noah and Connie and Duncan's 'baby'. Flaming Connie Watkins. She's always tried her best to love Lillian, but I suspect she's never quite forgiven her for being a half-Percy. But now she has Christie too, a grandchild with her beloved son's striking blue eyes, and I'm glad for her, even if she did look like a ridiculous blonde tart at the age of seventy-seven.

On the way to my bedroom, I glance into Theo's old chamber and grimly nod. Yes, that was the most distasteful thing I had to do in the name of love, unfortunately not just the once but several times in 1967 and again two years later. Did Theo enjoy puffing and plugging away at me to conceive his son and heir? His groans of pleasure might suggest so, but quite frankly the coupling repulsed me. And yet, paradoxically, it was an act of gritted-teeth selflessness I still have the most pride in. I gave Vivienne the chance of motherhood, of being called Mummy. Theo's venereal disease was cured by a round of strong antibiotics, but poor Viv didn't get off so lightly: through no fault of her own, the infection had already spread into her uterus and fallopian tubes, thus the miscarriages and ultimately a hysterectomy.

Did anyone beyond Rutherford guess I was Freddie and Imo's real red-headed, small-framed mother? Viv restyled and dyed my hair, so I don't think so, and who would take a second glance at an invisible servant anyway? Cook, the scullery maid, Honora and the whole household were privy to the secret, but no one broke the code of silence. Everyone wanted to hear the patter of little feet, and I think we all forgot Freddie and Imo were anyone's other than Vivienne's.

Deeply sighing, I close out the past. I was delighted to give my mistress and dear friend the gift of two beautiful children, but there's a sting in the happy tale I've never imparted to her or to anyone else. The only person who would have known was the housekeeper, Maggie Shaw, and of course she was dead by the time Freddie and Imo were born. The whole village, and not least Gran and me, were shocked that such a fit and indomitable woman would succumb to a huge heart attack and early death. But later, much later, I knew it had been the shock of Vivienne and Theo's surrogacy plans which brought it on. My realisation was slow, yet when Honora persisted with her 'fairy tales' of domestic abuse, sexual deviancy and forced intercourse, the dark conclusion that Henry Percy had also raped my mother in 1942 was inescapable. It made that man my father and Theo my half-brother, which meant poor little Freddie and Imogen were the product of incest.

The fluke of nature was cruel. Freddie didn't look right, but he was a good boy inside. Sadly, Imo was the opposite. Even now, I don't like to think about what I overheard her say to her brother the eve he died: '*If you want to be my friend again, you have to take a test.*' Did that include balancing on the bannister like a gymnast on his beam, something Imo was so proficient at? I don't know, and I really don't want to. That's the thing about motherhood: good or bad, you never stop loving your child, even if it involves washing the gloopy blood off your hands.

Will Imo 'dob' me and Viv in, as she put it all those years ago? She's maintained a dignified Percy silence to date, so I'm hopeful she won't, and she'll need someone to visit and take goodies when she's in a secure hospital, which surely she will be. As for the police's visits and probing questions in our front parlour thus far, me and Vivienne are just two confused and confounded elderly ladies, too shocked to register the astonishing turn of events.

Heedful not to wake my love, I remove my dressing gown and slide beneath the covers. Trauma always did make Viv sleepy, but she'll be fine with me to take care of her as always. Now her 'imprisonment' is over, she can blossom again, visit Lillian at the Ridings, walk into the village and perhaps even resume her church duties. After all, she's served her self-imposed sentence, paid her dues and done her 'Christian' time.

I look into the black night. Will I manage to sleep without the comforting sounds of Imo's midnight prowl around this beautiful old house? The nooks and crannies, the corridors and chambers, the furnishings and furniture we both love so dearly? Tears prick the back of my eyes. Goodness, I'll miss her. Yes, she was challenging when she had an episode, and at times we had to ply her with sedatives or sleeping pills, yet when she was well, she was the brightest and best company one could ever wish for. But I sniff away the emotion, turn to the orange couch and blow the usual kiss. Smiling his sunny smile, Freddie responds in kind.

I close my tired eyes. Who'd have thought my whispers about curses and bad blood would turn out to be prophecies. Yet I'm thankful I still have my boy. Within the majestic walls of Rutherford House, he'll always be here by my side.

A letter from CE Rose

Hello lovely reader!

Thank you so much for reading *The Shadows of Rutherford House*. I do hope you've enjoyed exploring the nooks and crannies of the big house, meeting Milly, Christie and Duncan, and discovering their dark, dark secrets.

If you'd like to read more twisty, chilling tales about ordinary, relatable characters who get caught up in extraordinary situations, dilemmas or crimes, please check out my other CE Rose gothic-tinged psychological thrillers, *The House of Hidden Secrets* and *The House on the Water's Edge*, or my Caroline England psychological suspense novels, *Beneath the Skin, My Husband's Lies, Betray Her, Truth Games* and *The Sinner*.

Book reviews are extremely helpful to authors, so if you have the time, I'd be really grateful if you'd pop one, however short, on Amazon or Goodreads, or your other preferred forum. If you'd like to chat in person, hear my latest news or see photos of my moggies and other random things, my website and social media details are below.

Thank you again,

Best wishes,

Caroline

Website: www.carolineenglandauthor.co.uk
Twitter: https://twitter.com/CazEngland

Facebook: https://www.facebook.com/CazEngland1/
Instagram: https://www.instagram.com/cazengland1/
TikTok: https://www.tiktok.com/@cazengland1
email: carolineenglandauthor@gmail.com

Acknowledgments

Huge thanks to: Keshini Naidoo, Jenny Warren and the rest of the Hera team for your top-notch editorial input and fabulous book covers.

My hubby Jonathan and my gorgeous daughters Elizabeth, Charlotte and Emily.

My brilliant family, friends, writing buddies and local bookshop, E J Morten Booksellers. Thanks so much for your love and support!

Every single blogger, reviewer, reader or online bookgroup member who has championed my books.

Last, but not least, you guys – the fantastic reading public! Thank you so much for buying my novels, investing hours of your time reading them and posting such heartwarming reviews.